2

The Guilt of a Sparrow

Jess B. Moore

A haunting and beautifully written story that will
stay with you long after you turn the last page.
Kate Armitage,
Author of The Wrong Side of Twenty-Five

CROOKED
CAT

Discover us online:
www.crookedcatbooks.com

Join us on facebook:
www.facebook.com/crookedcat

Tweet a photo of yourself holding
this book to **@crookedcatbooks**
and something nice will happen.

To my mom,
who probably thinks
this book is about her,
but really,
she was the one
who taught me
to be strong,
and set me free.

Acknowledgements

What is a book without readers? Big huge hats off to all of YOU for being the best!

Books don't write themselves. And although I wrote this book, I couldn't have done it alone.

Thank you Crooked Cat for taking a chance on me and for believing in my writing. Especially big thanks to Laurence for virtually holding my hand through the process, and for all the editing. All the CATS have been wonderfully supportive and helpful, and I couldn't have done it without them.

Hugs and love forever to Cindy, who after reading TGoaS told me it was important. That I HAD to share it with the world. Without that push, it might have lived forever as a document on my computer. All the love and hot tea in the world to Alisha for inviting me over to read the first few chapters. Out loud. I thought I might choke on my tongue or forget how to read when the time came, but I faced my fears and did it.

To Stella and Kelly, I wish I could give you hugs. I wish I could sit with you to talk books and writing for hours on end. But we must live within emails. Without you both the book would have been a big fat mess. A girl cannot write without fabulous critique partners.

I wouldn't be who I am if I hadn't been raised by a strong and compassionate woman. Thank you for trusting me to be myself. This one is for you.

Amanda, love til dentures.

My life isn't silent. I write with my kids around me, with music playing, with life being lived out loud. I wouldn't have it any other way. Elijah, I always think of you when I write, because I know you'll tell me the truth. I put Jerusalem Ridge in for you. Lincoln, you love books more than anyone, and I love that about you. Thanks for all the hugs when I needed them. Eric, I'm nothing without you. Your support is truly everything and I love you more than dark chocolate.

About the Author

Jess B Moore is a writer of love stories. When she's not writing, she's busy mothering her talented and stubborn children, reading obscene numbers of books, and knitting scarves she'll likely never finish.

Jess lives in small town North Carolina with her bluegrass obsessed family. She takes too many pictures of her cat, thinking the Internet loves him as much as she does. She is a firm believer of swapping stories over coffee or wine, and that there should always be dark chocolate involved.

The Guilt of a Sparrow is her debut novel combining her interests in family, music, and small towns into a thoughtful tale of growing up and falling in love. Her second book, *Fierce Grace,* follows similar themes in a whole new way, and will be available later in 2018.

Please leave a review to tell other readers what you thought. Reviews are everything for writers!

Look her up on social media **@authorjessb** - she'd be thrilled if you followed her on Twitter, overjoyed if you visited her on Facebook, and filled with glee if you liked her Instagram posts.

The Guilt of a Sparrow

to Rae
with love, ♡
Jess Z Moore

with love, ♥

Chapter One

Magnolia

Independence tasted of frozen grapes enjoyed beneath the relative shade of my favorite Dogwood tree in the city park. A sweet tart antidote to the oppressive heat. The strap of my worn bag chair dug into my shoulder and I switched it to the other side as I navigated the growing crowd along the sidewalk.

Freedom sounded like the rushed twang of bluegrass as it made its way around the circle during the weekly jam. Swift jangly songs familiar from routine exposure. Tunes plucked and shared by the members of our community and enjoyed by all that came out to the shady little park to listen.

Escaping to the jam was my quiet and desperate bid for deliverance from the stronghold of my mama's grasp on me. A hard-won fight, although a minor victory, if I was honest. I suspected she gave me this one small prize as an effort to assuage me, to keep me from wanting more.

More.

I couldn't put a name on what I wanted, other than, *more*.

If my mama was known for anything, it was her hard stance on avoiding anything to do with Fox River, the nowhere town in western North Carolina we called home. Not to mention her strong-arm rule over her daughter. Her quiet unnoticeable daughter.

Me.

She had her reasons. We all had our reasons for becoming who we were; for staying that way.

If our family was notorious in town, it all came down to my older brother, Luke. He took his role as troublemaker seriously, running with it until Mama was positively drowning in judgment. When he died, the gossip only seemed to get worse, a dark cloud hovering above our heads.

I longed to stay invisible, to shrink behind the shadow cast by my family. At first, it was my goal to skate by without raising attention, without causing trouble, without garnering disappointment. When Luke was alive, Mama was too busy to see me, and it wasn't such a bad line to walk. His death left me the only kid in the house, and I walked a minefield. Either I was so good it was seen as a mockery of my troubled brother, or I wasn't good enough and only caused more stress for my family. My desire to disappear only increased as time passed.

An advantage of living below the radar was that I could go out and rarely deal with people approaching me. The phenomenon helped to manage my social anxiety. In fact, it probably fostered it. When folks did speak to me, it was to ask after my mama, to poke a stick at our loss behind the guise of concern, or to share their surprise at having noticed me at all. Fox River was a small town of the sort that everyone knew everyone and there was not much chance at hiding completely.

It was my best friend Alyssa's idea to drag me to the weekly bluegrass jam. She helped convince me it was worth the effort; to win a battle would eventually help me win the war. Small victory in getting past my social anxiety, in getting past my mama's fear of town judgment, and in hoping I would see bluegrass music circles as super fun. So far the results were inconclusive. Yet I kept showing up near about every week.

In a town as microscopic as Fox River, meeting on Friday nights to play music was a capital-E Event. Food trucks lined the bordering streets. Exhaust mingled with food smells, heat churning the mix into the air so that it clung in a haze up and down the streets. Exotic spices, savory meats, over-salted snacks, snowy white sugared treats. Young and old alike came out. Families sprawled on blankets, plates balanced on knees, babies crawling into the grass to taste it in fistfuls, toddlers squealing and dashing as far away from safety as they dared to return in a hurry. Teens in tight groups meandered, cell phones in hands, snapping photos and swapping insults, calling to each other in brazen tones. Adults in work clothes, top button

4

released and sleeves rolled up, socialized and caught up on the past week in hushed voices, eyes tight in judgment when an offensive teen passed too near. Conversation flowed through the gathered crowd as swiftly as the music. People found comfort in the familiar faces and routines, excited another week was at a close, their ears turning to catch the songs playing in the background.

The evening was hot of the unrelenting sort. Late June in the mountains held astonishing heat levels and staggering humidity. The air was thick and my skin sticky. The scent of fried foods and cotton candy clung to me and turned my stomach. I could never eat in that sort of heat. I wrapped my thick hair into a knot on top of my head, anything to keep it off my sweat slicked neck.

Whomp. My uplifted elbows and downturned head smacked into a solid mass. As I braced my hands outward, the bag chair slung over my shoulder slid unceremoniously to the ground. As I braced my hand out in front of me, my hair fell free from my fingers, effectively shrouding my face.

"I am so sorry!" I blurted the words before I could assess the victim of my accidental run-in.

"Whoa. Hey, Maggie." Strong hands steadied me, thick fingers wrapping around my upper arms. Mint and something warm and sweet like cookies tickled my nose. I recognized his voice immediately.

Dominic MacKenna.

"Hi." I panted and stepped back to free myself from his grasp. "Sorry. Again."

"No worries." His smile was wide, his eyes mischievous, and his expression curious, as I finally looked him over.

I busied myself with my hair, allowing it to be a distraction, and securing it up and out of the way.

Dominic scooped up my chair, in a thoughtless motion, smile still stretching his lips. Rather than return the burden to me, he slung the worn strap over his own shoulder. He studied me as if he found me interesting, while I remained standing before him like an idiot.

"I haven't seen you in ages. How're you?"

Sure you've seen me; I'm here every week, same as you.
Difference being that I didn't typically smack right into him.
Rather than voice those thoughts, I smiled and focused on the
loose circle of men and women arranging chairs, tuning up
instruments, and preparing to jam.

"I'm good." My shoulders lifted in a shrug, going for
nonchalant, while my pulse hammered. "You?"

While avoiding looking too closely, I kept him in my
periphery. He was tall and broad, strawberry hair bright in the
sun, an undying smile on his lips. I could still picture the way
he looked as a little boy, lanky and gap toothed, friendly as
could be.

"I'm good, Maggie. May I carry this chair somewhere for
you?" His voice was smooth as silk, slow and distinctly
southern.

"No." My hand thrust out to snatch the chair back from
him.

"No?" I chanced a look at his face, at the amusement
painted there in his eyes and his smile. Mingled with disbelief
that I had turned down his simple offer.

The MacKenna clan was one short of a six pack of boys.
The five of them ranged from thirty-one to twenty-four years
old. Dominic being the youngest. My age. We'd gone to school
together. They were all well-known in the community, if only
by reputation. I knew him best of the bunch, though not well.
Some people loved them, for their good humor, musicality,
and generosity. Others hated the lot of them, for their pranks,
talent, and popularity. I had yet to know of anyone that didn't
agree they were each and every one of them highly attractive.
The general consensus was that Denver was the best looking
of them. He was also the oldest, and the most standoffish. He
was either brutally shy or plain anti-social, which I couldn't be
sure. Beau, the middle child, was outgoing to the point of
obnoxious.

Dominic was popular, quick with a smile, and known for
his rampant flirting. He attracted attention, people pulled into
his orbit, glances catching on him rather than sliding past. A
group of women in their early twenties paused at a polite

distance from us and pretended they weren't waiting to catch Dominic alone.

"No, thank you," I amended.

His laugh was good natured and infectious. A breath of laughter snuck past my own lips, and I gave in. No harm letting him carry my chair. Not that I needed the help, but that wasn't the point. He was a southern gentleman, and he would be insulted if I put up more of a fight.

"I usually sit under the Dogwood tree."

I looked at him again, not able to help myself. Soft azure blue eyes studied me, scanning my face. Perhaps hung up on my having said *usually*, pointing out that I had a regular spot and was therefore in regular attendance. I was hit with a wave of guilt. I hadn't meant to throw it in his face or make him feel bad for not having noticed me.

He led the way to the Dogwood tree, offset to the left of where the musicians set up. It was only marginally cooler under the shade of the tree, temperatures lowering only enough to be tolerable. Sweat had gone well past beading on my skin to sliding down between my breasts.

I stood aside while Dominic made quick work of setting up the chair, angling it to the best advantage to see the gathering players. I placed my small cooler beside the chair. With empty hands, I didn't know what to do with them, and my fingers entangled and twisted.

"Dom, man, you coming or what?"

Cotton MacKenna sauntered up to his brother. His long-legged stride and heavy sandals eating up the ground between us quickly. A couple years older than Dominic, all hard lines and no excuses. He was the scary one. No, not scary. Intense. Which is sometimes the same thing.

I couldn't stop my eyes from finding his. They were the most startling blue, with facets like cut stone, hard and sharp in his handsome face. How many times had I found my gaze trapped by the sharp edges and beauty of those eyes?

Chapter Two

Magnolia

I stood there in a beautifully strange alternate universe, in which I was flanked by not one, but two of the legendary MacKenna brothers. What the heck was happening?

Cotton had only come over to collect his brother. Who was only with me because I'd bumped into him and he'd insisted on carrying my chair after he collected it from where I'd dropped it on the ground. It was a series of accidents and didn't mean anything.

"Course I am." Dominic's smile didn't falter a bit. He looked to his brother, offering him an invitation to stay and be friendly. Then to me, in an apology for knowing his brother wouldn't do any such thing. "It was good to see you, Magnolia Porter."

I nodded. The words, *likewise Dominic MacKenna* caught in my throat, an easy reply ensnared by nerves.

He lingered, after his words, not stepping away quite yet.

I heard Cotton grunt and my eyes skipped back to him. He had the reddest hair of the bunch, the truest orange red. When I looked closely, finding it easier to study the strands of his hair than to look at his face, I saw every shade represented. Dark auburn, copper, blonde, everything in between. It made no sense comparing the individual strands to the overall head of hair. He cleared his throat, probably aware of my uncouth staring, and I shifted my eyes to the ground.

"Cotton, you remember Maggie?"

"Yes."

I could feel him looking at me, those eyes studying my downturned head. My scalp prickled under his scrutiny. Their exchange had been outwardly polite but hid something else underneath. I couldn't put my finger on why it struck me as odd.

Growing up, I had often gotten the impression that Cotton avoided me. I figured it all came back to the epic fights between him and my brother. Schoolyard quarrels through the years. But even after Luke died, Cotton was never in the same vicinity as me. So much that it seemed intentional, a careful avoidance. That or my infatuation with him made me spin fantasies to explain things that didn't exist.

"Hello, MacKennas four and five." A distinctly feminine, and decidedly playful voice rang out and broke the spell of awkward. "What are you two doing, ganging up on poor little Maggie?"

Alyssa's ability to crack a joke that was all-inclusive was one of her best qualities. She never laughed at me. Yet, she was nearly always laughing in a way that included me and made me laugh along with her. Also the way she pitched her voice, the delivery of her words. They were never mean.

"We were doing no such thing now, Lyss." Dominic was a joker as well. A flirty teasing type. He and Alyssa were friends of the sort that spent too much time trying to one up the other. I braced myself. "My mama raised me to help a lady in distress. Miss Maggie here needed a hand with her chair."

Alyssa released a peal of laughter to the sky. I rolled my eyes, swallowing my protest. Distress? Not quite. I hated the attention that gathered around me. As it built, my lungs shrank until they wouldn't accept the proper amount of air, my haywire brain turning my anxiety into something physical.

"You are a chronic flirt. If you helped her, with that little teeny chair, it was a ploy."

"Are you two done?" Cotton clearly had no patience for their verbal games. His gruff response pulled me out of twisting unease that tried to claim me. His words, not even directed at me, softened my lungs so that I could breathe again.

"Never." I answered for my friend. My lips pulled into a smile, a silent offering, a secret revealed for him.

Cotton directed his gaze my way again. That time I was ready and didn't look away. His lips pulled into an almost smile, which took me by surprise. I got hung up looking at his mouth, the fullness of his lips, and the way they twitched as if hiding away that smile.

"Not true." Alyssa stomped her foot and placed her hands on her hips. The picture of defiance wrapped up in mirth. "We are in fact done. It's time to jam, fellas."

"Where's that husband of yours?" Dominic asked Alyssa. "He promised me a *Jerusalem Ridge* showdown."

He and Alyssa fell into a conversation involving Dom's mandolin and Jacob's guitar, and a song I'd heard a thousand times yet couldn't quite place. If I was honest, most of the fiddle tunes sounded the same to me. They had a well-worn quality lent to sounding commonplace, each one plucking at familiarity, but they ran together.

Cotton and I stood there, accidentally thrown together for the moment. He could've walked away. Instead, he waited out his brother, and stood there with a scowl on his face. A scowling Cotton was still a thing of glory.

His version of quiet looked nothing like mine; eternally still, while I pulled at the hem of shirt, twisted my silver rings, then messed with my hair.

"You should sing." I blurted out of nowhere.

"What?"

"Sing. You should sing."

Where his gaze landed, there was a tingling left behind on my skin. Why did I open my mouth?

"I'm no good at singing."

"You have such a nice voice."

I watched his brows lift. Questioning. Or indignant. I blanched; my brain scrambled for a reasonable explanation for my being weird.

"It's just, when you speak, your voice is so ... resonant."

Impossibly, his brows lifted higher, toward his ginger hair which stood on end, sticking out every which way, with bends and waves, completely out of control. I had never seen it tamed. Indicative of something within him that couldn't be tamped down. A warning.

"I don't remember an occasion when you and I have talked beyond a polite greeting."

Talked enough for me to know his voice, he means, to think he should be singing. I swallowed my nerves, along with the cache of memories I had saved of hearing him speak in years past.

"We haven't talked."

Cotton's expression reflected questions, but before he could respond, we were interrupted.

"Good God man, stop flirting with my wife." Jacob Hunter approached with a smile and a faux snarl. He scooped Alyssa up off the ground and tossed her over his shoulder. She played her part and wailed in a good-natured way, then reached down to smack his butt. "We have a jam to attend, boys."

"Right you are, Jakey Boy." Dominic gave him a sharp nod, skipping out of reach. If Jacob hated being called Jake, he despised Jakey.

"Evening, Maggie. You going out with us later?" Jacob resolutely ignored Dominic and faced me instead.

"Yes! Her answer is yes." Alyssa called out, her voice from behind her husband. All I could see of her was a pair of legs, her hips propped at Jacob's shoulder.

"I don't know, I ..." I glanced at Cotton. Why? No idea why I looked his way, or why he remained standing at my side. It was the strangest thing. Stranger still that it seemed he belonged; I wanted him to belong in the same space as me.

"Alrighty, it's settled." When I looked back at Jacob, he gave me a wink. "Do you have your car here, or do you want to ride with us?"

"Jacob. Hunter. If you are going to stand around making conversation and plans, you put me down." Alyssa wailed.

Jacob laughed, chest shaking, in turn, making my friend shake. He slid her down his front, making a point to feel her up along the way.

"Sorry, Magpie." Alyssa shook her head and tried to make right her hair after being flipped upside down. Her eyes were alight, spirits high. "Did you drive tonight?"

11

"I walked."

Cotton's posture changed, stiffened, a movement I detected at my side, but I didn't dare look his way. I wasn't sure what I would find on his face, or if I wanted to see.

"Okey dokey. Ride with us." Alyssa grabbed one of my hands and gave it a squeeze. "Now, if you'll excuse us, we are actually heading over to play some music."

Cotton lingered. Only after his brother, my friend, and her goofy husband were halfway to the jam circle, and out of earshot, did he alter his position. The shift put him squarely facing me, and I was compelled to look up at him. My head tipped back, bending my neck to meet his height. I couldn't be sure what he was doing, or what my response was to be. Confusion and desire swirled deep within me.

"I'm sorry about Lucian."

I sucked in a breath. Four years had passed since my brother Luke died, and the apologies had all but dropped off these days. The direction Cotton steered the conversation was unexpected to say the least.

"Not about him dying," Cotton clarified, a swift utterance followed by a cleared throat. He was embarrassed, or uncomfortable. Then his face contorted, as if something like shame had hit him. "That was a terrible thing to say. I shouldn't have said that."

"It's okay, Cotton. Most people aren't sorry he's gone." The truth was right there; bitter on my tongue and something I normally swallowed. Until faced with freaking Cotton MacKenna, then it just spilled right out. His face did a fast-paced dance from shock to relief and finally landing on resolve.

"I meant, I'm sorry if I made things harder with him, when you were growing up."

A sigh escaped my lips. I tried for a smile, one that said it was in the past and I forgave him. One that I pulled out of my back pocket, always ready to don the polite mask of absolution.

"That was long time ago. And Luke would've ..." I wanted to assure him it was okay. Cotton used to pick fights with Luke

12

on the regular. Or the other way around. I had stopped caring why even longer ago. It never mattered. "Luke would've been Luke no matter what you did."

We both turned toward the folks circled up to play their music as a song started up, happy for the distraction. The song was fast and hard, started out by a fiddle setting an impossible standard. Denver MacKenna, I'd bet my life. A driven and downright impressive musician, even outside our little town. Still single at thirty-one, everyone said it was shame he was too shy to meet a nice girl. Only when they said *shy*, it sounded more like *stoic*. Unless it was my mama talking, then it sounded like *selfish*. She never understood why he put his fiddle playing first, instead of settling down like he was supposed to do. You'd think after Luke, she'd be more understanding about children not doing what people expected. But then I'd always suspected the reason she was so ought to compare Lucian and Denver was because she wished her son had been a whole lot more like the eldest MacKenna.

"Aren't you playing tonight?" I gestured toward the players, a loose circle of least twenty townsfolk. Anything to redirect and get us out the Swamp of Sorrows that was my brother and his past. Plus I was more than a little curious why he was lingering so long at my side when he'd normally have claimed his spot in the jam by now.

"I am."

I looked up just in time to see his solemn nod. Eyes trained on the players across the way, but not looking like he saw them. More like caught up in the space between, or in the years past.

"Don't look so excited now," I joked, my fingers reaching out to touch his forearm, to stop before they made their mark. I let them fall limply to my side.

He nearly smiled. Then he shoved his hands in his pockets and his eyes went tight. It was heady as well as strange to have him respond to my almost joke.

"I don't like when the jam is this big," he admitted in soft tones, drawing me in closer. "By the time each person takes a break playing, going around the circle, you end up playing the song two dozen times through. It takes forever. And playing rhythm that many times around isn't as fun as ..."

I watched his lips move as he talked, and found him adorable as he explained himself. I leaned in, without noticing, and my head tipped back, angled toward him. It was a sensation like falling into a gentle breeze, not scary but still yanking my stomach out of place with the motion. I watched his face, listening to his easy words, until he dropped off speaking.

"Don't look at me like that."

Immediately I shifted my eyes down. My face fell though I tried to keep a smile in place. Ever polite.

"I'm sorry."

"Don't be sorry." Anger colored his voice. I flinched as memories of a younger angrier Cotton flooded my mind. I could easily recall him throwing a punch at my brother, his anger a driving force to violence. Somehow, without realizing, I had relaxed with him while we talked. I had forgotten about his famous temper, because it was something I had buried in the past. "Are you scared of me?"

Cotton's anger ratcheted up as he ground out the question. Shame bubbled up inside me at my reaction to him. What had happened? The shift in dynamic was immediate and I couldn't find my footing.

"No. I ..." I looked up only so far as his chest, not able to bring myself to look all the way up to his surely stormy face. As if not seeing the anger there would lessen its reality. His fisted hands were enough evidence. "I don't know how I was looking at you, I was just ..."

I knew. It was with open adoration; my longing for him seeping out of me and coloring my expression. I could only imagine how ridiculous he found me, too young and naive, practically swooning over him while he talked about something so generic as the jam taking place around us.

Unable to complete a sentence was what I was. Good gracious. I shook my head and willed him to walk away. To go play his banjo and leave me there to sit under the little Dogwood tree, safe at a distance, observing. I wanted him to

14

walk away and stay away because that's what he did. Cotton never came too close to me; it's the way it was for us.

For a suspended moment he stood there, body inclined my way, and I wasn't sure what he would do next.

"I should go."

With that he stalked away with fast stiff steps. I watched the hard line of his shoulders, a glutton for punishment, always appreciative of his strength and build.

My mama had always said to avoid Cotton. I figured that was the best explanation for my massive and stupid crush on him. It was a silent rebellion to let myself covet him. It had always been from a distance. Whether or not I harbored fantasies of him in my head made no matter. Then he was standing there, so close I could smell the soap and musky dark man scent of him, oddly comforting and impossibly familiar. He had stayed beside me too long and we'd shared an almost conversation.

It was something.

In the end he walked away anyway leaving me feeling more alone than usual.

I settled into my saggy bag chair to snack on ice-cold grapes with nothing but my rampant thoughts for company. The heat of the evening was relentless, getting worse rather than better as time wore on and sunset beckoned. I watched Cotton sit in a position that rendered it impossible for me to see more than the back of his head. I watched the musicians jam, and the community mingle around them at the park. I sat and I watched, doing what was expected of me: staying out of sight and out of mind.

Chapter Three

Cotton

Nothing was going the way it should.

Not in the jam. I broke a string during *Foggy Mountain Breakdown*. Shouldn't be a big deal as I had extra strings. It riled me up for no good reason.

Not at work. I had put off hiring someone to help part time for too long and worked too many damn hours in the meantime.

Not at home. Denver was in a mood, worse than usual, and it was lasting for next to forever. Beau couldn't make up his mind if he wanted to ask Elliot to move in with him, or if he'd give in and move in with Elliot. I was sick to death of the back and forth. Dominic was on my last nerve. More so tonight than ever. Too many brothers was my problem.

Not in my head. Magnolia Porter circled my brain, infiltrating my every thought, and it was frustrating as hell. I couldn't shake the image of her gravitating to me, her face a clear picture of her fascination with me. I was certain I had done nothing to warrant her bald interest, yet there it was, plain as day. My head was a war, torn between dashing her hopes and tracking her down to fist my hand in her gorgeous hair.

"Hey, so that Magnolia Porter is looking good. Huh?" Dom elbowed me. His voice a loud whisper; loud enough to be overheard. And it was filled with jest.

I did not punch him in the face. There's that.

Across the circle, Alyssa Hunter and old man Donovan were debating which key to play *Minor Swing* in. I was ready to kick the song off myself and play it in a key no one would

16

know it in, because I felt like being an asshole.

"I didn't notice." I lied through my teeth. More to myself than to Dominic.

"Whatever. You are a terrible liar, brother."

I gave Dominic a look. There it was. He was calling me out on my shit. My teeth ground together as my eyes flashed their warning at him. Rather than intimidate him, it served to make him laugh. He had stopped being scared of my threats or my fists by the time he could hold his own in a fight. We were well matched, really, only he didn't care much for fighting.

It rankled that Maggie had been afraid. That split second when she'd flinched away replayed in my head again and again. Her eyes, deep chocolate brown, framed by thick lashes that fluttered too quickly as she'd tried to catch hold of her fear. Still, she had looked up with those eyes, expressive and open, begging me to give in to her every desire.

Her reaction - the fear, not the glimpse of want before I'd been a jackass - made perfect sense. She ought to be afraid of me and my temper. I knew that better than anyone, and it was exactly why I stuck to hook ups. If I didn't trust myself, why should I risk another person or ask them to trust me?

"I'm just saying is all." Dominic tossed the words out, pretending they were innocent. His lips curled in a Cheshire Cat grin. "She grew up nice."

"Who are we talking about?" Ryan Felty leaned across me to aim his question at Dominic.

I heaved in a breath, not ready to unclench my teeth lest I bite someone.

"Maggie Porter. I was talking to her before the jam. She was wearing these short shorts and this little ..." Dom was pinching his fingers together at his shoulder to indicate the barely-there straps of Maggie's tank top. I hit him before he could finish. "Damn it, Cotton. Not while I'm holding my mandolin."

"She is a person. A real decent one. Our mama taught us better than to reduce her to nice legs in short shorts. So you shut your mouth right now."

Ryan sat back in a hurry. Smart boy.

17

My infatuation with Maggie in years past had bordered on unhealthy. That is a lie. It was nuts. I had put forth a good deal of effort to not think about her since those days. Dominic laughed, his eyes lit with knowing the truth of how I felt about the girl.

"Oh, this is gonna be fun. Real fun, Cotton." It was a promise, his impending enjoyment at my expense.

It had been foolish to sit with my back to Maggie. I had thought stubbornly it would keep me from thinking about her. It would keep me from watching her. Keep me from checking on her and waiting to see if she'd look at me. Turns out, all it did was ramp up my obsessive thoughts of her. Without being able to see her, I didn't know if she was all right. The need to know crawled under my skin, an itch I could never satisfy unless I was in close proximity with her. Which I hadn't been for a long time before this evening. The itch had become a chronic ache over the years, something I could never forget, but that I was able to ignore on occasion.

My fingers rolled over my banjo strings, sure without much effort as we played through *Old Joe Clark*. I was only half invested, if that much. A shame I didn't have my head in the game. Luckily I could pull off that old song from muscle memory and it didn't require my head. It left room for my thoughts to churn.

God, it was ancient history, the drama with her brother. Lucian Porter. A slimy no good jerk of a kid. I'd kept my distance. Until I couldn't stomach the way he picked on his sweet too good little sister. It became something of an obsession to keep an eye on her and step in when Luke bullied her.

Then the truth came out -- every time I intervened, Luke went home and took it out on her worse. I had kept my distance from Magnolia Porter as much as possible since she was fourteen, when I'd learned I was hurting more than helping. Somehow that was ten years ago, and now she was a beautiful woman.

Not as if I hadn't seen her all over our minuscule town. Not like I hadn't noticed her sit under that Dogwood tree near 'bout every week. I had merely perfected not looking in her direction, not allowing myself to fall into the trap that was my unnecessary and crazy feelings for Maggie Porter.

"Hey, so the Hunters are going to Prissy Polly's for a drink."

"And you're telling me this, why?"

I was bent over my banjo case, snapping latches and taking too long on account of my avoidance of people at the moment. Namely my little brother and a pretty little girl across the way. I knew precisely why he dropped the information: to taunt me. He knew why, and knew that I knew why. It wasn't my favorite game.

"Oh, no reason. I thought we might like to join 'em."

"We?"

"That's right, Cotton Alexander MacKenna." He full-named me with a smirk I could hear in his voice. He might as well have his hands on his hips, cocking that much attitude, channeling our mama. "I thought we might like to go out. To the local dive bar. For a drink, or twenty, with friends."

"I am not friends with them."

Dominic's laughter was loud and full. It drew attention because he was so awake and so alive. People longed to be near him if to know his secret. To know how to live, too. Like he had cornered the market on happiness.

"You most certainly are friends with Jacob Hunter. Granted maybe not Alyssa, seeing as she's my age."

No mention of Maggie, which we both knew was the reason he was running his mouth and goading me to go to Polly's. Whether he was teasing me or setting me up for some other purpose, I hadn't figured.

"Whatever." I stood, banjo case weighing me down on one side. My eyes scanned the remains of the crowd. Not looking for Maggie so much as making sure she was gone, and I could avoid her more easily. She was nowhere in sight. Neither were the Hunters, so most likely she'd gone with them to the bar already.

"Come on, Cotton. Seriously." Dom's voice was level. He dropped the showman's face. "You can't avoid her forever."

"Yes, I can."

"Why?" His astonishment was genuine. "Lucian died ... what, like, four years ago?"

"This has nothing to do with him."

"Doesn't it?"

My conversation with Maggie flashed bright hot in my brain, a branding iron. I had brought up Luke to her, placing my foot in my mouth, and broaching the very topic my brother thought I was hung up on. My ability to hide my thoughts from him was apparently nil. Didn't stop me from continuing the farce.

"No, Dominic, it doesn't. I stopped fighting with him ten years ago."

I didn't have to say I wasn't sorry when he died. No one was sorry. Except his own mama; she was sorry enough for all of us. Otherwise the town was caught in a torturous place of being relieved he was gone, and feeling a healthy dose of guilt over not missing him. When his name came up, people would mutter *God rest his soul*, but it always sounded more like *good riddance*. It was a tired tale that had thankfully become old news as years wore on.

"You stopped being a lunatic about Maggie ten years ago. But no way did you stop caring about her."

"Shut up, Dom."

Only a few stragglers remained at the park. Moms folding blankets and wiping dirty hands. Teen girls running around in too little clothes, showing off miles of leg and pretending they didn't notice when you noticed. The tail ends of conversations - well wishes for the weekend, hopes the weather would hold or conversely prayers for rain, last minute plans made for grilling and outings. It all faded into the background of our town, of the central park, of the normal Friday night after jam wrap up. The Hunters and Maggie wouldn't be the only ones to follow up the jam with a trip to Prissy Polly's.

"Why are you fighting this? Just go out with us. Be there, at the same place as this girl, and see what happens."

"Why are you pushing this?" I roared at him before I reined it in. I clamped down the flood of anger. The bloom of red in my brain that left unchecked would haze my eyes. The automatic tightening of muscles, tensed and ready to fight. It had become vitally important I keep control of myself and I had spent a lifetime learning to not lose my temper. "You know good and well I don't date. And you know why. I am not going there."

"I know you think you're a monster. An out of control raging person. I also know that isn't true. You have yourself under control. Never mind which you spent so many years looking out for that girl, there's not a chance in hell you'd hurt her. You'd beat your own ass before you let yourself hurt her."

He had a point. Didn't Dominic MacKenna always have a god damn point? I would rather die than hurt her. A primal protective instinct came into play with her, and it included shielding her from the likes of me. I couldn't risk it.

I sighed, a slow thin exhale of stale air through my nose. I hated the self-doubt. I hated the seclusion. Not that I was a social person by nature. But going home and having a drink by my lonesome wasn't always appealing. On occasion I did want to go out, relax and have a good time, and do it with friends. It had been too long, and the idea of going out started looking good. It tugged at me, urging me to give in.

"I'm pushing this because I know how you feel about her."

"Does everyone know?" And by everyone, I meant our brothers. I meant Maggie.

"Nah. Denver never pays attention to anyone but himself. Joe knew back in the day, but he thinks you got over her. Especially after you were with Haley for so long. Beau knows, of course."

I sighed again, a faster rush of air forcing its way out. I did not wish to discuss this. I wasn't the least bit surprised Beau knew; he always knew everything about everything.

"Maggie doesn't know." The way he said it was like he had a whole lot more to say about it. But he didn't elaborate. Quiet assurance that was strangely full of secrets.

Questions pressed up my throat and I swallowed them down. How did Dominic know what Maggie knew? Did I want to know?

"Fine, Dom. I'll go."

Fighting my own damn self was exhausting. Even as we walked toward the parking lot, I was kicking myself. It was wrong to put myself in her path. She had looked at me like ... like she wanted to keep looking at me. Like she wanted me to keep talking to her. Like she wouldn't mind if I stood there at her side a bit longer. Like I was something. Then I'd gone and scared her. It was probably a good thing, a reminder she ought to keep her distance. A reminder for myself that she was afraid of me, and she darn well should be. But it hurt. Stabbed right between my ribs and deep into my chest to see her flinch away from me. I never wanted to see fear in her eyes. I hated the reminder that she had reason to be afraid of men; that she had grown up with a bully of a brother that instilled fear in her. I hated stupid fucking Lucian Porter all over again whenever I thought about Maggie.

Chapter Four

Cotton

I trailed into Prissy Polly's behind Dominic. Hulking broad shoulders, smooth but bold walk, full of confidence. A bright light in any place, happy to lend that easy assurance to others. A magnet that snagged attention, heads turning to watch him, hands lifting to say hello, greetings called out across the wide room.

I was content to stay out of the spotlight, following behind and not responding to the bevy of *hellos* and *how the heck are yous?* as we passed.

Prissy Polly's was originally an old farmhouse on the outskirts of town; a squat wooden building with a deep front porch. The place had been a spectacular dive bar since as long as anyone could remember. The current owner was a gal named Iris, not that folks much remembered that detail. Far as I knew every owner of the establishment through the years had been a woman that went by the name of Polly.

Scuffed smooth wood floors spread wide and deep. Darkness clung to the corners, offering cover for less savory deeds. Hand jobs, drug deals, mess I stayed clear of and didn't want to know about and ignored gossip about. Tables scrubbed shiny over too many years pocked the space, circled with mismatched chairs prone to wobbling. Country music played a touch too loud competing with the myriad of voices in the packed bar. Beer, sweat, perfume, all tinged with an edge of anticipation permeated every inch.

At a table halfway to the back, Jacob and Alyssa sat with their chairs pushed close together. He had one hand over hers and waved the other in accordance to whatever story he told.

23

Maggie sat across from them, her elbows braced on the edge of the round table. Her smile wide and free, unlike I usually witnessed, and I was entranced by her.

"Jakey Poo." Dominic leaned in and clapped Jacob on the back. Jacob gave him the bird as soon as he pulled back. "Alyssa. Maggie."

"Holy MacKenna Brothers, Batman." Alyssa hopped up and threw her arms around Dominic for a quick hug. She paused in front of me, looked me over, and then gave me a small side hug. My smile was inevitable. She was impossible to dislike. "Twice in one night, Cotton. Color me shocked."

"Mm hmm."

Maggie looked like she'd swallowed her tongue and she on purpose didn't look directly at me. When I went to move toward the chair nearer to Jacob, Dominic shoved me out of the way and stole the seat. He laughed uttering a string of happy curse words. I shot him daggers with my eyes then turned to the open chair beside Maggie. Hands gripping the seat back with too much force, I did not take the seat. My back was too straight, a rod down my back, a dead giveaway to my sudden discomfort. I expended as much effort not looking at Maggie as she did not looking at me.

"I'll get the next round. What's everyone having?"

My generosity a ploy to escape the scene. I chose to walk to the bar and be busy rather than to sit beside Maggie. At the bar I relayed the order. *Fucking coward, Cotton.* Jacob, Alyssa, and Dom were all having beer. Maggie wanted nothing, so I ordered her soda water with a twist. I ordered two whiskeys for myself; downed one at the bar letting it burn my throat and warm my stomach, and brought the other back to the table.

"I am not even kidding! She said that." Alyssa snorted through her laughter, animated by her tale.

I passed out drinks and reluctantly took my place in the vacant chair. All without looking toward Maggie. I didn't need to look to know she was there. Her presence at my side was a pulse that beckoned to me; begged me to slide closer and lean my mouth to her ear and neck. No, I didn't look at her. My fingers wrapped firmly around my glass and I concentrated on

24

not chugging the whiskey.

"She did not. No way. No one is that awful." Dominic laughed and took a long swig of his dark beer. A coffee porter from a brewery a few towns over, the mocha scent encircled him.

"No, it's true. Tell the story, Magpie." Alyssa urged her friend to speak, with a tilted head and pleading smile. A knowing glance passed between them, speaking volumes.

It was harder to not look at Maggie after the story was tossed her way. Alyssa kept laughing and she moved in a way that looked like she kicked her friend beneath the table. Jacob hid behind his beer. Dominic watched me, waiting for me to give in and turn toward the beautiful girl at my side.

"We were at Darlene's for coffee." Maggie's voice was soft. We all had to quiet down and lean in to catch her words. She did that, sank into herself so far that you had to work at staying with her. "It was stupid o'clock in the morning, so I hadn't bothered with real clothes. Anyway, I was walking up to the counter for a muffin to go along with my coffee, and Mrs. Albright was there at the front counter."

I was having trouble following because I didn't know what real clothes meant versus not. I was thinking about the proximity of Darlene's Coffee Shop to my studio, and how close that put Maggie to me. Mrs. Albright. A horrible old biddy. White blue hair, deep set wrinkles, and an affinity at spreading ignorance.

"She looked me up and down, and said, "I didn't even see you back there, which is surprising seeing as you're dressed like a homeless tramp." So, naturally, Darlene was working and overheard, which was so embarrassing. But she sure gave Mrs. Albright an earful."

See now, this is what happens; this is the problem for me. I cannot endure this sort of casual story. Knowing that someone was awful to Maggie. Then knowing she didn't stand up for herself, and instead someone else stepped in. Someone that wasn't me. I was grateful to Darlene, but hated she had to get involved. I wished Maggie had the backbone needed to stand up for herself. I clamped my mouth shut and stared hard at the single cube of ice in my whiskey. The edges had softened, melted into the drink. I made a list of words to describe the color of the whiskey to occupy my mind and stop thinking about the injustice in the world. Gold. Russet. Burnished. Mahogany. Henna. Burnt Umber.

"Oh my God, for real though," Alyssa went on, indignant on her friend's behalf. A quality I admired about the outspoken girl. "And she was wearing yoga pants and a t-shirt. Not trampy in the least."

"Are you saying I looked homeless?" Maggie's voice was light, playful even, not caring. Maybe that was why she didn't say anything to the old lady who had insulted her. Maybe she just didn't care. Her lips curled into a relaxed smile, as she shifted in her rickety chair to aim her body my way. A subtle movement that sent the signal to my own body, turning me slightly so that my knees bumped into her, hot skin on hot skin.

In my mind, Maggie should have been upset with old Mrs. Albright, ready to defend herself. In reality, she told the story with a laugh and seemingly without a care. Truth was, no matter how much I had convinced myself I knew Maggie, I didn't really. What she thought remained a mystery to me. One that drew me to her, wanting to know more.

"Oh, yeah, for sure. You look homeless right now." Alyssa barely got the words out with a straight face.

The girls continued their conversation and I was still hung up on my efforts at unraveling the sweet mahogany haired girl with the shy smile. I had to scramble to keep up. Had to work to keep my face calm, only showing a minor level of interest rather my intense and growing regard.

I glanced over at Maggie before I could stop myself. Her shorts were cut offs, and had ridden up her thighs to expose the length of her legs. Her tank top was pretty and feminine, silky with a floral print, draped neatly over her perky breasts. Her hair was a mess, but it was always a mess. Her curls were out of control even when she worked to get them under control. The effect was that I wanted to thread my fingers into the mess of curls and get stuck there. I wanted to control the tilt of her head when I kissed her.

"I have to go." I stood up so suddenly my chair rocked. I spoke too loudly and people turned to look at the disruption.

"You haven't finished your drink, man. You okay?" Dominic leaned back heavy in his chair, tipping the front legs up off the ground, and gave me a look that said exactly what he thought of my erratic behavior. My brother was able to pass a message in a look, and he wasn't impressed with my showing.

I picked up the glass, downed the amber liquid, then slammed it back to the table. I lifted my brows in challenge to my meddling brother. I could pass a look right back with as much ease.

Five steps, maybe six, summer sandals slapping on the wood floor, and I heard Dominic send Maggie after me. Shit.

I slowed my pace so she would catch me. I wanted to be caught. Running away, I still wanted her to catch me. There were moments when I couldn't remember why I bothered running. I blamed the whiskey for pickling my brain and bolstering my bravado.

She didn't say anything or try to stop me, stepping softly in time behind me, so I kept walking. I held the door for her, and we stepped out to the porch. The night remained thick with heat and humidity, suffocating within seconds. It only served to further drown my resolve.

"You okay, Cotton?"

Good lord, my name from her mouth was something else. The slow spread of poison through my body. I wanted to fall to my knees and beg her to say it again. Instead I looked out toward the parking lot, carefully avoiding looking down the loose tank that Maggie wore.

"I'm fine."

"You don't have to go. I'll go."

"What?"

"Well, you're leaving because of me, right?" Her small shoulders lifted, and she was brave looking up at me, meeting my insolence head on. "I'll go, so you can stay."

"Why would you say that?" My anger was getting the better

27

of me once again. I was in control enough to keep my voice fairly level, but I still noticed the spark of worry that drained the color from Maggie's face.

"It's okay. I know you don't like to be around me."

So simple. The way she said it made it sound uncomplicated. She had no idea what she was saying. Maggie couldn't be further from the truth.

"What makes you think I don't like being around you?"

I shouldn't have asked, because I didn't want to hear the answer. I didn't want to hear her say that she knew I had been avoiding her for a good ten years. I didn't want her to leave on the grounds of making things easier for me. I hated every second that was passing because it was all wrong.

"Because it's true." She shrugged again, like she didn't care. Like, no big deal. But I could see past the small sweet smile and the motion of her shoulders. I could see the pain in her eyes, the hurt that welled up there coupled with confusion.

Without letting myself think, knowing if I did I wouldn't go through with it, I stepped into her space. I placed my body too close for polite conversation. I looked down at her, and I liked the way she tipped her head back to look at me, the way her neck bent and begged to be touched and licked. Her waist invited my hand to take hold and drag her ever closer.

"That is not true, Magnolia Porter."

She swallowed, and I watched the nervous movement. Her eyes were big, and she shivered. This wasn't the same as her earlier edge of fear. Maggie wasn't scared of me hurting her, yelling at her, or picking a fight. This was longing, and a frustrating fear of rejection. As if I might turn her away. All of which made perfect sense, seeing as she was correct and I'd spent a good many years turning away from her.

"I don't allow myself to be around you. That isn't the same thing as not liking it."

Because I was crossing all the lines I'd drawn, I touched her. I placed one hand around her arm, securing her in place. I used my other hand to tuck a thick lock of hair behind her ear, and let my fingers linger, moving slowly, trailing down her neck and to her collarbone. Chills erupted along her skin despite the heat, a reaction to my touch. Her eyes drifted closed. She wanted me to kiss her, body swaying into mine. Her lips were luscious and promising, waiting for me. I could kiss her. I could let myself taste her, then go home with the taste of her still on my mouth. Because I was a greedy bastard I pushed reason out of my head, and leaned down to devour her.

There was no gentleness, not like there should have been. My hands shook as I held her to me. Maggie's soft warm body flush against mine. My lips pressed hard into hers and took from her. She was supple and giving. I nipped her lower lip with my teeth, and she gasped her mouth open. I took full advantage and entered her mouth with a lashing of my tongue. Her hands went to my head, my neck, my shoulders, down to my waist. Small fingers grasping and clinging; searching. In the end they settled on my arms, gripping tightly, like she was afraid I'd leave.

Maggie was soft, trusting, open to me. She was sweet. Her mouth tasted of the tang of lime from her drink, and I licked the far corners of her mouth to claim it for my own. I wanted more. As I continued to kiss her right there on the front porch of Prissy Polly's, my head spun ahead to possible outcomes. I could bring her to my car and lay her across the back seat. I could bring her 'round the side of the building and press her up against the wall. No way could I stop kissing her long enough to bring her home to a bed.

But it was all wrong. I wasn't supposed to be kissing Maggie. I wasn't supposed to have her. She wasn't mine. She would never be mine. I had no idea her level of sexual experience, and I refused to think too hard about it. Either way, she wasn't the kind of girl you took in a back seat or on the sidewall of the bar. She was too good for that. She deserved better.

I ripped myself free from her, panting, and forced my feet to put space between us. Back. And back again.

She worked to catch her breath, chest heaving with effort. She had one slim hand cupped around her throat, and the other reaching into the space I had vacated, fingers clasping open air where they wanted to find my body. Her eyes watched me carefully, anticipating my next move. I could see how she braced herself for me to walk away. She was a smart girl, and she knew already that I would hurt her.

"This is why I stay away from you. I'm not good for you." I snarled the words at her. I threw them at her, then turned and walked away.

When I looked back she was gone. I drove home, my hands trying their darnedest to tear the steering wheel apart, and my head going a million miles an hour.

I was stupid. Mean. Terrible. What had I done?

Chapter Five

Magnolia

I trailed back into Prissy Polly's with an ache in my chest and trembling fingers. I could barely remember how to walk, but somehow managed to slap a neutral look on my face when I sat with my friends at the table. Alyssa watched me, her eyes carefully scanning my demeanor, while Jacob told a story about some guy he worked with that habitually stole food from the office fridge. Dominic didn't take long to make his assessment; suspicion giving away to something like shock and anger, jaw tight and eyes squinted. I looked away before I started comparing one MacKenna face to another, picking apart each detail and learning to read them.

My friends were little more than a blur before me. My brain caught on a loop reliving the previous moments. I had been outside for maybe ten minutes, and it was as if hours or days had passed. Everything was different inside me, my heart pounding a staccato beat against my rib cage still caught up in the thrill, my stomach clenched in the aftermath of rejection, and my traitorous lips wanting nothing more than another taste of Cotton's mouth.

He had kissed me. Cotton MacKenna kissed me. Not a simple thing. Not an accidental slip of lips across lips. A forceful and hungry kiss. I would've sworn it was filled with longing and possession. If I didn't know better, I would've thought it meant something.

But he had been able to stop, to pull away from me, like it was nothing. Left me standing there, cold despite the heat of the night, and frantic with longing for him. I had never wanted anything as much as I didn't want him to stop kissing me.

But I'd known. I had known he'd stop. Logically speaking he couldn't kiss me forever. Even so, I knew he'd come to his senses long before forever, and once he did that, I knew he'd stop kissing me.

My fingertips lighted gently on my lips, a pressure nothing like the kiss, and a sore remembrance.

"Magpie? Hello?" Alyssa was looking at me like she'd called me name more than once. Her little elfin face was pinched with concern, a furrow deep between her brows and her lips pursed.

"Hmm?" I had spaced out, my mind wandering down the road where Cotton ran away from me.

"What happened? You're being ... weird."

"Nothing." I forced my lips to smile, the muscles not entirely cooperating. They still tingled from the pressure of Cotton's mouth. I shook my head and hoped it was convincing. "I'm always weird."

"Uh huh. You are a terrible liar! I don't know why you bother." Alyssa sighed and set her chin in her hand. She blinked at me, waiting for me to spill the truth.

I had little choice; Lyss would never let it drop. My mouth didn't open, not yet. My gaze skipped to Dominic. The last person I wanted to bear witness to the truth was Cotton's brother. Embarrassed heat rushed up and colored my face, and I knew even as I dipped my head it was too late to hide my reaction from Dominic.

"Hey, look, if Cotton did something. Or said something. I'm real sorry." Dominic placed a hand on my arm, his fingers warm and surprisingly soft. The muscles in my arm jumped, startled by his contact, and poor guy immediately removed his hand.

He looked at me like I was a frightened bunny, and like it might be Cotton's fault.

"No. Of course not." I waved a hand toward the door, toward the setting of Cotton's departure, and pretended I didn't care. "He just, you know, left."

I drank the fizzy water that Cotton had brought me from the bar. Sharp with the tang of lime, filling my mouth with bubbles, so that it almost burned. It had been so sweet of him to bring me something fun to drink when I'd told him I wasn't drinking. That small gesture that meant he had thought about me and gone out of his way for me. It was the water's fault I had the guts to follow Cotton out of the bar when he stormed away from the table. Stupid sparkling water was to blame for me kissing him back.

"Yeah. I'm gonna call my brother. Excuse me just a sec." Dominic got up and headed toward the back hallway with the bathrooms and storage. His shoulders a stiff line atop his straight spine. He was past curious and onto pissed in an awful hurry.

What would Cotton say to him? How would the story be translated from Cotton's point of view and for his brother's hearing?

"Shit." Alyssa was excited and leaned farther forward, chin still resting in hand. Wide eyes sparkled at me, going in the opposite direction of concern and leaping to thrilled. "What happened? Say it quick before he comes back!"

"He kissed me."

"Holy shit. Cotton kissed you?" She didn't do a good job at keeping her voice down. I urged her with my eyes to keep it quiet. Her laugh was a wide-open thing, not a bit worried about her volume.

"Yes. But then he just ... left. Like ravished me with his mouth, then pushed away and left."

Ravished. Yes, that was how it felt, like he had ravished me. It played again in my mind, a constant thing, each replay less and less real until it was a whisper of a kiss. A memory kiss that held nothing of the real thing. Ghostly in the end.

"Wow!" Alyssa glanced at Jacob who, bless him, was doing a good job looking uninterested. "This is huge! You think he knows you've had a crush on him for like your whole life?"

"Oh my lord. Stop talking." Panic bubbled in my chest and pushed up my throat. I might choke and die on it. "No, I do not think he knows that. I wish you didn't know that."

"Oh please." She rolled her eyes and sat back hard in her chair. "There isn't a girl in town that doesn't have a crush on at least one of the MacKennas."

"You don't." Jacob intoned. His lips had moved to one side, almost smiling almost stern, as he looked to his wife.

Happy for the reprieve I let them steer the conversation. Alyssa wasn't wrong. The MacKennas were something of a fantasy for all of us. With five of them, each so different and yet so alike, there was something for everyone. Teenage years, filled with slumber parties and whispered secrets, hours spent dissecting each boy we crushed on. For so many girls it was one of the MacKenna boys. We each had our favorite.

"Yes, I do." Alyssa laughed easily, not at all embarrassed by her confession, and Jacob dropped his act to stare harder at his wife. "Have you seen Denver? Ooh wee, that boy is fine. And with a fiddle in his hands he's a God."

My lips twitched into an easier smile. Content to sit back and watch, hard wood chair back pressing into my spine, last sip of fizzy water on my tongue.

"Calm down, woman." Her husband grumbled, a look of jealousy flashed across his features. One that said he was content to let it exist without fight. Acceptance. But he downed the remainder of his beer and slammed the bottle down a little too hard.

"Whatever. You have a crush on him too."

"That is not entirely accurate. Besides which we're both straight so it would never work out."

They bantered, and I knew all was right in their world. Faces slipped back into being relaxed, their easy trust winning out.

"Honey, I promise, Denver will never notice I exist."

"That is not the point."

She leaned in and kissed him on the cheek and did something unseemly under the table involving her hand and his lap. I looked away, and saw Dominic pacing the hallway, appearing at the end I could see every few seconds. Was he still on the phone with Cotton? I didn't want to face Dominic after that conversation. No thank you.

"I'm gonna call it a night." I shoved my glass toward the center of the table and pushed my chair back. The noise in the bar rushed in, no longer in the background, a jumble of voices, glasses clinking with ice, country music threaded through it all, fans droning in a wobbly pattern.

"Nooo! Don't go."

"It's okay. I'm okay." I stood and offered my usual small smile coupled with a small shrug. I was still reeling from that kiss, and I needed time alone to sort it out. More than that, I didn't want to know what story Dominic was getting from his brother or face him after they'd talked.

"I'll walk you out." Alyssa hopped up fast and offered me her hand. She held fast to me as she walked with me to the entrance, weaving our way through the tables packed with patrons, all people I could have recognized if I had taken the time to look.

"I can't believe Cotton kissed you." Alyssa shrieked at me, spinning me around to face her, as soon as we were down the steps of the front porch. Shoes crunching gravel, our movement slow.

"Me neither." The memory was beginning to be painful; squeezing my heart and making my whole chest burn. Yes, it was beginning to hurt, the shock of it wearing thin and leaving behind something awful.

"Jerk." Only she didn't mean it. Her voice was still touched with happiness, on my behalf, because she knew all about my silly crush on said jerk.

"Tell me to forget about him."

"Forget about him." She braced her hands on my shoulders as we came to a standstill in the parking lot. "I have an idea. Go out with someone, and take your mind off him."

"Go out with who? I don't see anyone here asking."

"Hmm." Her lips twisted as she put some thought into the issue.

"No. I was kidding."

Alyssa rarely put effort into setting me up or pressuring me to date. She knew better. I was not interested. When placed in front of a guy, I became incoherent. A guy I liked? Off the charts awkward. Not to mention the complications with my mama's expectations when it came to my dating. As in I

35

shouldn't.

"My brother." I watched the dim outline of my best friend's head nodding. Satisfied with her suggestion. "Kent will take you out. Why haven't I thought of this before? It's brilliant."

"Um, no, it's not brilliant. It is the complete opposite of brilliant." I recognized the quality in my voice that indicated I was halfway to a panic attack. Sometimes working myself into a frenzy was easy as breathing. I shook myself out of it, calmed by the obvious truth. "Doesn't matter. Kent would never go out with me. Does he even date?"

Kent Garner. Nice enough, if not also incredibly boring, and more importantly not interested in me. He was in love with Olivia Hamilton and everyone knew it. Her daddy was full of pride for his daughter, and as such made an edict many years ago about the sort of boys his Olivia could date. Kent wasn't on the short list. Olivia was a sweet thing, pretty in a porcelain doll sort of way, and she was madly devoted to pleasing her parents. Poor girl didn't have any of her own ideas as far as I could tell and only did what her crazy father said she should. It was a sad tale, but I knew Kent well enough by proxy of his being my best friend's older brother, to know that he was still hung up on Olivia and therefore not interested in me.

"He dates." Alyssa nodded her head quickly and her voice turned hard. I knew she was thinking of unrequited love, same as me. "Kent's smart enough to know he'll never get through Mr. Hamilton and being in love with Sweetheart Olivia Grace is dumb. On second thought, my brother is a dummy. But he does date."

"That does not imply he would date me. He's known me next to forever and he has never been interested in me. It's a bad idea."

Alyssa threw her arms up, exasperated with my logic.

A group of girls exited a large SUV, laughter ringing through the night air, and it was clear they were already tipsy if not drunk. Arms were linked to keep from falling as they walked en-masse toward the door. Alyssa and I both watched them go, at an impasse with the date thing.

"Ooh! Vincent."

My jaw slipped open a degree in response. I closed it with a slight rattle of my teeth. I gave my friend a look that she likely couldn't get the full effect of in the weird light of the parking lot. Dark night pressed around us, with yellow streetlights at the edges of the lot casting long shadows toward where we stood near the middle.

"Are you drunk? Did you get high in the bathroom?"

At this Alyssa cackled and flicked my upper arm. I muttered an *ouch* and she laughed harder.

"First off, you need to stop doubting yourself. Kent would go out with you. Vincent would go out with you." Her voice was strong and sure and she was ramping up for a good old-fashioned pep talk on my self-esteem. I put up a hand, a universal sign for her to stop and she flicked my palm. "Magpie, you are pretty and smart and funny and weird, and those are all good things. All you lack is confidence."

"I am going home now. Give me your keys." As much as I loved my best friend and her confidence on my behalf, I wasn't able to hear it. Not when my head and heart were trapped in a fight between what I wanted and what really happened.

"What? No." She slapped at my hand as I reached for her front pocket. "I'll get Jacob and we'll all go. Just hold on a sec."

I sighed and shifted my weight to the other foot, flat sandal sole sliding across the knobs of the rough gravel. I was tired. That bone weary sort of tired that hits all of the sudden and offers no release. Tired of being in the hot parking lot - why was it so blessed hot after the sun went down? Ugh. Of people in general. It was past time for me to hide my head and pretend people didn't exist until I could face them again. Alyssa meant well. But her meddling made me crazy.

"I'll call a cab."

"Puh-lease. You will do no such thing. A cab? What is this, New York City? You aren't calling Wesley Donovan to come pick you up."

"It's a legit business." Giggles were trying awful hard to let loose, softening my mouth. I tamped them down, barely, to get through my diatribe. "He uses his daddy's car and offers a safe sober ride home."

At which point, we both succumbed to laughter. It was mean. He was a good kid. Doing a good thing. Wes worked at the Fox River Auto Shop, which his daddy owned. They kept a few older cars, super clean no frills cars, for people to use when they had to leave their own at the shop. After a drunk driver ran Wes off the road one night, he got it in his head that our little town needed a designated driver. He volunteered as driver for the whole entire town. The best part was that he stayed busy. People called him, and I heard that his brother Seth was driving a second car now. Fox River was full of drunken fools - fool enough to drink too much on such a regular basis they required a driver. That was the part that got me. I loved that people weren't driving drunk. Duh. I loved that Wes was willing to provide such a service. I hated that people couldn't control themselves one iota and arrange to have a sober member in their party, or not drink to delirium. It was like the small town version of Uber, without the fancy app, and usually free of charge.

"You are not drunk."

"I'm sure Wes would drive me home regardless."

She harrumphed. She also texted Jacob that we would all leave. Guilt punched through my gut and settled low and heavy. Lead belly, that was my guilt. I didn't want to ruin their night. I shouldn't have come in the first place.

"Back to Vin." Alyssa cleared her throat in a way that indicated how hot she found Vincent Berry. "Have you seen him lately? With the tattoos and all. Boy is rocking his rebel whatever look."

Fox River, like many small towns, was woefully behind the times. Tattoos were still for bikers and prisoners. Usually both at once. Acceptable only if you were in the military. They weren't for art or expression. Unless you were Vincent Berry. He took off when he turned eighteen, about a minute after graduating high school, and went to Asheville. No place in North Carolina is known for being proud of their weird like Asheville. Music on the streets, art on every corner, expressing yourself freely, yoga studios all over town, all the good stuff including tattoos resided in Asheville. We resided a three hour drive and a million galaxies away from Asheville. Vincent had come home two years ago, when his daddy got sick. He took care of him until he died, and he stayed after to take care of his mama and his little sister. No one had it in their right mind to judge Vin for all his colorful ink or the piercings in his face when he'd devoted himself to caring for his family. Actions speak louder than tattoos and all that.

"He's a great guy." I could say that surely, because everyone knew it was true.

"It's settled. I'll talk to him on Monday."

"What? No. Not settled!"

"What's settled?" Jacob's converse sneakers crunched along the gravel of the parking lot. He slung an arm around Alyssa when he reached us, tucking her into his side. She fit there, her head at his shoulder, her arm snaking around his back with her hand coming to his waist. He supported her weight, for no reason other than he loved her and he could. Almost like he didn't think about it, his body slid into hers out of habit and comfort, their coming together a natural part of their being together.

"Vincent Berry taking Maggie out."

"When did this happen?" Curiosity spiked in Jacob's tone. He kept himself well guarded, careful not to laugh at me or point out the unlikelihood of any such thing.

"It hasn't happened yet. I'm setting them up."

"Alyssa Dianne Garner Hunter." That was a mouthful. "You stop meddling. Maggie can take care of herself."

The look she turned on her husband was brutal. I could see it in the dark, and up close as he was to her face, it must have hit like a slap. She remained attached to his side, twisting to aim her glare at him.

"Did you just full name me? What the hell?"

Uh oh.

"Yes, I did, and I'll do it again. Now stay out of this and don't go around setting people up. If Maggie wants to go out with Vincent, she can ask him out."

"Oh, right." My friend's harsh sarcastic tone needled. I

tensed, ready for the pain of having it pointed out how inadequate I was at dating. "Like you asked me out?"

Damn. She turned it around on him. Ha. I leaned against their spectacularly old station wagon, prepared to wait this out. The night sky was growing heavy, rain clouds and humidity gathering around the perimeter.

"I should have seen that coming. Walked right into it." Jacob threw his hands up. Then lowered his head to Alyssa's height and looked her in the eye. "You're right. You are absolutely right."

"Damn straight I am. You be supportive. I am talking to Vincent on Monday, and he'll ask her out, and before you know it they'll have little tattooed kids running around."

"Tattooed kids?" I asked because I couldn't help it. The idea was too funny.

"He can't have plain ol' regular kids." She deadpanned, and I couldn't decide how serious she was being about the matter. It served to let us all laugh, to pull me into the mix.

"Good, you're still here." Dominic approached. How had I forgotten he was still in Prissy Polly's? "Maggie, can I take you home?"

His face was beautiful and dangerous. Tinged with worry and more than a little bit of regret. Seeing it there, my own humiliation reflected in his expression - and that's what I had decided the drive by kiss had been - hit me hard. My head ached behind my eyes, my throat wanted to collapse and choke me, my fingers curled in so that my nails bit my palms. An overreaction that I struggled to contain, to cover with a blank look.

"Uh."

"Yes. Of course you can." Alyssa pushed me, literally with her hands shoved me into Dominic. "She'd love a ride home. Come on, Jacob baby, let's go."

"Are you leaving me here?" What in the hell was happening? Alyssa dragged Jacob away and they got into their car in record speed.

"I'm not abandoning you. Dominic is here with you!" She called out her last words before slamming the door.

40

In their impending absence, I looked up at Dominic. He stood with practiced calm, obviously trying to be approachable, not that he had to try very hard. I would swear he was regarding me with pity, like he felt sorry for me. Shame burned in my veins, hissing through my body.

I sighed and pulled my lips into something close to a smile.

Dominic pointed toward his truck and I followed after him. He opened the door and gave me a hand up, which turned out was necessary because you had to be six feet something to step into the damn thing. A behemoth black Ford, jacked up with rugged tires, sides splattered with dried mud from some past adventure. Stupid raised up high monster truck.

I had a few seconds alone in the cab as Dominic walked around to his door. It smelled like mint and stale French fries. It was a mess, stuff everywhere, but it was too dark to inspect. I smiled, to find myself in this personal space, shrouded in darkness that helped me pretend I could hide, and I relaxed slightly. This was Dominic MacKenna. He was friendly. Nice. A charming flirt that smart girls everywhere knew better than to fall for. Not scary.

"I'm sorry about Cotton. He's a jerk."

I fiddled with the hem of my cut off shorts, thick threads tugged between my fingers ripping free without effort. Sorry about Cotton. My chest squeezed tight for a beat, before I shoved that pain away.

"You don't have to apologize for him."

He backed out of the parking spot and angled toward the main road. A classic rock station played in the background and I liked that it wasn't bluegrass or country. The night grew darker, the threat of rain becoming a promise, hot and heavy, biding its time.

"I don't have to apologize because I am not responsible for what he did? Or because he didn't do anything that needs apologizing?"

Then he didn't know the details? I turned to observe him, his profile gray against the night, barely lit by the dash and radio of his truck. Strong. Sure. Sorry. A long sigh escaped my nose.

41

"I think that's the longest sentence you've ever said to me. I guess it was a question, not a sentence. You know what I mean."

I heard his breath release in a huff of soft laughter. Not too put off by my rambling. He drove toward town and we bumped along in his ancient model truck.

"Yeah. That's probably true. But you didn't answer me."

"Both." I cleared my throat. Our town blurred outside the windows and I pretended I wasn't nervous enough to hurl in his messy truck cab. "You certainly don't need to apologize for anything Cotton does, in general. I learned pretty early on that it was a waste to try and apologize for another person's actions."

The truth of my brother settled there in the cab with us. As soon as the words were out, the implication clear, I wished I could take it back. I was always saying the wrong thing. My next breath was shaky as I pulled it in and Dominic turned to look at me for a second. His light eyes white in the darkness, his teeth a ghost's smile.

"He wouldn't say what happened when I talked to him. He was plenty riled up though. Which tells me he did something stupid."

Kissing me was stupid. Yep. Without meaning to, I brought my fingertips to my lips. My lips that still burned with the aftermath of having been kissed so thoroughly. My lips that I pretended still tasted like Cotton.

"I'm not very good at ..." I passed my hand in the space between Dominic and me. "I'm awkward and I always say the wrong thing. I don't know what I'm doing."

Dominic was quiet for a minute. Lost in his thoughts and holding onto some residual upset from the mess Cotton had made with me. Dominic's knuckles were white from how tight he held onto the steering wheel, as I waited him out. He turned off the main road and toward my mama's house, weaving through the quiet suburban roads.

The silence felt like a real thing, something swimming in the air that I could grab at and come away with evidence in my hands. It pressed on my ears along with the rumble of the truck engine and the familiar melody of a seventies rock song. The silence between us won out over the truck and music as dominant. I could only focus on how many seconds passed without either of us breaking the silence.

We rode that way until Dominic pulled into the driveway of my mama's house and shifted the truck into park. It idled in a way that shook the truck and my resolve.

"Dominic." I tried to speak over the sound of the silence and the engine to be heard. "Alyssa thinks I should go out with ... well, go out on dates, and I don't know how."

Of all the stupid words to fall out of my mouth, those were the ones I said to Dominic MacKenna. My lungs failed to hold onto the air I sucked in and I was struck with a need to run away. But Dominic sat there, calm and thoughtful, hands falling away from the steering wheel to rest in his lap. Why had I told him about my dating issues?

My dating experience was pathetic. A few guys that had asked me out over the course of many years, none of which blossomed into something more than an awkward first date. Stilted conversations, sweaty palms, cumbersome shared meals.

None of the guys was ever good enough according to my mama, which never helped set me at ease in getting to know a person. After a particularly tense date with a man that had insulted my wild curly hair and had talked only of himself for a solid two hours, home and washing the light makeup from my face, Mama had admitted that she was worried I'd leave her. I could still recall with vivid accuracy the panic in her voice that had pulled my gaze to her face, wide eyes and wobbly chin indicative of her deep rooted fear coming loose at the ends. She was debilitated at times by her own worries, one of which was my moving away from home and leaving her alone. It had been nothing to assure her then and there that I wasn't going anywhere any time soon. I distracted her, pulling her mood up by telling her the horrors of the date.

Alyssa had set me up a couple times, urging me to get out, and encouraging me to be more open. Despite her best intentions, when it came down to it, I was lost when it came to knowing what to do or say on a date. Or with men in general. If I were to dissect the reasons, I'd be left with pulpy mess of childhood trauma involving my absentee father, my abusive brother, and a generalized fear and distrust of men. I preferred not to look at it so closely.

Now, with Vincent Berry as a possible option, I was struck with debilitating nerves.

"What are you asking me, Maggie?" He turned to face me, shifting so that his back was toward his door.

What was I asking him? God, I wasn't sure.

"You're good at dating."

He laughed, and it was a sweet good-natured thing. I smiled a little and looked up at his face. He smiled back at me, with soft eyes and a sweet expression on his handsome face. I was aware I had not asked him a question at all, yet he had gussied it out.

"I am." Dominic nodded, sure of his skills in that arena. He was the type that was sure of everything he did. Maybe because he was good at everything he did. I couldn't remember him ever failing. "But it's not because I learned how. It comes natural to me. But look at Denver, or even Cotton. Neither of them is a lick of good at dating."

People were different. Denver was too wrapped up in his own stuff, playing music and touring. He had been with a few women, discreetly, and with no strings attached. Cotton could have his pick, much like his brothers, with plenty of women interested in him. But he was too serious to date casually. He held himself apart, watching, quiet, too reserved. Like me but with more brooding and darkness.

"So it's not genetic?" I went for the joke.

He laughed again and agreed with me. Neither of us mentioned Cotton, not willing to bring him up again.

"Alyssa thinks I should go out with Vincent Berry."

Dominic nodded his head, a smile still present on his lips.

"Do you want to go out with Berry?"

If he was frustrated talking to me, he was doing a good job hiding it. I was still being awkward, but I wasn't in a state of panic. The reality of that hit me hard, knocking some of the wind from me. He was right there, all huge and marvelously good looking, and we were talking - and I wasn't freaking out. I mean, I was freaking out about not freaking out. But I wasn't freaking out about Dom. He didn't scare me. Huh.

"Sure. I guess." I was ambivalent about Vincent. He was an idea, not a real thing to me at that point. It remained to be seen how I would feel about him up close and personal. "I'm scared."

"Of dating? Of Vin? Of what?"

"Embarrassing myself."

"Ah." His smile had slipped away. "You can't worry about that. Honestly, everyone is afraid of that, Maggie."

"I'll let you go home. Thanks for the ride." I moved to open the door, but he placed a hand on my thigh nearest to him.

"Wait."

I sat, and I waited, watching him retreat from me with a knowing smile. He walked around and opened the door for me, a sweet albeit old-fashioned gesture.

"You didn't have to do that."

"Did you know my mother?" He let out a dark laugh. It was filled with love more than anything, and I kind of liked that it could be both dark and light. That he could love his mother so much, but also joke about her expectations. "Molly MacKenna would smite my ass if I didn't open the door for a lady."

"We aren't on a date."

"You're right, but that is beside the point." Dominic came up short and took a moment to think. "It would be wrong. Never mind what my mama would think, I'd kick my own ass if I didn't open the door for a lady."

I laughed; it was a sweet light thing that let my heart float in my chest. It felt nice. Dominic calling me a lady. Talking to him and joking with him. It was nice.

The smell of impending storm tickled my nose. Crickets chirped and mosquitoes buzzed joining a symphony of night noises around us. My house stood small and ordinary before us, front window glowing with the lamp left on for me. It occurred to me too late to be embarrassed by the overgrown lawn and the shutters that desperately needed repainting.

45

"Well, thanks."

"Hey, Maggie?"

I turned back, halfway up the walk to the front door of my house. Dominic stood in the lights of his truck, his silhouette bold and large, with his hands stuffed into his pockets.

"What?"

"I could take you out."

I took a step toward him. Then stopped.

"What do you mean?"

The sound of his breathy laughter helped calm my pounding heart.

"I could take you out, and I don't know, help you. So you get used to what it's like. When Berry takes you out, you won't be so nervous."

"Oh." I couldn't decide if I was disappointed. I hadn't thought that Dominic would ask me out. Not for real. Then he did, and for one second my brain had tried to sort through how I might feel about that fact. I hadn't gotten around to figuring out how I felt about a fake date.

"I'm sorry. That was presumptuous," he amended, a nervousness coloring his words. Not something I would've thought I'd hear from him. But then I didn't know him all that well, and of course he was a real person and not just the poster boy for friendly that he was in my head. "I shouldn't assume that you would want to go out with me."

"You think I wouldn't want to go out with you?" I took a step forward, and another, until I was in front of him. His body blocked the light, so it wasn't in my eyes, but it shined bright around him like an aura. "Goody goody Magnolia wouldn't go out with the notorious serial dater Dominic MacKenna?"

I loved the sound of his laughter. I joined him, laughing too. There wasn't an attraction there, despite looking at him and knowing he was a fine specimen of a man. I was elated and disappointed at once.

"I did not say that, Miss Maggie." He ran a hand through his hair that in the weird light looked darker than normal. "I know you're too good for me, but it's a practice date after all."

"I'm not too good for you. That was my point." I sighed and

tipped my head back to look at the stark outline of him. "But I'll go out with you. I find that I'm not a wreck with you, and I'm not sure why exactly. It's kind of nice."

"I'm glad I don't scare you." His voice was unusually solemn. Another side to him, another facet of Dominic I would learn about. "I'm not going to think about why that is, because I'm not sure I'd like the reason."

He knew. He knew I wasn't into him. I didn't think he'd really care. But I was okay with not looking too hard at it and just accepting that I was moderately comfortable with him.

"How about tomorrow night? You free?"

"I am free, but I'm surprised you are. How is it you don't already have a date lined up for a Saturday night?"

"To tell the truth, I'm tired of the whole thing." He shrugged and looked past me into the dark or at nothing at all. "I'm getting old."

"You are twenty-four. That is not old." I lightly smacked him with my hand and his eyes immediately moved to me.

"Serial dating is getting old."

"I'm sorry I said that. I shouldn't have."

"No, you were right." We had slipped into something serious. His tone was dark, heavier than I expected from him. It drew us closer, both of us stepping in that last little bit until we were so close we could have fallen together. "I am good at dating. I'm a flirt, and I take out a different girl every other week, and it's all fun and games. The skill I lack is taking it to the next step."

"You just haven't met the right girl. When you do, it will be easy. You'll keep asking that girl out rather than finding a new one."

"Do you have my number?"

I had to scramble to catch up with the change in direction. I shook my head and he handed me his phone. I opened his texts and sent myself a message. I felt my phone vibrate in my back pocket.

"Good, now you do. I'll text you tomorrow and we'll make plans."

"Okay, yeah." Turning, I began walking to my front door

again. "Good night, Dominic."

"Good night, Maggie."

I let myself in. The lamp on the table beside the couch lit, on a timer that let it burn from sundown until about midnight, meant to be a deterrent to burglars. Somehow the idea of a light on meaning we were home and not to be taken advantage of. My mama would be asleep in her bedroom. She took sleeping pills every night and nothing could wake her. She would never know if I didn't come back home at night. For all her worrying, she wouldn't know. There was a freedom in that, but it was coupled with sadness. Course I was too old for her to keep a close watch on me anyway. I had saved up enough to move out, and I had been itching to move out for years. But when it came down to telling my mama that I was leaving her alone, I could never do it. After Luke died, she leaned on me, she told me frequently I was all she had and that she would fall apart without me, and I stayed.

My phone vibrated again, reminding me I had Dominic MacKenna's number.

I was going out with Dominic the next day.

Cotton had kissed me. Then I had made plans to go out with his brother.

Alyssa was setting me up with Vincent. Maybe. Probably.

My head was a mess. I fell into bed, confused about what had happened and what was coming.

I dreamt of forests and streams in the mountains - my favorite places to go, filled with dappled light and waterfalls. I dreamt of running and stumbling, loss urging me into motion, but all the while with sure hands there to catch me. When I turned to look at who was there with me, I could never catch sight of his face. I woke frustrated along with confused.

Chapter Six

Cotton

I had to put the incident out of mind. That was all there was for it. Nothing to be done. No way to undo the damage. I couldn't very well rewind back to the moment I leaned in and put my mouth on hers and make the other choice, the one in which I walked away before tasting her. I'd spent the last five hours throwing paint at canvas in angry strokes while fanatically combing over my poor decisions, unable to truly put it out of my mind.

I should never have kissed her. But let's go farther back and get to the root. I knew better than to have gone to Prissy Polly's to start with - it had bad idea written all over it. That girl was a temptation, one I clearly could not be trusted with.

The barn where I stabbed my paintbrush against the tooth of the canvas was ominous in the middle of the night. An owl in the rafters, his every hoot a reminder that my problems with Magnolia Porter went back a helluva lot further. I picked my way through a lifetime of memories, going back and back until she was a tiny sprite of a girl, and I was doing what seemed like the right thing protecting her. Heat rushed up my neck, anger taking its tight hold on me, even all these years later. She was small, innocent, and afraid of her own brother as he yelled at her. Did I go all the way back to those moments? And let her brother holler at her and push her around?

No. Hell no.

I quit painting about the time I came to the conclusion I wouldn't change things. At least not those things. In fact, if I could go back, I would've done more. Punched Luke in the face, then instead of walking away, I would take Maggie's hand and glue her to my side. For all my faults, she would have been better off with me there to protect her better than I had. But there's no going back.

Damn it.

Friday night had passed, and we were on into Saturday, if you were technical about the time. The storm that had hung heavy in the sky, pressing in around Fox River, was finally breaking. The distant heat lightning crackling closer, with real intent, as the first drops began to fall. Large splats of rain creating a cacophony of noise on the barn roof and surrounding land.

"Shit, Cotton. You sure are making a mess of things."

I looked around the barn, at the paint on every single thing in the vicinity, while Dominic looked at me. He'd snuck up on me; sound of his foot falls lost in the rain. I dropped my brush into a bucket of tepid gray-brown water, my hands knowing they needed to be free.

"That is my specialty. What do you want?"

"I drove Maggie home tonight. After you stormed off like an asshole."

Dominic wasn't one to point fingers. Not one to call names. He was lightest easiest one of us, with the jokes and free love. The way he stared at me was harsh. Those fat raindrops had hit him hard on his way in and dripped from his hair and nose, soaked his shirt, slicked his arms.

"Good. That's good." I nodded and wished I had one iota of control over my own mind. The warring clash of jealousy and gratitude in my head, translated into the jerk of muscles in my arms asking for release.

No, that wasn't right. I did have some control - it was the reason I spent an inordinate amount of time running, doing mundane tasks like chopping firewood, throwing myself into painting. Hell, one time I'd built a tiny house out on the back of the property down by the stream. I kept my body busy and willed it to settle my mind. I had learned control. The thing I wished I had was the ability to change. To not fixate on things to the point of sacrificing my sanity. I would have to talk with Denver. He had the same issue; only he had managed to fully turn it toward his fiddle playing. That hadn't always been the case. And I knew for a fact he wasn't always happy about it. He was lonely even if he didn't know how to be around people. Of all my brothers, I was the most like Denver, only I was still afraid of the hair trigger on my temper.

"You know what? We'll come back to that." Dom moved in closer and examined the frenzy of angry creative energy. "I can't remember the last time you painted something."

"Yes, well, I prefer to take photographs. Cameras don't make near the mess paint does. However, I can't slam my camera with force. I needed to expel a few demons." My voice remained calm. It was a wonder.

"You done?"

"Can't say."

He nodded at me, a slight and tense movement. His jaw was tight; teeth grinding together. I noticed the curl of his fingers, hands fisted. Oh yeah, he was good and pissed. I fed off him and caught up in no time, ready for him.

"You gonna hit me, brother?" I asked with a tip of my chin, almost an invitation.

Dom recognized the challenge in my tone. He met my gaze with one of his own, a conversation that needed few words. The fight was right there, and we were skimming the surface. The joy that stood side by side with the hunger to fight in me was the reason I avoided physical altercations. I liked it too much. Dominic wasn't an unsuspecting stranger. If he picked a fight, he knew what he was getting into, and he wanted me to let loose. I was given a free pass.

Just then, I wanted it.

"Nah, but I reckon you'll hit me."

"Why's that?"

"I'm taking Maggie out. Tomorrow night." He pulled out his cell, checked the time, and one side of his mouth pulled into a mischievous smile. My brother checked the time, feigning interest in it, even as he shifted his weight between both his feet, ready. "Tonight."

I hit him. Square in the jaw. Fuck. The release called to me and begged for more. This, it was a lot more effective than all

51

the damn painting I'd done. It pushed Maggie from my mind and let me focus on Dominic. He shook off the blow and came at me with a gleam in his eye. A wicked enjoyment that he'd pushed me over the edge, that he had something to hang over my head.

We were a physical family. Affectionate. Hugs were given freely, hands clapped on shoulders, elbows nudged into ribs, hair tousled in loving jest. Aggressive. Punches thrown to prove nothing or something, wrestling matches for no good reason, powerful outbursts to settle disputes. Since we were little, it was always that way, and we'd never outgrown it.

Every punch, elbow, and kick Dominic landed on me, I took. Taking my punishment for being a shitty person was something I did well. The pain was real and alive and it anchored me. Not one to stand still, I gave him as good as I got, answering his call. In the end we'd unsettled all the paint and canvases, and we were both smeared with wet paint. Our abrasions a work of art. Paint covered skin that would ripen into equally colorful bruises.

It was a draw. Neither of us willing to annihilate the other.

I offered him my hand and tugged to pull him to his feet. Chests heaved in the aftermath, breaths coming quick as reality caught up with us. Some of the fire had gone from his eyes.

"Cancel your date, D."

"It's not like that." He was breathless, panting, but his lips tugged into that damn smile. Like he knew more than me, like he wanted to dangle it in front of me. Taunting and playful, even now.

"Explain yourself."

"I offered to take her out," Dominic lifted both hands, a sign of surrender, a means to keep me from laying him out again. "As a means of helping her feel comfortable going out with a man."

I let his words settle. The straw that covered the floor of the barn was striped in colors, disheveled as the two of us, and when the sun rose I would take pictures of it. The aftereffects held something of beauty in the chaos. Keeping my head down, I considered his words. I had to assume she had told him as much, that she was uncomfortable going out. The aggressive way I kissed her would be one more reason she was fearful, distrustful. The truth of that shot pain, white hot, through my chest.

"You're going to fake date Magnolia Porter?"

It was impossible to keep the rage from coloring my voice. I didn't bother trying for my earlier false calm. No need with Dom. We were the closest of all of us, and being such, he knew all sides of my fucked-up-ness.

"Listen, Cotton, she's not into me. Not like that. The way I figure, it's win-win." I lifted my face and glared at him. It encouraged him to keep speaking and explaining his plan. "I am tired of vapid girls and putting another notch in my bedpost."

Good Lord, the mention of his bedpost in semi-reference to Maggie had me seeing red again. Thankfully, I had become adept at taking all that kicking screaming rage and balling into something else. Like framing the shots I could take of the barn in the morning and imagining the slant of the morning's sunrays across the now dark space.

"I think taking her out will explain to the ladies of Fox River why I'm not out flirting and serial dating." He sneered the words serial dating, like it was the utmost insult. Huh. "And I think I can help her. I noticed this evening, when I was driving her home, that she relaxed with me. She wasn't looking for an escape or trying to turn invisible. I don't know that I can say that of any other guy."

"I hear what you're saying. Rationally, I agree it's a good idea. I trust you enough to not hurt her."

"But?"

"Ah. The but. There's always a but." I shook my head and shook out my sore hands. My knuckles were split and bloody. "Irrationally, the idea of it makes it difficult not to kill you."

Dominic laughed. It was a heavy dark thing, not his charming endearing public laugh. It helped remind me how much I loved him. He was my brother, and my family was everything.

"I feel I should mention this line of talk came up in particular because Alyssa plans to set Maggie up with Vincent Berry."

"Fuck no." I spit the words. They were a waste because there was no one else to hit and I was done hitting my brother. I contemplated throwing things around, and even allowed myself a few seconds of imagining it. The feel of the wooden easels in my hands, the fantastic crack of splitting wood and tearing canvas as I mauled them. Then I pulled a thin breath in through my nose, and let that impulse go. "That is not happening."

"Why? You have something against Berry?"

"I have something against ..." I was brought up short, of course, because I didn't have a damn leg to stand on. Maggie was not mine. I was nothing to her. I needed to let this go. "I need to not know about this shit."

"You could ask her out. Then she'd be going out with you, Cotton."

"No."

"You're a damn broken record. I think I'll pass on the Cotton is Worthless conversation." He walked to where I stood and gave me a hearty pat on the back. A peace offering that I accepted with a nod. "I'll let you know how it goes."

He laughed on his way out. It was meant to hurt me. No, not to hurt me. Dominic didn't want to hurt me. It was meant to spur me into action. To convince me I should bypass my morals and date like a normal person. Not happening.

***

I didn't sleep. I counted the minutes as they passed until the sun began to rise. Then I took my camera out and took a few hundred shots of nothing. Of light and shadows, of angles and curves, of anything that wasn't alive. I preferred to shoot subjects that I could manipulate, rather than people that always thought they knew how to stand and pose. Family sessions and weddings were the bread and butter, and being the only professional photographer in Fox River meant that I was

54

sought after for such things. On my own time, when it was my preferred way to focus my thoughts, I wandered the mountain paths and captured nature.

That night, when I knew Dominic was out with Maggie, I went full boar stupid. I had little choice. I texted Emily Doyle. I met her at her place, the little apartment above Doyle's Flowers and Gifts. I went into Emily's apartment above her daddy's flower shop where she begrudgingly worked days, and I pretended being with her would satisfy me. Like the jerk I knew I was, for the first hour I pretended I was with Maggie. Then I gave up on that fantasy because it was too far-fetched to believe. Emily was lovely, curvy and willing, and easy to please. She welcomed me into her bed, and happily escorted me to her door when she was done with me. It was an arrangement that worked for the both of us. Until that night. Despite the way I made her squirm and scream, she wasn't Maggie. Her body was wrong. Her voice was wrong. My touching her was all wrong.

I went home and punched a hole in the wall of my bedroom in the family homestead. Then I texted Dominic and told him under no uncertain terms what I thought of his plan. I threatened his life and mine and leveraged to give up everything for another taste of Maggie's sweet mouth.

Chapter Seven

Magnolia

Coffee was already made, scenting the sleepy house with its warm bitterness. Ready, as expected, when I made my way to the kitchen. My mama prepped the coffee the night before, without fail, taking comfort in her routines. Come morning, she would hover around me waiting to clean the pot. She woke early each and every morning, and had one cup of coffee. I poured two cups for myself, one in a mug and the other in a thermos that I covertly delivered to my bedroom for later consumption. My coffee procured, she was obviously relieved and set to cleanup. I had learned to live within her system. We all had our quirks.

"You have any plans today?" Mama asked with a look at me over her shoulder, hands busy washing up in the sink. Pale yellow light filled the room, the window over the sink east facing and making the little room perfect for mornings.

"No." Then I remembered that wasn't true. I had a date that evening, though I wasn't sure yet what that would involve. "Or, yes. But not until tonight."

I watched her rinse the coffee pot and scrub the counters, her back to me where I sat at the bar. Her hair was like mine, a thick tangle of dark brown curls. Her body was softer with age, worn down by her life. Otherwise we looked very much alike.

"I'm replanting the tomatoes this morning. They shot up overnight and got too big for their pots. They'll need little cages, if I can manage it, or I might use bamboo stakes and twist-ties."

I smiled into my coffee as she spoke. Every year she did a

little container garden. Tomatoes, bell peppers, and basil. I had offered to help her with a bed in the yard, but she liked to do it her way. Partly because with pots, she could have them up on a table and not have to bend over the work. Mostly, though she would never admit it, because she had a collection of beautiful flowerpots and she liked the look of the way she arranged them all out front. Stella Mae Porter was known for her artful eye and eccentric tendencies. I liked when I was reminded of those qualities, rather than feeling bogged down by being her daughter.

She hadn't asked about my possible plans. I hadn't expected her to, because I knew she wanted to tell me about her own plans. But I would have to fill her in, or she'd be upset when I left later without having informed her.

"Just use the bamboo stakes. They worked last year."

Her morning cleanup complete, she turned and leaned the back of her hips against the counter. I dug into the fridge and found a cup of yogurt, then pulled almonds from the pantry, and a banana from the bunch on the counter. I combined my ingredients into a bowl while I felt my mama's eyes on me. She often studied me. Like she might miss something, or like I might disappear. It was a tendency that came about only after Luke had died, when suddenly the house had only one child remaining, and I was understanding of the habit.

"Let's go shopping this afternoon," she suggested. "You could use a few new summer dresses. I need shorts that don't cut into my waist all day."

"Just give it up and go with the elastic waistband."

She hated denim, loathed wearing it, and complained about the uncomfortable nature of the material. I had always loved jeans, but she told me it was because I was thinner than her. I didn't know what to say about that, so I didn't say anything. I wasn't especially thin, but I was two sizes smaller than my mama.

"I am not ready to be a grandma yet."

I turned and smiled at her while she rolled her eyes. Elastic waist = grandma pants, or some such thing.

"Yoga pants are for everyone."

57

"Not me. And that wasn't the issue at hand."

She was right. Elastic waist shorts were not yoga pants, but if I was picking comfortable waistbands, I was going with yoga pants. I couldn't help myself either, picking on her about the issue. She hated yoga pants too, as everyday wear. They were for lounging at home - if not for actual yoga - not for wearing in public. Again, it came back the weight thing. I assured her she wasn't too big for yoga pants, and in fact I had yet to see anyone too fat for stretchy comfortable pants. The only caveat was in finding the right size and a material that wasn't transparent when stretched. But that was true for all sizes and shapes.

"I'd be happy to go shopping with you, Mama." I began to eat my yogurt nut fruit mix. This would be a good time to mention my plans again. "I'm not sure what time my plans are tonight. I'll need to be back in time to get ready."

"What are you doing tonight?" Her tone was sharp, like this was the first she was hearing of my plans.

"I'm going out with Dominic. MacKenna." I swallowed another bite while she gathered her thoughts and looked me over. "As friends."

"Dominic. He's the youngest one?"

"Yes. He was in my class at school. I've known him forever."

"I didn't realize you were friends."

We aren't, or weren't, and it was complicated as of yet.

"Oh, well, you know, I ran into him last night at the jam." My words jostled free the memory of having actually run into him. "Like I literally ran right smack into him."

"Nice of him to ask you out after." I couldn't tell if she was amused or on the verge of judgment.

"We all went to Prissy Polly's after the jam, and he drove me home. He asked me out then."

The gears in her head were turning, and I was disinclined to watch. My food was suddenly interesting; I stirred the thick yogurt to fully coat the remaining nuts.

"You went to Prissy Polly's? That place is trashy. A girl like you shouldn't be hanging around a dirty bar. Now you've given this MacKenna boy the wrong idea."

Laughter fought to come up with my throat. Problem was it would bring my breakfast up with it, and that would be a mess.

"I was with Alyssa and Jacob. It's not trashy."

"You think I haven't spent my fair share of time at Polly's?" Oh, I was in for it now. I sighed and scraped my last bite free from the walls of my bowl. A handmade pottery bowl, my favorite of her collection. "I know exactly the type of place it is and the type of people that frequent it."

It couldn't be said that I frequented the establishment. I did not point that out to her. I abandoned my empty bowl and looked at my mama. She was disappointed in me. Worried about me. She wasn't a bad person, a fact I bore in mind as I heard her out.

"Good girls like you, shouldn't be in places like that." She was completely serious. "Magnolia, you are too sweet and innocent."

Alyssa had given me a bumper sticker the day I got my car that read: I only look sweet and innocent. Obviously, I couldn't put it on my car. I kept it in the glove box, and wished I had the guts to display it. I was the good girl, and I made good choices. I was sweet and arguably too innocent. However, I wasn't completely naive.

"I didn't stay long. That's why Dominic offered to drive me home."

That was true. Mostly. Sort of.

"I want to meet him."

"Oh my God." I settled my head into my hands, elbows braced on her spotless counter top. I could feel her eyes on me, and I knew she wouldn't tolerate me throwing a fit. Not that I ever dared. "I feel certain you have met him. Fox River is the size of a shopping mall and we've met every single shopper."

I heard her huff at my lame comparison. Fact was we were too small a town to have a shopping mall. It was ironic, what I said. No less true. There was no chance she hadn't met Dominic at some point. Our families had ties, even if they were mostly related to the days when Cotton and Luke would get into fights and the subsequent fall out.

"I don't remember meeting him. If I did, it wasn't when he was taking my only child out."

I bit my tongue. Held it between my teeth to keep from saying something, anything, to her. I had to take three full breaths before I could get past the *only child* jab she threw my way and the immediate effect it had on me.

"We're going out as friends. It's no big deal."

"I know your friends, Magnolia. I do not know this boy."

"Okay. Okay. You can meet him."

I mean, what was the big deal, right? I got up and walked away, leaving her there to think about having an only child, and to distract herself with her tomato plants. Somehow, no matter what, I always felt like a terrible daughter.

When I checked my phone, I had a text from Dominic. More than one. I couldn't help smiling at my phone because he was adorable even in text.

Dominic: *Good morning, sunshine.*

First thing I noticed was that he texted without text speak. He wrote out words, and used a comma as well as a period. Nary an abbreviation. I was pleased by this discovery because I detested sifting through the gobbledygook that was meant to pass as words and sentences in some texts. Rather than an inner child, I had an inner old lady that liked her real words and (mostly) correct grammar.

Dominic: *Is it too early? I don't know what time you wake up. I was up late last night dealing with ... well, things. A particular thing. Rhymes with Rotten. Ahem.*
Dominic: *So, tonight. Hmm. What shall we do pretty girl?*

Next thing I noticed was that he was cute and flirty even while texting. How was that possible? It made no sense to me that his short electronic snippets could color my cheeks pink.

Me: *Good morning, D.*
Me: *I wake up early. It's my mama's fault. She has the*

coffee pot set to brew at 5:45 every morning, and if I don't go get some, she'll dump it by 6:30.

That was true. She announced one day she would give me an hour. Turned out she could only last 45 minutes before giving in to the call to clean up the coffee pot and put things right. I would hear the coffee maker beep at 5:51, it's work complete, and I would spend the next few minutes convincing myself I wanted to get up if for no other reason than to secure my coffee. By the time I got up and moved around, I was up for the day.

Dominic: *Then it's a matter of life and death.*

He responded before I could tap out any suggestions for our friend-date. I laughed. He sent an emoji of a skull and crossbones.

Me: *You are so cute. How do you manage to be adorable in text? It's unfair to the rest of us.*

I hit send, then forgot how to breathe. The air in my lungs struggled to release or pull in something fresh, burning behind my rib cage. What was wrong with me? I was always saying the wrong thing, or too much, or something ridiculous in real life. I could blame any number of things: nerves, inexperience, whacky lack of thinking before speaking. I had no such excuses in texting. I was given the opportunity to think and compose. Ugh.

Dominic: *You think my text skills are adorable? I think it's wonderfully fair to you - perhaps unfair to my competition.*
Dominic: *Not that I have competition. As you and I are friends. I do worry I'm setting you up to be disappointed by future text dialogue.*

I was giggling and blushing. A desire to fall for Dominic struck me so fully; I sat on the edge of the bed, clutching my phone. I should try to fall for him, to harbor a massive crush on this wonderful boy. But even as I tried to change my heart, I could only think of his brother. I knew that Dominic knew that I would be thinking of Cotton, and that it was precisely his brother he worried would fail to excite me via simple texting. I didn't worry about how Dominic knew I liked Cotton - I knew he knew. I suppose it was possible he was thinking about Vincent Berry. Assuming Alyssa could pull off the set up, I might be communicating with him soon. He struck me as a sweet texter, based on nothing but his generally sweet reputation.

Me: *You are setting the bar unfairly high. It's true. I will compare all future texting with boys to this.*
Me: *(I'd recommend you scale it back, but I am too selfish, and I won't deny myself your full abilities).*

Again. I did it again. I hit send. Then two seconds later I realized what I said, and I cringed. I lay on my back and held my phone over my face. Holy hell. I won't deny myself your full abilities? What was that?

Me: *Ignore that. What are we doing tonight?*

Dominic: *No chance. I'm basking in your praise.*
Dominic: *Tonight. Yes. I say we go traditional. Dinner and movie.*

Me: *Where? I'll meet you.*

Last ditch effort to thwart my mama meeting Dominic. It would stir up trouble in my house, but I could deal with it. I could deal with her disappointment better than I could deal with living through the moments of her speaking to him.

Dominic: *What? No way, no how. This is a "date." I will pick you up. Six.*

I groaned and dropped the phone to my bed. It was twin size, covered with an old quilt we'd gotten at a craft fair when I was a kid. I'd seen the quilt across the room and fell madly in love with it. Crisp white, butter yellow, and sky blue, in a wedding ring pattern; and I needed it. I coveted it. Luke was being terrible that day, using a loud voice to announce his disdain of homemade things to the building. He stalked around acting like he was better than the people there displaying their carefully crafted goods. I didn't ask for the quilt, knowing better. I swiped at tears as we walked away and kept my mouth shut. Two months later, at Christmas, I woke up with the quilt over me. My hands gathered the worn soft fabric and held tight, a solid good memory, proof that sometimes good things could come my way.

Me. *Nice use of air quotes for our "date." See you later, D.*

Chapter Eight

Magnolia

I stuffed my phone under my pillow and refused to look at it again. Instead, I went outside and helped my mama repot her tomatoes. We fell into fits of laughter as we tried to secure the bendy stalks to the bamboo stakes. I loved gardening and yard work, the sun hot on my skin, dirt beneath my nails. With my mama, there was always to be some mishaps and resulting laughter.

After we cleaned up and ate a simple lunch, we went shopping in the neighboring towns, hitting up thrift shops as well as boutiques. I found a couple light summer dresses that I liked, and was pleased to buy them. We came home feeling accomplished and it went a long way to distracting me from being nervous about my upcoming friend-date.

Back home, there was only time to get ready, then Dominic would be arriving to pick me up.

"You'll wear one of your dresses tonight?" Mama asked, likely anticipating my answer.

"Um, yeah. I was thinking I'd wear the boho one."

"I agree. The seersucker is nice, but perhaps too nice for a casual evening with a friend."

When she said *friend*, it sounded like she meant *date*. But not just date, more like *why the hell isn't it a date*. I sighed and finished pinning my hair back. We were both in my bathroom, while I tried to secure my hair up off my neck, and to do it in a manner that looked pretty. It involved a lot of tiny braids and a lot of Bobby pins. On the one hand, my mama wanted me to date, to find love and happiness, to get married and give her loads of grandchildren. On the other hand, the one most often seen, she wanted to protect me from getting hurt, and she wanted to keep me at home as long as possible. Drawing out the years and our time together, holding tighter the older I got, knowing it wouldn't be long before the future was now.

She smiled at my reflection. I used to watch her get ready. In the mornings, when I was little, I would go into her bathroom in the mornings and watch her do her hair and makeup. I would sometimes read storybooks to her. Other times we would talk back and forth. There were days we were silent, just together. It was a strange reversal to be an adult, to be the one getting ready to go out, and for her to watch me.

"I'll let you get dressed."

I detected sadness in her tone. Unsure if it was because I was grown up, and she was remembering the same things I was from when I was a little girl. Or if she had reservations about my non-date, sending me out with a boy and trusting I would behave. My heart ached in a way that was dull and familiar, as I thought about Luke. She was possibly thinking about my brother, and that he would never date again, that he wasn't here with us, and how I was all she had. I took all those gloomy thoughts and shoved them into a box in the back of my head. The one I kept under lock and key and stuff full of all things Lucian Ezra Porter.

The doorbell rang only a second after I had pulled my dress on. I hurried to the front door to intercept, only to be too late.

"Nice to meet you. Please come inside."

I rounded the corner from the hallway that led to my bedroom in time to see my mama step back and usher my "date" inside our house. The house was okay. I had always liked that it was small and that my mama was weird. Art hung on every wall, paintings and photographs, hung with frames that matched nothing. Pottery sculptures and bowls, glass orbs and figurines, wood carved creatures and abstract nothings, settled along every flat surface. There were books everywhere, trinkets collected over my mama's lifetime tucked into every nook, and people said it was like being in a museum. It was warm and real and very true to Stella Mae Porter.

Dominic came in with an open smile on his face, his gaze

promptly landing on me. His dark blue eyes were rich with good humor, and they stayed on me rather than examine the room around us. He wore jeans and a salmon colored t-shirt that looked amazing with his skin and clashed horribly with his strawberry blonde hair.

I did notice the way his size impacted his clothing. It wasn't something you could look at him and not notice. Jeans that hung low on his trim waist, shirt that stretched across his broad chest with fabric taut around his enormous arms. Boy clearly worked out on the regular. I also noticed that there was no skip in my heartbeat and no clenching in my gut. I could appreciate the beauty of him, but it wasn't for me. I found, once again, I was disappointed.

There was nothing I could do to prevent the immediate longing I had for Cotton. How it obliterated any chance of attraction to another guy. Dominic, here to take me out. The idea of Vincent asking me out. Cotton's kiss. It was all too much, a toxic mix of stress in my stomach, swirling and threatening to make me sick.

Still, I recognized that the reason for my relative calm with Dominic had everything to do with not being attracted to him. I would take it. It wasn't a bad thing to have friendly feelings for this particular MacKenna.

"Hi."

"Evening, Maggie. You look good enough to eat." He pulled me closer to him, grabbing my hands and tugging until I was at his side. He smelled like cinnamon and sugar with a touch of coffee. He smelled good enough to eat.

"That is hardly polite. What would your mama think?"

I went red, embarrassed she would bring up his mother, who had died five or six years ago. The town had taken it hard, Molly MacKenna having been highly respected and an active supporter of the festivals that took over downtown on the weekends. The boys had taken it harder, their mama having been their only parent as long as anyone could remember. Every one of those boys worshipped their mama. She was strict, kind, patient, expected her boys to be gentlemen, and loved by all. With the notable exception of my own mother; to be fair she didn't like much of anyone.

"She'd agree with my assessment, I'm sure." Dominic had an innocent expression on his face as he responded to my mama. Not a trace of concern marred his features, like he wasn't bothered by my mama's words. "We'll bake her into a Maggie Pie."

He winked. My mama scoffed and made a point to not respond to that line of talk.

"What are your plans for the night?"

Now, my mama was always polite to people. Without fail. Sometimes it was passive aggressive polite, with a *bless your heart* tacked onto the end. Or it was said in a tone that painted a picture different than her words. The sugary syrupy consistency of her words were too much when she was displeased with a person. She stood there, head cocked gently to one side, looking up at Dominic MacKenna, and her words were politely inquiring. Yet, you couldn't miss the undertone of warning and skepticism. I stiffened and held my tongue.

"Dinner and a movie, Ma'am." With a sympathetic squeeze to my hand, Dominic gave his obliging answers to her mock-pleasant inquiry.

"That sounds lovely. What time will you have Magnolia home?"

"Okay." I stepped up, putting myself between the two of them. Enough was enough. "I don't have a curfew. I'll be home when I'm home."

For one second her eyes went wide, and her lips went thin. I held my breath and waited.

"Have fun." Her voice was schooled. But she couldn't stop talking, couldn't let us go with that. As Dominic held the door open for me and I stepped through, she called, "Be good. Don't do anything I wouldn't do."

"Oh God. Go, just go." I pushed Dominic with both hands and closed the door behind myself.

"What's that supposed to mean?"

"She's had her share of drunken one-night stands. She expects better of me."

The look on Dom's face was priceless. Truly worth seeing. I

wish I had thought to pull out my phone and snap a picture. I ignored the punch of guilt that followed my words.

"I am not going to comment on that."

"Good idea."

I shouldn't have said it. That was a terrible thing to say. Thing was, my mama was single from the time I was ten. She wasted no time going out, usually outside of Fox River, looking for a good time. Other than a couple semi-long term relationships with impressively repulsive jerks, most of the years since my daddy took off, she slept around no strings attached. Not that I blamed her. Maybe I had judged her when I was younger, but as an adult, I could understand her reasons. Single mom, working multiple jobs, struggling with a particularly challenging child, of course she needed an escape from those parts of her life.

Trouble was she was unrelenting in her strict standards for her daughter. Me? I was not to date certain types of boys. There were places she would never want me to go because of the way it would tarnish my reputation. Mostly she didn't have to say these things to me, it all came wrapped up in the tidy box of expectations of my being a Good Girl.

Every so often she felt the need to drop reminders. Things like never letting a man give me a hickey, because it's tacky and announces to the world a girl is easy. No public displays of affection, showing off what should be private, because it was nasty. My mama considered it a joke to remind me when I did go out, not to be her. She could be wild, reckless, and without consequence. I was afforded no such liberties.

Chapter Nine

Cotton

Not like I was going to obsess about it. (Any longer than I already had done). Grown man, with a life, moving on.

Dominic could take Maggie Porter out all he wanted. He was a good guy, and they were friends, or "friends," whatever. She should have someone taking her out. As far as guys go, my brother was a damn good one. That was that.

Trouble was, I didn't believe my own good advice.

I went to the studio to work. I was about six photo shoots backlogged on editing. That was the way of it. The wedding I shot on Sunday had to sit and wait until I finished editing all the other photos that came before it.

Three years earlier I had found a space downtown Fox River and set up shop. Before that, working from home was, well, not working. I lived at the homestead because it was big enough to have space for all of us without feeling crowded, it afforded us time together, and let us help out our mama when that had been a necessity. Joseph was the only one that had moved out, and he had done so for college and never come back. He lived on the other side of town with his prissy no good wife and his beautiful squishy children. The rest of us stayed at home. Denver would never leave - he inherited the house when Mama passed. It was his. But he had no interest in living in the place alone, and I couldn't blame him. It couldn't be said Denver was much into having people around, but he loved us and he would be swallowed up in that big old house all on his own. If he ever settled down to start a family, the rest of us would find other places. Until then, Beau, Dominic, and I, we enjoyed being a big rambunctious family.

That being said, home wasn't an ideal work environment.

The space I leased was in the oldest building downtown. The Fox River Hardware Store resided below me. The building was originally bank slash mayor's office slash government official offices. They all split and went their separate ways a century ago, at which time the Lawson's set up shop and have since run the hardware store. Brian Lawson had taken over for his daddy back when I was a kid, and he brought life back to the shop and to downtown. He was a go-getter and organizer. Once a month we did a Third Thursday event, all the downtown shops staying open late, and the townspeople all coming out. I wasn't much into the events, and left business cards on the doorstep for anyone interested. My space was reached by an ancient wrought iron set of stairs on the outside wall of the building, topped with the smallest balcony space ever conceived that threatened to pitch you off, and was likely never meant to be usable space. I loved it. Once inside, there were walls where there shouldn't be, with archways carved too low for my height. There was a loft reachable by a wooden ladder I had made myself. It was all bricks, the walls and the flooring, and they were all uneven and a tripping hazard. It had become my sanctuary. I had a little office to work. I had a room set up for clients to come in and see their prints.

"You working or avoiding people in here?"

Beau. My big brother let himself in - I shouldn't have given him a key and trusted him not to drop by - and called out to me. I groaned, but despite wishing he'd left me alone, I couldn't rally any real venom toward him.

"Both."

He cropped up in the awkward doorway from the viewing room into my office. He was the shortest of us, but he was taller than average and had to stoop to enter fully. People referred to him as a Golden Boy, with his thick blonde hair and topaz eyes, full red lips, and bringing his own light into every space. Perpetually up-lifting.

"Hiya, Little."

I let out a dismissive grunt, while waving him into the

room.

Story went, he had called me Baby Brother, and simply Baby, until Dominic was born. At which point Dom became Baby, and I became Little Brother. And just, Little.

"Hey, Beau. What's up?" I hugged him, one arm wrapped around his steady shoulders, my nose assaulted with his sharp citrus soap and cologne scent.

Of all my siblings, wrong may it seem, he was my favorite. By a long shot. I wasn't sure I loved him more so much as different than the others. I was closest to Dominic, but it was Beau I turned to most and whose presence was always a balm.

"Nothing." His smile was wide, and he batted his eyelashes at me. I sat back down and rolled my eyes at his mockingly flamboyant gesture. "I need you to house sit for me."

"Sure." Beau didn't have a house, but I knew he meant Elliot's house.

"God, I love you." He sank down into the other chair in the room. The one he had brought himself and put in the office because he hated when I gave him my chair and stood while he sat. An antique wingback chair, with buttons tucking the fabric and making it uncomfortable to sit in for any length of time. "It's this weekend. Elliot made plans for us to go to a hot air balloon show."

"And that is why Elliot wins at life. He's phenomenal."

"I know, right?" Beau lived every day fully, and as such he was newly in love with his wonderful boyfriend on a daily basis. They were quite the pair and if they weren't both so loud all the time, I'd never want to leave their company. "God. Who thinks of that? Anyway, he'll worry about the African Violets all weekend if you don't go sit with them."

There were pets to consider as well as the plants.

Beau had a cat that lived at the homestead with us. A scrappy calico monster that needed nothing other than food in her bowl. Between Denver and Dominic, one of them would keep her fed with Beau away. Birdie - yes, the cat's name was Birdie - would howl incessantly until someone catered to her simple needs, which left Beau satisfied she wouldn't starve to death in his absence.

71

Elliot and Beau had adopted a cat together three years ago. Jango was a behemoth orange cat they guessed was a Maine Coon. He was affectionate in as much as he would purr at your feet and wanted to be petted under the chin for perhaps a minute. Then he'd follow you around and stay close but not require any additional attention from you. It was a happy agreement as far as I was concerned.

The biggest job at Elliot's house was his plants. Checking the soil was simple enough, and it shouldn't have been a job that caused me any stress, especially over the course of two to three days. But then I would remember how important these plants were to Elliot, how much time and energy he devoted to them, and I was terrified they would die on my watch.

Beau went over the care of Jango and the plants, all of which I was familiar with because it wasn't my first time house sitting. Somehow, I was the responsible one of us. Denver could handle ill-tempered Birdie at home, and tolerated Jango if need be, but he flat out refused to get involved with the plants. I knew it was because he worried about killing them, and hurting Elliot in the process. Joey would never give up his time to help out. But we let him get away with that because he had a family to take care of and knew his kids should come first. Dominic had volunteered in the past, and loved the cats, but he was unreliable. Dom was likely to forget to shut the door, to over water the flowers, or forget about them entirely. He was good for willingness, not so good with the follow through. That left me. I wasn't particularly fond of plant care in general, but I liked Beau and Elliot enough to lend them a hand.

"You're upset about something. What's going on with you?" Housesitting job settled, Beau got down to the business.

"Nothing."

Beau's eyes inspected my face. He didn't believe me, as I knew he wouldn't.

"You'll tell me eventually."

"Not this time." I assured him. Would I admit how hurtful I'd been with Maggie? How careless? No, I'd much rather not.

He swallowed, and I knew I'd hurt him with my omission.

Beau didn't like it when we kept secrets from him. I figured it was middle child syndrome that made him mind being left out more than the rest of us.

I'd been kidding myself thinking I could forget my state of despair, forget the way it ate at my insides, and how the agony of it showed on my face. I was the brooding one, the serious one with the fuck-off face. With most people, I could hide my inner turmoil behind that veneer. Not with Beau. *Inner turmoil?* I was an emo jerk wallowing in a vat of nothing; nothing but trouble of my own making. I had determined, through experience, that hooking up with a different girl wouldn't work. It would not purge Maggie from my system. I would need to find something else, a hobby that occupied all facilities mental and physical, as an outlet. I was lacking ideas.

"If you change your mind, you know where to find me." He clasped a hand over my shoulder, giving a meaningful squeeze, before heading out.

"In a hot air balloon?" I called the joking words out too late, after he already closed the door, locking it behind him.

Sealed inside my studio, I turned back to my work. Loneliness gnawed at me, pressing in on all sides, and I found myself looking out the window over Main Street. Hiding away up here wasn't doing me any favors. Doing what I'd always done wasn't working.

I thought about Dominic, his confession that he was tired of meaningless hookups. We were going through quarter life crises or some shit. I was sick of the white painted bricks that imprisoned me, sick of my self-imposed solitude, sick of avoiding life. I had my reasons for distancing myself from people. Namely my hair trigger temper.

I was doing the community of Fox River a favor by not exposing them to my brand of crazy. But I couldn't bear it anymore.

Chapter Ten

Magnolia

At twenty-four, I still didn't know what I wanted to be when I grew up. I had ideas about being a wife and mother, and the kind of person I'd like to be, but not career wise.

Growing up, I remembered those kids who were sure and never wavered. Those same folks who now worked jobs in their chosen field. Alyssa, for example, always knew she wanted to be a nurse. After high school, she went to Western Carolina University, got her BSN and now happily worked at the Fox River Medical Park. The town was entirely too small for its own hospital, and for most of its existence there were only two doctors in town. About fifteen years ago with another doc moving into town, and a desire for something more, they pooled their resources to create a central location. Over the years, they'd grown to have a radiologist, a nutritionist, and a separate children's and elder center. Alyssa's goals were clear-cut and she didn't hesitate to make them happen. Maybe it was because her older brother Kent always knew he'd be an accountant and he did exactly that, and in record time because he finished college courses before he finished high school. Whereas my brother had no goals, worked pretty darn hard at sabotaging anything good along his path, and I had no example. No positive role model or good influence.

My mama had gone to college for a couple years, before dropping out to have Lucian. After that she stayed home with us kids. It wasn't until my daddy took off that she needed to find work - something made more challenging due to her lack of education and lack of job experience and being a single mother of two kids. She settled for working jobs that paid the bills rather than doing what she wanted. I wasn't sure she knew what she wanted to do when she grew up any more than I did.

I couldn't blame my lack of ambition on my family, but there it was an obvious influence, and I was floundering.

I wound up working in the Fox River High School front office because at the time taking the job was a practical and good choice. I'd always told myself it was temporary, something to give me a paycheck until I found something better. By better I meant utilizing my degree in birth to kindergarten education. When I chose my major, it was for lack of a better idea. After my mama pointed out that it was ridiculous to waste four years of college to work in a daycare, I stuck with my major as a form of standing up for myself. Alyssa told me one time that I was only able to stand up for myself in that arena for the fact that I didn't actually care. It was something that didn't matter to me, and therefore it wasn't too scary to stick to my guns about the issue. She wasn't wrong. I had lived at home during college because it made more financial sense to stay local. It was a forty-five minute drive to Spencer Community College in a neighboring and slightly larger town for classes, and I opted to take as many online/distance classes as possible. When the high school's principal, Mr. Nesbit, offered me the job in the office, as an administrative assistant, it was a good opportunity. My plan was to keep the job as long as it took me to get a job at a preschool. The reason I kept the job was twofold. One, I hated the preschool in town, finding their philosophies on childcare and education outdated and stifling. Two, my mama insisted that working with preschool aged children didn't constitute a real job.

During the summer months, I worked part time. There was enough to do with summer school and preparations for the coming school year, to keep me on staff. All these years later and I still found it weird being at school during the summer. At first I thought it was a residual feeling after a lifetime as a student. I came to realize that it had more to do with the school itself and the smaller population of staff and students. It was strange to be one of three in the office rather than one of six or more. It was odd to walk the hallways with so few people milling around. The students behaved differently too, responding to the summer themselves, so the mood of the place was altered. It was the high school version of a ghost town.

The phone on my desk rang, and I knew before I answered it would be Alyssa. Shortly after I took the job we found the loophole in the no cell phones rule. I kept the calls short, and we bypassed having to go without talking.

"Fox River High. Maggie Porter speaking."

"Maggie Porter speaking." Alyssa lightly mocked my professional tone.

"Ha. Ha." I rolled my eyes and twiddled with the phone cord. Phone. Cord. Such a throwback. "What's up?"

"Bring me lunch."

"You're so bossy." My laugh gave away my feelings on the matter, being that I wasn't put off by her bossy pants demand. "It will be late. I'm off at one."

"Ugh. I'm starving!"

"Vending machine, Lyss."

"Yuck. Okay. I'll see you in a few hours."

As soon as I hung up the phone, Mr. Nesbit left his private office and approached my desk. Slick gray hair parted on the side and swept over his shiny balding head, sharp eyes and sharper nose. One of those voices that stopped students in their tracks.

"Ms. Porter." He was a good principal. An all-around good guy. He was stiff and formal. It was off putting. Which was maybe the point. "Need I remind you that you are not to take private calls during work hours?"

I stifled a snort. My eyes managed not to roll. If I could do anything, it was keep a straight and sweet face while falsely agreeing with a person. It was a skill I had honed over a lifetime of going along with whatever my mom said/wanted/expected.

"Yes, sir."

He lifted his bushy brows and gave me his stern face. I wanted to not care. Instead, my stomach ached. Guilt or shame, I could rarely distinguish between the two, made itself known. My head said, *I kept it short and I am allowed to take a five minute call,* while my gut said, *why would you break the rules and put yourself in this position to disappoint Mr. Nesbit?* I was sick from the back and forth of it.

Thankfully Mr. Nesbit was a man of few words. He shut himself back in his office for the remainder of the day. I fielded calls from parents, worked on a few schedules that needed rearranging, and filed paperwork. There was never a lack of paperwork in the front office.

Egg salad croissant sandwiches in hand, I went to the Fox River Medical Park. Alyssa worked in the urgent care, and as such her schedule was sometimes difficult to coordinate lunch breaks. I shot off a text and sat with our lunch at our regular spot at the picnic table off the southwest corner of the building. It was too hot to be outside mid-afternoon in the summer. Not that such a thing as heat would stop us. A large oak provided shade, and I secured my hair up off my neck. Following hours in an office with windows that looked out into the school hallways, I craved the outdoors and sunshine.

"Lunch is a decoy."

I jumped when Alyssa joined me at the table. She yanked her food out and eyed me over the paper bag. She wore lavender scrubs, and her hair was pinned up in a severe bun.

"Um. For what?"

"I talked to Vincent."

Her smile gave away enough for me to know she was pleased. I couldn't pinpoint what that meant for me. I licked my lips and pretended to be busy drinking my sacrilegious unsweet tea.

"I kind of forgot about that."

It was a testament to how much I was preoccupied with Cotton, and to my efforts to not be preoccupied with Cotton, that I had forgotten about Alyssa's plan to set me up for even a minute.

"What!?"

"Sorry."

"You, my dear, are hopeless." She spoke with sandwich in her mouth. "But, look, it's all set up. Friday night. Plus it gets you out of going to the jam."

Did I want to get out of going to the jam? Granted bluegrass wasn't my favorite thing, but I went nearly every week because despite myself I did like getting out and being a member of my community. I wouldn't see Cotton if I missed the jam.

"Oh God." She didn't just give him my number. She didn't encourage him to ask me out. She planned a date. "What am I doing with Vincent on Friday?"

"Getting tattoos?" She laughed and swallowed her last bit of lunch. Her break was short, and she had gotten in the habit of eating at least twice as fast as me. "I don't know. He'll call you."

"Call me?" I pressed the heel of my hand into my forehead. I hated the phone. I hated answering the phone, talking on the phone, making calls. I did it for work, but somehow that was different.

"I'll tell him to text you."

"Please! I can't answer the phone and have a conversation with Vincent Berry. Can. Not."

"Hopeless, sweetie." She took my hand across the table and gave it a squeeze. "It's hot as balls out here."

"I'm ignoring that." I picked at my food and sipped at my tea. The paper cup was sweating profusely in the heat, and the ice was melting into my tea and watering it down. Alyssa was crude generally because she found it funny, but also to see the looks on people's faces.

"Jacob and I are out of town this weekend. Do not back out of this date."

"I won't." I might have had a history of doing that exact thing. Only after an established history of horrible dates.

"Promise me you will go out with Vin. Give him a chance."

"I said I'd go."

"Promise."

I sighed dramatically, but nodded my head.

"I promise."

78

"Good. I have to get back in there." She stood, came to my side of the table, and wrapped me in a loose and sweaty hug. "Let me know when you hear from him. We'll dish."

I nodded my agreement. I was tired of speaking. My best friend walked away and disappeared through a side door. I stayed and finished my lunch. Rough wood scratching beneath my thighs, the sun brutal in midday, yet nothing to prevent me from staying right where I sat. I stayed to eat, but mostly I stayed to work out how I felt about my upcoming possible date with Vincent.

For lack of a better plan, I texted Dominic.

Me: *I'm going out with Vincent on Friday. So Alyssa says.*

Dominic: *He's a good guy. It will be fine.*

I wanted better than fine. But I knew what he meant. I didn't have to be so worried. A gnawing in my lower abdomen accompanied memories of Cotton kissing me. There was no need for feeling bad about going out with a different guy. I was not with Cotton. I would not be with Cotton. He wasn't an option. Still, that kiss had been wonderful while it lasted. I worried it had ruined me for other guys, that I would compare all future kisses to the one I had shared with Cotton. Much as I would compare all text interactions with future guys to those with Dominic.

Dominic: *Be yourself. He'll like you or he won't. In the end, how much does that even matter?*
Dominic: *Speaking of which, let's hang out. When is our next date?*

Speaking of which? Were we speaking of which? My lips smiled, and my queasy stomach settled to some degree. Dominic was my new platonic boyfriend and it was an agreeable arrangement. For both of us. I didn't understand why he liked hanging out with me, but I was going with it.

Me: *I'm free whenever. Except Friday, obviously.*

Dominic: *Come over for dinner Thursday night.*

I rolled my eyes. I considered texting him that I was rolling my eyes since he couldn't see me do it. I highly doubted this would go well. I had never been to the MacKenna's house before. I knew Denver had inherited it, and that all of them but Joe still lived there. Denver might be there. He would probably ignore me. Beau might be there, and maybe his long-term boyfriend Elliot. I liked them both, but worried they were too extroverted for me. Just as likely those two wouldn't be present, as they had active social lives.

Cotton. My brain flickered, not up to full working capacity, at the thought of him. Cotton might be there at the MacKenna place. Dominic knew this, and it was part and parcel with the invite.

Dominic: *You don't have to if you'd be too uncomfortable. I'll cook, and I promise everyone will be nice to you.*

Me: *Me? Uncomfortable? As if.*
Me: *I'll help you cook. I'll bring crates of alcohol.*

If I helped him cook, I would have an excuse to hide in the kitchen. Not that master chef Dominic would need my help, but I was happy to offer my services. I was already a low level of sorry for the way I planned to use strong adhesive and secure myself to Dom's side.

As for the plan to bring alcohol, it seemed a joke-worthy coping mechanism. I didn't drink often, and when I did I didn't drink much. I had never been interested in getting drunk. My mama threw up when she had too much to drink, and I had listened to her puking too many times to risk it myself. Luke had been a sneering nasty drunk, more prone than usual - which was damn prone - to treat me poorly. I used to lock my door and put on headphones to block out the sounds of my life. Still, the prospect of being in the MacKenna house with multiple MacKennas was enough for my brain to advise alcohol consumption. Not enough to get drunk, just enough that I wasn't on edge and crazy the whole evening.

Dominic: *Magnolia Peach Porter! (What is your middle name, btw?)*

Me: *My middle name is not in fact Peach. But I kind of like it better, so I might change my name. Thanks for the suggestion.*

Dominic: *Alright, alright. I will aid and abet the alcohol drinking plan. I'll even hold your hair at the end of the night.*

He was joking. I knew full well he was joking. Dominic wasn't aware how my thoughts had just gone to a dark place recalling too many nights of hearing the expulsion of a plethora of mixed drinks from my mama. Still, I cringed at the thought of being in that position, and of Dominic - much less any other member of his family - bearing witness. Not happening.

Dominic was hilarious and relentless in teasing me. It was fun. I enjoyed him. I chose to cling to the happy side of his playfulness with me.

Rather than obsess about when Cotton kissed me, his lips searing against mine and his hands greedy to have me, I played at being friends with his brother. It was easier to talk to Dom. I made plans and I kept busy. Who was I kidding? All the while, on a repeat reel in the background, ran the footage of that kiss. Of Cotton, domineering and passionate, kissing me the way I figure all people ought to be kissed at some point in their lives. Of Cotton, panicked and full of his stupid martyrdom, as he pulled away and abruptly ended that kiss. Of Cotton leaving, just leaving me there to put all the pieces of myself back together after he rearranged them so that they fit only with him.

Chapter Eleven

Magnolia

A factor that made it easy to continue living with my mom, was that we got along well and she was easy to live with. Or if I looked at it from another angle, I might say that I was so used to living with her, that I knew how to do so easily. I knew her routines and quirks. When to be in her space, and when to make myself scarce and give her space. We learned to coexist peacefully. That was the way of it, and the way of me. Peacemaker Extraordinaire. At first, when Daddy left, it was tough. The new dynamics of a single mom struggling to make ends meet, an older brother intent on destroying his own life and taking us out with him, and me trying to not rock the boat.

No. That wasn't it. I wasn't only trying to not rock the boat, because I never rocked the boat. My intent was to calm the already rocking boat. To still the turbulent waters that surrounded the boat.

It was an insurmountable task, and I became a very quietly anxious child. Sharing a house with Lucian was tremendously stressful for me, and had been as far back as I could remember. I never adapted to it; instead drowning in shame and effort. After Lucian died, it was just Mama and me, and suddenly it was easy. Every day. She was still working too many jobs and we still had to stretch each dollar. But gone was a constant source of worry and stress. I would think how much better it was without Luke around, then my belly would ache for hours as I succumbed to the guilt of being a bad sister. It was hard in new ways, knowing Luke would never step through the door again, and my role as the surviving child a heavy burden. Easy in other ways, with Mama and me able to live companionably with the other.

From the time I was eighteen, my mama had encouraged me to date. If *date* was defined clearly by her guidelines. Primarily a steady income and a strong lack of desire to ever leave western North Carolina. My mama had been making me promise not to move away for as long as I could remember. Yet, she was insistent that I couldn't support myself, and needed a man to take care of me, at least financially. She wanted better for me, I knew; she didn't want me to be poor like she had been. One of her reasons for having such high standards for the men I should date was wrapped up in her excuses for keeping me at home. It was a hopeless tangle. No matter, each date had been a dead end, with no attraction on my part. I had stopped dating and declared myself happily single more than a year ago.

I was happily single. I could say that with a straight face. There was no one I wanted to date of my own choosing. I didn't count the secret and fanatical crush I harbored for Cotton MacKenna. I knew better than to think there was a chance of that becoming reality. I disliked dating enough that I convinced myself I preferred being single. If truthfully, as of late single had become synonymous with lonely. If I was brutally honest with myself, and didn't think about what anyone else thought or wanted for me, I longed for a connection with another person. Specifically one that delved deeper emotionally - as well as physically - than friendship.

Dominic taking me out had been a loophole. We weren't dating, and none of the standard rules need apply. There was no use kidding myself that I could get away with our *only friends* bit forever. Hints had already been dropped that it wasn't proper for a girl of my age to become close friends with a boy, especially one with Dominic's reputation. My mama wasn't one to hold back, and she'd put a foot down sooner rather than later.

The date with Vincent, however, was a date. No getting around telling my mama of my plans, and opening myself up to her ideas of dating in the process. I couldn't imagine her approving of Vincent, at least not when it came to his love for places outside of Fox River, and his propensity for inking his skin. It would be a nod in his favor that he had come home to help his family, and that he had stuck around.

Thursday rolled around, and Alyssa came by on an afternoon off to check in and catch up. At least until Jacob would be home from work. It never failed to remind me of high school when we shared my otherwise empty house, talking for hours and not noticing the time as it passed.

"Have you told her yet? It's tomorrow."

Alyssa drummed her fingers on the gray swirled laminate countertop. She was small and golden and somehow managed to come across bigger and brighter than she was. I stared past her out the small square window over the stainless kitchen sink. No, I had not told my mama about my upcoming date with Vincent Berry. I was putting it off until the last minute because I was a big dumb coward.

"No."

"I predict she will be excited for forty-five seconds. Until she remembers who Vincent is, that he isn't made of money, that he is prone to up and leaving Fox River, and that he isn't a stuffy boring accountant."

I laughed until I snorted. Her prediction was sadly hitting on the mark, but that wasn't the part I found amusing.

"Kent is an accountant. I'm telling him you said he's stuffy and boring."

"First off, he knows I think that about him." Her smile was wide and showed a mouth of straight white teeth. Her brother Kent was neither stuffy nor boring, but when he was standing beside his shining sister he could come off that way. "Second, no way you're saying that to him. You clam up when he's around."

She waved away my threat. I nodded and quieted my laugh. It was true and I couldn't deny it. Kent was older than us, super cute in a classic clean-cut way, and kind of adorable the way he was still hung up on Olivia Hamilton. Therefore, I couldn't form two words in a row if I was faced with him.

"Okay, okay, back to my predictions." She pitched her voice to be mock serious. "Your mama will then put two and two together, because she is a smart lady, and point out that you should not be gallivanting over to the MacKenna's when you are dating another boy."

Alyssa had a point. I could see my mama saying that to me.

"Cross that bridge if and when I come to it." I couldn't worry about my dinner non-date with Dominic at his house that evening. I was going, it was settled, I was not stressing about my mama's opinion over it. I was stressing dinner enough on my own, over thinking how I would handle being with most of his family at once.

"She'll cave on you going out with Vincent the one time. So that you are officially back on the market and open to dating. Then she will line up a string of men willing to marry you. Where she finds them, I'll never know."

"I'm trying to decide if I'm insulted by what you said."

Her head cocked to one side and her eyes squinted as she thought back over her words. The afternoon sun slanted in the window and lit up the room with a golden glow.

"Oh. No. There are loads of guys that would marry you. Fantastic ones." She smiled and muttered something that sounded an awful lot like Cotton under her breath, followed by something terribly like Vincent. I ignored her. "I meant, I don't know where she finds all the moderately wealthy scumbags."

"I blame you for this. I'm just saying, you set me up and it's your fault if my life is ruined."

"You're welcome." I glared at her false words and wicked smile. "I'm out. I promised Jacob I would make lasagna tonight."

"You're going to Bella's and buying a lasagna?"

"Oh, totally." She nodded, and we walked toward the front door. "I have an arrangement with Lewis Rossi. He makes it for me, but doesn't bake it. That way I can technically cook it myself in my own oven."

Lewis was the fifth or sixth of the eight Rossi kids. They were by far the largest family in number of kids, and all ran Bella's together. The oldest ones already had families with multiple kids each. I could recognize them, with their olive skin and shiny dark hair, but I struggled to keep them apart, as they looked uncannily similar. They only one I sort of knew was Lewis, and that was by proxy of Alyssa.

"Diabolical."

"Right?" She laughed. I hugged her and sighed into her familiar body. "I hate that we're going out of town tomorrow. I won't get to hear all the details until we get back."

"I'll text you." I let her out the door and shrugged my shoulders. We texted far more than we talked on the phone, and it would suffice as a means of information exchange.

"You can try. I doubt my cell will work. You know how bad service is the more north we go into the mountains."

"In that case, I'm coming over Monday night. I'll bring ice cream."

"Don't plan for it to go poorly!" She smacked my shoulder.

"Celebratory ice cream." I said it like, duh. She didn't buy it, of course, knowing I had already considered my mama's reaction as well as my date a forgone conclusion. One that didn't pan out in my favor.

"Love you, Magpie."

"You too, Lyss."

The house to myself, I kept myself distracted until my mama got home by playing loud music and forgetting the world. When given the choice, I had a strong preference for sad music. Townes van Zandt. Joe Purdy. Not sad. Real. Soulful. Troubadours. I put on Anais Mitchell and let her voice warble through the house. I dusted already clean knick knacks in the living room and did not think about what I would say to my mama.

A tap on my shoulder startled me. I jumped and clutched my frantic heart. The jasmine scent told me it was my mama, and there was no need to panic.

"You scared me."

"If someone can come in the house without you hearing, your music is too loud." With that my mama turned the dial and quieted the lyrical ramblings carried on my idea of vocal perfection.

"Uh huh." I was inclined to agree with her. Lesson learned.

I was too busy calming my rapid pulse to argue. "I'm glad you're home. I need to talk to you about something."

"Figured as much."

"Why?"

"You were dusting."

I learned my "clean away the stress" habit from her, so she would find it familiar. Huh. I would have to come back to that and work out how much it bothered me that I did the same thing as my mama, and that she knew it.

She went through her after work routine of changing clothes, pulling her hair up off her neck and shoulders, washing the makeup off her face. When she came home, she meant it. Once the bra and makeup were removed, she wasn't going back out again. I listened as she talked about her day, and waited for an opening.

"I'm starved. What are we doing for dinner?"

It was an hour before I was to be at the MacKenna's house.

"I'm going to Dominic's."

"Oh, right." Her eyes narrowed on me for a second, then she shook her head. "In that case, I think I'll do something simple."

I helped her pull out what she needed to fill a plate with bits of finger foods. Meat, cheese, olives, pickles, crackers, grapes, berries, anything small that fit on her plate. It was a fairly typical meal for either one of us.

"I have a date on Friday. Tomorrow." I blurted the words out. They had been sitting on the back of my tongue for so long I couldn't hold them back any longer. "Alyssa set me up."

"Hmm." She thoughtfully arranged the last items on her plate. Everything in neat rows that spoked out from the center, like sunrays.

As much as I wanted to urge her to spill her opinion, to get it over with, I gave her a second to process. I followed her to the sofa, where she balanced her plate on her knees. Not a few seconds later she shifted and moved the plate to the coffee table. I endured her direct gaze at me, sat still while she studied me, and I smiled back at her.

"Give me all the details." The practiced patience in her

voice grated on my nerves, but I told myself I was being too sensitive.

"I'm going to Bella's with Vincent Berry." I wasn't sure what to share. There were no details, other than the particulars of our planned meeting. "He works with Alyssa. Sort of. Or she knows him from work. It was her idea to set me up. She thinks I should start dating."

For lack of anything specific to say, I rambled and dropped random useless tidbits. My smile had slipped, so I pulled it back into place. She watched me, and I tried to understand the level of worry on her face.

"What does this Vincent think of your friendship with the MacKenna boy?"

Nice. Don't even call him by name. Sheesh.

"I don't know. I haven't talked to Vin much. We haven't gone out yet." I said it was for Friday, right?

"Well." That one word held a whole host of judgment. "You go out on your date, and have a good time. Not too good a time, mind you."

I nodded. My teeth didn't want to come apart, so I didn't bother with words.

"I'll be thinking on who else you might like to go out with, now you're amenable to dating." Her mouth was a small smile, and her eyes were innocent, but I recognized the sly maneuver for what it was. Someone she approved of rather than the guy I had a date with. Not that I could fault her when I knew she wanted me to be happy, and she thought she had my best interest at heart.

"I'm hoping that I'll continue to date Vincent." I already worried I was using him. Before the first date. But, no, I did honestly and for the right reasons hope it went well. I just sort of also hoped it went well to keep my mama off my back when it came to finding a proper suitor.

"Let's not jump the gun." She tsk'd.

I nodded. I wanted to say the same back to her but knew better.

"I need to go. I don't want to be late for dinner."

"I'm very uncomfortable with you being unsupervised in

88

that house full of boys."

"They're all grown-ups, Mama." Unsupervised. Please. "I am a grown up. Plus, we're friends, and it's no different than if I go to Alyssa's house."

"It's very different, Magnolia. The very fact that you can't see that is what worries me."

And on that note, I was officially over it, no longer interested in talking to my mother. I nodded. Again. Like I was incapable of any other response. Her eyes stayed on me, serious and worried, as I got my bag and headed for the door. She seemed to seriously marvel at my guileless trust, like I was walking into a tank of sharks rather than an old farmhouse of boys.

Chapter Twelve

Cotton

I had a decision to make. Did I stay? Or did I go?

My insufferable brother invited Maggie to our house for dinner. He could have gone to her house. He could have taken her out. He could have done any number of things that in no way involved me. Instead, he was having her over to eat with the family. That's the way he said it, *with the family*. He made sure to look me right in the eye when he said family.

The thing was, the others were excited. I hadn't expected any one of them to care. But when I thought about it, it was kind of a big deal. The four of us still living at the homestead, we were close and we were selective who we brought home. Denver had people over occasionally that played music with him. Never a date, or even a close friend. He didn't do close friendships. As far as he was concerned having four little brothers constituted all the friendships he needed. Beau had Elliot, who came over so often the new had worn off for us a good four years ago. At this point Elliot was part of the family, and we didn't think to extend an invite because there was already an understood inclusion. I certainly didn't have people over. Not the girls I met with when the mood called, and not my friends. I kept my private life private. Dominic had a whole host of girls and friends. He was the least homebody of any of us, happy to go out more often than not. The thing with him, none of those girls he dated or the friends he hung out with were close, none were important enough to bring home.

Then there was Maggie Porter.

Dominic had befriended her all of two seconds ago. They had gone out once, texted with enough frequency that even I noticed the constancy of it, and all of the sudden they were best friends forever. I didn't care that he had made a friend, or that he was compelled to invite said friend over. I cared that it was Maggie. My Maggie.

If I stayed, it would be awkward as hell. For me. For Dom. For Maggie. That was sure to leak over to Denver, Beau, and Elliot. I couldn't stay.

If I took off and skipped dinner, it would be obvious. My not being in attendance would be noticed, talked about, and it would come back to bite my ass. It was a good way to raise a flag on the situation and tell everyone I was messed up over Maggie. I would never live it down with my family. Then there was Maggie to consider, and she would blame herself for my absence. I didn't want to do that to her. I had to stay.

I started day drinking to prepare for the evening.

In an effort to be technically at home, yet out of the way, I sat on the back deck an hour before she was supposed to show up. I would stay until one of my jackass brothers finally called me indoors. No one bothered me. It was hot, the shade unable to counteract the high temps. I took long slow drags of bitter IPAs and let time swim past me. It was a coward move, and I wouldn't get away with it all night, but for the time being I couldn't think of a better plan.

"What's with you?" Denver stepped through the French doors and onto the deck. We had built it together three summers back; it was wide as the house and deep enough to hold a large table, the grill, and an outdoor bar, with extra room for a scattering of chairs.

He leaned against the doorjamb with his arms crossed over his chest. He'd let his hair grow out, probably not on purpose so much as he hadn't made it to the barber in too long, and it curled around his ears and neck. He was the biggest of us, which had always made some sort of sense to me since he's the oldest. Only he didn't look thirty-one, he looked the same as always, which was outwardly aloof with too much going on behind his eyes. People said I was intense, but for me that title went to Denver.

"Nothing." I claimed.

"Bullshit." He countered.

I lifted my eyes to his face and flipped him the bird. His lips pulled up on one side into a half-amused smirk.

"Let me rephrase: is there a reason you're avoiding that girl?" He hooked a thumb back toward the house.

"Nope."

"Okay. Don't tell me." He shrugged. Denver could do without knowing personal stuff. Still, he stood there and stared at me. "Dom will be all kinds of pissed if you don't get in there."

"He'll be more pissed if I say the wrong thing to ... her." At the last minute I swallowed her name. To let it pass my lips was wrong. The pain of not saying it was less strong, still I winced. I hid my reaction behind another drink of my beer.

"You have a thing for Maggie Porter?" He sounded honestly surprised, and more curious than I would have thought. He didn't laugh. His calm reaction wasn't one of disbelief or mocking, only mild intrigue.

"I didn't say that."

"You didn't have to." He didn't care about relationships, but he was observant. "Still, you better come in."

I nodded and sighed. I drained the last of my beer and grabbed another. Denver took one as well. So much for the Hide on the Deck plan.

We found Dominic in the kitchen. No surprise there. He was in his element in the midst of the organized chaos of meal prep. Telling myself not to look for or at Maggie was futile. My eyes weren't listening to me, and went directly to where she sat perched on a tall stool on the far side of the island.

"What do you do at the high school? You enjoy your job?" Beau stood a step away from her and peered at her with a benign smile. He was curious about everyone and always asked too many questions. No one ever seemed to mind.

"Oh. Um." She paused speaking, like she had to consider her answer carefully. Her eyes darted around the room at all of us, and I knew she was nervous. We made her uncomfortable, not us specifically, but as a group of people giving her their full attention. "No. I mean, yes."

Beau reached out a hand and patted her shoulder. It was an innocent move, and still I found I had to restrain myself from marching over there and tearing his hand off her.

"Which is it, Maggie Baby?" Dominic called the words over his shoulder as he rinsed berries in the sink.

Another strong dose of jealousy coursed through my system. I answered it with more silent restraint. Baby?

Maggie smiled at him, an easy natural thing, and when she looked at only Dom she relaxed a little.

"I don't hate working there. It's a good job, and the hours are great." She shrugged and continued to look toward Dominic. He gave her a wink when he caught her focusing solely on him.

The food was almost ready. Elliot was helping, stacking plates on the butcher block counter and pulling out silverware. Dominic was drying his hands on a worn thin flour sack towel. Our mama had embroidered it when we were kids, or even longer ago, and none of us could bear replacing it.

"But?" Beau blinked down at her, but she didn't look at him.

"But it's not what I want to do."

"What do you want to do?"

"I don't know."

Denver made a sound, like *huh*, likely because he had always known what he wanted to do. An all-consuming interest in the fiddle had been the core of his life for about as long as any of us could remember. Beau looked like he had about a hundred more questions. Elliot rounded the island and flanked Maggie on the opposite of where Beau stood. He put an arm around her shoulders and pulled her in.

"Don't worry about it, doll. I still don't know what I want to be when I grow up either."

Rather than shy away from him, she turned her head and looked at him with a relieved smile.

"But you're good at ... everything." Her admission was sweet and simple. It was clear she knew about Elliot, even if she had never officially met him.

Elliot and Beau both laughed.

"That's not entirely accurate." Elliot's smile was a thousand watts and his affection for Maggie was obvious. He smiled at the group, and then directed it down toward the shy trusting girl tucked to his side. "I like you."

"It is true." Beau said it like he found it aggravating, but we all knew different.

"You don't have to suck up, B. I already like you." Elliot gave his boyfriend a wink, and Beau answered simply by rolling his eyes.

"Alright, alright, food is ready." Dominic pulled all attention to himself and gestured at the food lining the countertops. "Maggie, would you like to eat in the dining room or out on the deck?"

Denver groaned. He hated the deck this time of year because it was so brutally hot. He didn't hate the deck; he hated being outside. I chuckled at his reaction. I already knew what Maggie would choose.

"On the deck." Her voice was quiet, and I wasn't sure how many in the room caught it. "If that's okay?"

"Load your plates, boys." Dominic took Maggie's hand, pulled her up and around the island. "But ladies first."

Her face went immediately and delicately red. Her anxiety with people watching her, with going first when she didn't know what she was doing, was at a high. I shifted forward, debating helping her. I could push my way through and go first, and it would take the attention off her.

But Dominic knew. He picked up a plate and put it in her hands. He took one for himself. They walked along the row of prepared food together, all the while he told her what each dish was and helped himself to the food alongside her. Her cheeks cooled. I watched her take small portions of each dish.

Dominic had made all his favorite Cajun dishes. The kitchen reeked of spice in a way that made my mouth water and my stomach growl. Beau had concocted spiked lemonade for the occasion and carried a pitcher along with glasses out to the deck.

We gathered there, on that deck with plates of food and glasses of sugary tart alcohol, and it was perfect. The rightness of it exquisite and painful. Maggie sat beside Dominic, not hiding her desire to stay attached to him. Elliot sat on her other side and bent over to whisper to her frequently. As the two non-MacKennas they bonded. I watched her find her place and the anxiety in her slip away.

She didn't have much family. I couldn't remember exactly when her dad had skipped town, only that he had never been around. It was Mrs. Porter raising Luke and Maggie for about as long as I could remember. The last few years, it was just the two of them, mother and daughter holding together their little family.

Our dad had left too, shortly after Dom was born, leaving our mama with five boys and a massive house to care for on her own. Joseph put himself in charge, acting the part of whatever he thought a dad would do, bossing us around. By the time he was in high school, he was so used to playing the Dad card and laying out orders, we were all sick to death of him. He was more tolerable married and living across town; in small doses. Even without our parents these last few years, we were a tight knit family.

Maggie fit, sitting there with her shy smile growing, and her interest peaked each time one of us shared a story. This girl with hardly any family to speak of, found herself surrounded on all sides with us brothers. It seemed to me she liked it, she liked being part of our family.

"Who's going to the Super Summer Slip'n Slide whatever next weekend?"

I had ignored the signage for the event with tenacity. It was the thirtieth anniversary of the event, which in itself was ludicrous. Thirty years of the townspeople of Fox River showing up to the city park in their swimsuits and setting up an obscene number of Slip'n Slides. I had gone as a kid - we all had - and it was a day of wicked sunburns, laughter, and exhaustion. Since about the time I turned thirteen, I skipped the day festivities, and showed up for the bonfire. It was held on the far west side of the Wakefield's land, down by the Fox River itself. The land dipped there, formed a bowl of a field. Mr. Wakefield would clear it out and a few able bodies would spend the afternoon hauling in firewood. While everyone, young and old and middle aged, spent the day at the ridiculous Slip'n Slide event, only the late teens and the under thirties were at the bonfire.

"No." Maggie's answer was tinged with sadness, but also resignation.

"Why on earth not?" Elliot sat back and asked the question like he was personally offended by her lack of attendance. "Where else in the world can you find an entire town of folks walking around in swimsuits and embarrassing themselves sliding across wet plastic?"

I knew she wouldn't go. She had only gone twice that I remembered, when she was still pretty young, and her brother was meant to keep an eye on her. Lucian ran off and did his own thing, and I watched her from a distance, hoping she wouldn't notice me. Maybe hoping that she would notice. She wouldn't go now because her mama hated all town events. I would have thought everyone knew that already.

"Our town is so strange." She let out a small laugh and shook her head.

Dominic opened his mouth, like he might say something. To change the subject. Or to convince her to go. Who knows.

"Her mama won't let her." Denver chimed in, and as soon as he said the words his face went stony. He had the bad habit of speaking words that were in his head, that he found obvious, without thinking through how other people might feel. He was right. It was a simple truth. Unfortunately it effectively silenced the whole group of us, and Maggie looked like she might cry.

Damn it.

"Maggie Blue is a twenty-four-year-old woman and can make her own decisions." Dominic stood up for her with a reassuring but solemn voice, and patted her knee in a caring gesture.

I ground my teeth together. Blue? What the hell was with Dom and the interchangeable middle names? He was making me crazy.

"Yeah." I watched her steady her chin and sit up taller. She

96

nodded her head and said the word as if she were convincing herself more than us. "Yeah, you're right. I'm an adult."

"Damn straight, sweetie." Elliot gave her a wink and lifted his glass of high gravity lemonade to her.

"What's your mama got against town events?" Beau asked, head cocked to one side, curiosity eating him up.

I glared at Beau. He wasn't looking at me and didn't notice my disdain. I moved to set my beer bottle down before I threw it at a wall. Then decided empty hands were a bad idea, and clutched the glass too tight in my fist. Was he trying to make her uncomfortable?

Maggie dipped her head, gathered her wits, then looked to Beau. Oddly enough she wasn't upset. She had that same resolve from seconds before when she had declared herself a grown up.

"She used to go. We all did, as a family." She did that thing where he voice was too quiet. I didn't think she was aware of it. We all went silent, and leaned in to catch hold of her words. I studied her face, and her warm brown eyes. "Then after my dad left, Mama was always working. And Luke, I mean, you guys know, he was always in trouble. If she took us, or if she let us go, he'd wreck something. After a while she was just too embarrassed."

I was floored by her response. I had the feeling my brothers were the same. The honesty of it stung, because we did know. We knew Luke and his antics, and we understood why her mama would be embarrassed. Maggie's place in all that, missing out because she was too good and quiet to speak up, made it painful. The air was bitter with the facts of her life. Then it shifted, because we all as a whole took her in. Just like that, in silent agreement, she was ours. Dominic had already laid claim to her, and I knew then why he'd wanted us all there for dinner. Beau and Elliot rallied at her other side, and looked at her with such love and acceptance. They spoke to her, and I didn't hear their words. My heart pounded too hard in my chest, and my ears only heard a high-pitched keening. Probably my brain disintegrating; or my heart exploding. Even Denver looked abashed, and softened toward her. I was proud of my brothers; pleased they would fall so easily in love with this sweet bit of girl. I was equally angry that they were able to love her so freely. I pushed up from my chair and stalked down the steps into the yard.

"Cotton!"

Dominic called after me. I didn't turn. In fact, I walked faster, going nowhere except away from my family and the girl I couldn't get out of my head.

"Cotton. Alexander. MacKenna." He fully yelled each piece of my name.

I tuned him out and stalked past the barn. On the other side, the land sloped down, and I was able to disappear from their sightline. I didn't stop there. I had no destination in mind, but whatever I was looking for, I hadn't found it yet. That was the problem with running away, when your only goal was to leave something behind, but never to find something ahead.

Chapter Thirteen

Magnolia

The sun was setting behind the thick rows of trees that circled the MacKenna property. I had never been to the house before, and when I arrived it took my breath away. It was a big old farmhouse, two stories, white washed clapboard siding, stark black shutters that looked functional rather than decorative, and a deep porch that ran the length of the house and then turned the corners to go along the sides. I'd spent the first half hour adjusting to the size of the house and how small it became after all those boys were in the same room. Dominic wouldn't let me help him with dinner, so I'd sat there useless on a too tall barstool. I hadn't followed through on bringing alcohol, because I wasn't sure how to drink and I was less sure what they would like to drink. Thankfully Beau had made an obscene amount of spiked lemonade and he'd poured me a glass as soon as he'd officially met me.

I noticed the lack of one brother in particular right off the bat. All I could think about as the others talked around me and bless them tried to pull me into the conversation, was that Cotton wasn't there and it was because of me. I had driven him out of his own house.

Dominic cooked with an ease and that belied hidden skill. He kept surprising me. The food was all rich with spice, and leveled with a subtle creaminess, and there was something about the scent that made me crave the taste.

Eventually Cotton came in, following Denver who'd gone to fetch him from the back deck. I wasn't sure if it was better that I had not pushed him from his house, but that he hated being near me so much that he hid when I arrived. The sting of it wasn't any less.

Though Beau kept peppering me with questions, and Elliot kept giving me easy assurances, I was wound up tight. Elliot, being an outsider, latched onto me, and whispered answers to the riddles that were the MacKennas. He told me we had to stick together. I didn't tell him there was no point because I would never belong to them the way he did.

Beau and Elliot were leaving the next day to go to the hot air balloon festival. It was such a funny coincidence they were going to the same place as Alyssa and Jacob. I urged them to try and find one another. It was such a small world sometimes, even outside our small town.

Out on the deck, with the land rolling away from us as far as the eye could see and only the tree line to set a boundary, it was easier. After a couple hours with the boys, and allowing myself to enjoy each of them, it was easier.

I had survived and I was having fun, and I had let myself believe that I would walk away from the night not only unscathed but willing to do it again. The key was pretending Cotton wasn't sulking off to the side, or at least to pretend I didn't care.

Then someone brought up the town's upcoming Slip'n Slide event. It had been an innocent enough thing, an across the board inquiry as to who would be going. I laughed into my second glass of Beau's Magical Lemonade that tasted like honey and tartness and heaven. I couldn't believe they were planning to go. It was such a silly event, and these were grown-ups for all intents and purposes. The youngest of us here were Dom and me, and even we weren't all that young.

My answer was a simple no, because no I hadn't planned to go. Inside my head, I didn't care. It was dumb, and why would I want to be in a swimsuit in front of the whole town and throw myself down a wet sheet of plastic? But when the word left my mouth, it sounded sad. I realized I was maybe a little sad. I blamed my brother. I could vividly recall the last time I had gone to the Slip'n Slide event. I was twelve; scrawny and wishing I had boobs. Lucian was fifteen, uninterested in anything and supposed to keep an eye on me. We walked over together, then I didn't see him again. He disappeared for hours and I had no idea where he'd gone. Once Alyssa arrived, I spent the day with her and Kent who exemplified what an older brother should and could do. I was there, surrounded by all those people, and I was alone. I noticed people staring at me, and an increase in whispering. Turned out Luke had broken into the bakery, taken all the pastries he liked and destroyed the rest. Later, when asked why he did it, he simply stated because he could, no one was watching and he knew he could get away with it. The irony of course being his not getting away with it. He had also taken the Sheriff's car, covered it in shaving cream, and no one could prove it was him so he did get away with that. A few years before, he'd put dye in the water hoses so that everyone walked away from slip n sliding a colorful rainbow. He was young, and enough people found it funny, that he had gotten away with that as well. No. No, I wasn't planning to go to the event.

I tried to play it off like *ha-ha Fox River is weird*. It was true, and we all knew it.

Denver didn't let it go. He had a tendency to speak before thinking, or to speak what he thought without considering other's feelings. Or he had a tendency to be an asshole and bludgeon people with the truth. Something like that.

"Her mama won't let her."

The others stood up for me, and tried to convince me that I was an adult and could make up my own mind. All the while I shrank under the heavy weight of the truth. I was easily and highly influenced by what my mama did or did not do. When she stopped bothering with town events, I understood her reasoning, and I followed suit. The last few years, as Alyssa insisted I get out more, she and Jacob would drag me to these things. As the years passed, my reasons to stay behind made less and less sense.

I agreed with my status as a fully functioning adult responsible for her own decisions, half determined it would be true, half wishing we could talk about anything else.

Beau's question was innocent enough, coming from his genuine curiosity. He wanted to understand when he asked

101

what my mama had against town events. The explanation came out in jumbled thoughts and memories and left a salty sad taste in my mouth.

Something happened when I spoke. When I told them what it was like for us, to live with Luke's choices, especially for my mama to be judged for them. There was a shift, and it rocked me. All those MacKenna blue eyes looked at me, and saw me differently than a half second before. It wasn't with judgment or pity, but acceptance and longing. Like they wanted to help me, to lift me up, and to care for me. Dominic's hand squeezed my thigh, the warmth of him grounding me.

"You ought to come with us. It will be real fun." Beau smiled his promise. I blushed under the intensity of the moment but couldn't deny the relief and belonging that cocooned me with them.

I loved this family. Every one of them there that night, they were special to me. Just like that, in one instant. I had never seen such trust looking back at me, trust that I could make my own decisions, and more importantly trust that they wouldn't stop loving me if I messed up.

One time, years ago, I'd thought *I wish I had a sibling*. There was a certain loneliness in growing up how I had, hidden in Luke's shadow. And we'd never been close, not at any point in our lives. I'd been a sort of only child long before my brother died. I realized when I'd had the errant thought, that of course I had a sibling. What I wanted was a different one. I wanted this, a troupe of people that looked out for one another, that saw me and accepted me.

"Pack a picnic and spend the afternoon with us. Saint Joe will even show up."

I gave Elliot a sideways look and his smile was full of mischief.

"Joseph. He's the do-gooder super responsible one, you know? He hates it when I call him Saint Joe, which of course is why I do it." He winked at me and I hid my laugh behind my hand. Elliot was a riot. "His wife, Missy, thinks we're all a bunch of loser misfits. If it wasn't for the kids I wouldn't bother to put up with either of them."

"That is my brother you're talking about." Beau acted offended, but I didn't buy it.

I knew who Missy Douglass MacKenna was, and had never been a fan. When I had dated her little brother Tiny back in high school, she had been awful to me. She would say terrible things about Luke, which weren't too far off base, but it was still rude. Tiny always took up for me, and we made an effort to never be around her when we could help it. I always kind of figured he broke up with me because of her constant barrage of my lesser qualities to him. Tiny had moved away after high school, and cut ties with his sister, evidently sick of her behavior. I saw her around town, in her high fashion clothes and hair that she drove an hour to get cut in a fancy salon, but we never spoke. They had two kids, a boy and a girl, both young enough to still have chubby cheeks.

"We'll all go to the bonfire after."

I nodded, and for no good reason looked toward Cotton. Every so often I tortured myself by sneaking a glance his way, usually to find him looking at the deck flooring or out at the pasture. He was fuming. I sucked in a breath at the harsh glare he shot my way. Before I could think through why he was upset, he stood and stalked away. His boots heavy and loud on the deck and down the stairs. I stared at his back as he went, watching the power of his movements, and his hair orange as the sunset.

Dominic called after him, to no avail.

"This is my fault." The words escaped me on a whisper, before I could stop them.

"Of course it's not." Dom assured me, but we knew better. His grimace was an apology and annoyance at his brother all in one.

"Don't be ridiculous. You're a doll. Cotton just has his panties in a wad." Elliot joked, and I snorted at his glib words.

"Still, it's about me. The panty wadding, it's my fault." I sucked in another long breath, then released it in a sharp sigh. I heard their laughter in a distant way.

I pushed up to my feet, and before I could tell myself to stop being stupid, I left. I followed the path Cotton had taken

103

away from the house and toward the barn. I wasn't sure where to go from there, as the land dropped away and I couldn't see him. The grass was taller back there, tickled my legs, and I waded through it like a sea. There were probably snakes hidden in the grass, and I was probably very stupid to follow Cotton. Again. It didn't end well the first time, and who was I kidding thinking it would go differently this time. Only, I wasn't thinking about any of that, I was answering the call to follow him, responding to the pull of my heart to him.

Just when I was cursing my terrible bad decision to gallivant back there while the sun slipped away and cast the land in a thick gray darkness, I saw him. The dark silhouette of him. He stood still; too still.

"Go back." His voice was gruff and reached me before I reached him. "I don't want to talk."

"Cotton, I'm ..." My voice was so soft, so weak. I cleared my throat. His shoulders tensed at the sound of my voice, like maybe he hadn't known it was me coming up behind him. For lack of anything else to say, I said the all too familiar words, "I'm sorry."

"God damn it, Maggie." He spun to face me, and I was glad I couldn't see his face, as he yelled at me. It was surely scary. "Stop apologizing to me."

I flinched but stood my ground. He muttered a curse under his breath.

"Why did you leave?" Again. I wanted to ask why he left again. The pain of his leaving after kissing me last Friday resurfaced, an open wound.

"You don't want to know. Just ..." He stepped in my direction, but kept his distance. "I'll walk you back."

"I do want to know." When I didn't move from where I stood, he stopped and stared. His eyes glinted in the dim remaining light.

"Should I have not been here tonight?" He asked, clearly worried and taking the blame himself. We weren't so different in that way.

"It's your house, Cotton."

"All I can do is hurt you. I see you and I can't ..." He

stepped closer; he smelled of the acrid beers he'd been downing. "I stood a chance at doing the right thing, up there, with my brothers all around you. You shouldn't keep following me when I leave, Magnolia. All my resolve goes away when there you are looking at me like ..."

He was right, I had followed him. Last week, before he kissed me. Tonight. I kept throwing myself in his path. He kept reminding me he would hurt me. It was stupid to think he cared for me, or that he wouldn't hold true to his words when he promised being near him would cause pain. But whatever was there between us, it was a connection I couldn't possibly deny or ignore, and I had to trust my heart to lead me true. I blinked up at him, barely visible as more than the shape of Cotton as the last of the light died and darkness fully cloaked us.

"Like what?"

"You should tell me to walk you back to the house." I recognized the plea for what it was; my last chance to escape unscathed.

I shook my head. He was right, of course, that was exactly what I should have done. I was tired of doing what I should. When I was so near to him, the only thing I could be certain of was how much I wanted him. It was a powerful drug that controlled me and pushed me to him.

He stepped closer still, closing the space between us. I lifted one hand and placed it on his chest. He was hot to the touch, and his heart was pounding against his ribs. I relished the feel of it beneath my hand, proof that he was affected as much as me by our proximity.

Cotton's hands went to my hips, fingers gripping me tight, pulling me to him. I gasped when I found myself pressed hard against his body. He took advantage of my surprise and kissed me. He wasted no time on being gentle or warming up, instead moving his tongue directly into my mouth. He stole my breath. My mouth moved with his and met his kiss with fervor. All that pent up anger at him leaving me mixed with the years of crushing on him, and I wanted to devour him. I had no idea what I was doing and I didn't slow down to think about it. One

105

hand was caught between us, with the other hand I ran my fingers through his thick hair and settled it behind his neck. I held him to me. He bent me backward as he kissed me and held me to his body. I was his. For as long as it lasted, I submitted to his hunger for me, and I belonged to him.

Never letting an inch of space open between our bodies, he ran his hands up my waist and up my ribs then back down. His mouth moved to my jaw, trailing kisses then down my neck, and gently biting the sensitive skin below my ear. I pulled oxygen into my lungs and moved my free hand over the firm muscles of his shoulder and down his side. When I reached the hem of his shirt, I slipped my hand beneath the soft cotton to his skin. He paused, releasing a breath with a groan, then impossibly pulled me closer to him.

He said my name, again and again, each time like a prayer. With such reverence, I cracked open and knew there was no turning back from him. Not from the way he held me, not from the way he worshipped me. I whimpered and lost myself to his touch.

"Cotton." I didn't know what I was saying. I knew why he had repeated my name, because to speak his name was enough. It was a statement of my desire, of the wing flapping thing happening to my heart, of my brain giving way and accepting him as a necessary part of me.

Instead of encouraging him, at the sound of his name, he stopped. He held me tight to his body, his fingers hard on my soft skin, his lips grazed my collarbone, but he stilled. In reaction, I stilled too. The only movement was the frantic pounding of our hearts and the panting of our breaths. Then he stood up and straightened me with him, and released me. I was left cold in the heat of the summer night, with only the phantom memory of his hands on me. A tingling ache for more the only thing that remained in each place he'd touched me.

He didn't say a word. Cotton took my hand, and pulled me along back up to the house. When we reached the edge of the light that shone from the deck into the yard, he stopped. His big hand squeezed mine, like he didn't want to let go. The way he held tight to me told me this was more than a kiss, more than a physical thing. But he was still fighting it. I willed words to come out of my mouth. I begged my tongue to cooperate and ask him to stay. He let me go; he dropped my hand and walked the wrong way from the inviting house.

My feet knew what they should do, and they moved my body closer to the house. Three steps into the yellow spill of light on the gray green of the night grass, and I was seen.

"Maggie. Thank God." Dominic bounded to me and scooped me into his arms. I fell into him and clung to him. He tensed and shifted, and that's when I knew that he knew that I was broken. He didn't let go.

"You want me to bring you inside? You can stay here tonight."

"No." I didn't move, I stayed there wrapped up in Dom's embrace and my hands fisted the back of his shirt.

"You want me to drive you home?"

"No." I spoke into his chest. He was warm. He was not Cotton. But just then I didn't care. I wanted the broad chest to place my cheek on, the thick strong arms to hold me together, and the comfort it provided. I should have let go. It was wrong after kissing Cotton, to run into his brother's arms.

"What did he do, Maggie?" Dom's words were a soft whisper that rumbled in his chest and in his breath. They were laced with a subtle threat that both startled and soothed me.

I was dimly aware that Denver passed in my peripheral. He slipped by silent as a ghost and was swallowed by the night. What would Cotton tell him?

"Why doesn't he want me?"

"What do you mean?" He reached around behind himself and pulled my hands loose of their hold on him. He held my hands, so that we were tethered, but put space between us so that he could look into my face.

"I'm doing something wrong." Hot streaks of tears moved down my face and dripped from my jaw. A silent assault from torn emotions that poured over my cheeks. "He kisses me, and holds me like he wants me, then he leaves. He's able to walk away. While I'm ..."

I couldn't explain it right. Not even to myself, much less to

107

Dominic. His hands around mine tightened and when I finally looked up into his face it reflected back an all too familiar anger. He looked too much like Cotton just then, with the subtle differences melted away by the lack of light, with the efforts at controlling a temper evident in his face.

"Maggie. Listen to me." His words were strained. I found the things that made him Dominic and focused on them. "You aren't doing anything wrong. Never think that. Cotton, he ... he doesn't think he should ever let anyone love him because he's so sure he'll hurt them."

There was more to it than that. I could feel the way Dom warred with himself about how much to say, and the careful selection of words. It didn't matter what he told me. I knew that Cotton wanted me, but that when he kissed me it was a slip up. I'd been wrong to think it meant anything to him. After his brain caught up with what his body was doing, he pulled away, and he put as much distance as possible between us. He had shifted from the boy I wasn't supposed to like, that I crushed on, to the man I longed for, but could never have. The rejection hurt. I hated that it hurt. A burning orb in my chest that bumped up against my heart and my lungs and my stomach, and made me ill.

When I finally pulled myself together, I wasn't hurt so much as embarrassed. The pain evolved into shame of being such a fool. I drove myself home, threw myself into bed, and wallowed in my own idiocy.

Chapter Fourteen

Magnolia

I called Alyssa's phone at least a dozen times. I texted her repeatedly. At some point I called Jacob's phone. I was desperate to contact my best friend and tell her I was queen of all stupid girls. My redundant efforts suggested a stubborn streak and a touch of insanity. She had warned me they lacked phone service at the hot air balloon slash music slash camping thing. The mountains were spotty at best for cell phones.

I had to tell someone about the kiss. My fingers kept doing stupid things like touching my lips and making me remember the pressure of Cotton's lips on mine. I refused to gush to Dominic about it. He was Cotton's brother, and as such not an impartial confidant. Plus I was mortified about the way I'd clung to him and cried on him after the incident.

With no one to talk to, and a full day stretched out before me, I did what any mildly neurotic person would do. I cleaned.

My mama was out for the day. She was driving up the Blueridge Parkway to meet some old friend vacationing near enough to warrant a get together. They were doing lunch or some such thing. She had divulged all the details to me that morning over coffee, and I had tried to pay attention, but walked away with nothing but my head swimming with my own problems.

While I ran the vacuum and scrubbed the kitchen tiles, I let my mind drift to Vincent. Vincent Berry, with his tattoos, his playing electric guitar when that was the antithesis of our bluegrass prone town, and his sweet devotion to his family that brought him home. I wondered if he'd rather go back to Asheville. He'd been there for like six years before he came home to Fox River. After his dad died, he stayed to take care of his mama and his sister. Louisa was sixteen or seventeen, and as such still lived at home. For a second I considered it unlikely his mama needed that much help, for him to uproot his life and stay here long term. Asheville wasn't so far away, and he could come home on the weekends.

Then I reflected on my own mama. After Lucian died, she needed me. Four years later, and she still needed me. Her dependency on me was sometimes a burden, and I suffered waves of guilt when I thought of it that way. I couldn't place my own issues and perceptions onto his situation with his family. Likely, Vincent was happy to stay home and help out, or he wouldn't be doing it.

Vincent was a couple years older than me, and I had always thought he was hot. Even back in school, before all the tattoos, he would dye his hair blue or pink, he hung out with the drama kids and seemed to be the leader of the misfits, he found clothes at thrift shops and altered them so that they were his own brand of rebellious. But he never got in trouble. His grades were good, and when he left after graduation and didn't go to college, it was a big deal. People talked about him throwing his life away. I wasn't sure when he went, but at some point he did attend college because he was a radiology tech, which was at least a two year degree. Alyssa knew him at work, but they weren't friends and didn't talk enough for her to have the details.

I dusted, I cleaned windows, and I scrubbed bathrooms. I filled hours with busy work. Every time my thoughts drifted toward Cotton, I forced them to cease and desist. I focused on Vincent and our upcoming date.

The house was clean. It was midafternoon.

To fill the remainder of my time before the date, I showered, obsessively changed my clothes seeking the perfect date outfit, and flat ironed my naturally wavy hair. I ended up looking not like myself, in the seersucker dress, and with abnormally straight hair. I even put on makeup, which I rarely bothered to do, saving the effort for special occasions.

I played loud music while I got ready, and spent all my time convincing myself that I would fall madly in love with Vincent Berry. I would show up for our date, we would have a wonderful time, and I wouldn't think about Cotton MacKenna. Nope, he was not allowed in my head. I convinced myself that I didn't care if he kissed me - twice, and walked away from me - twice, and left me bereft. Nope, he could do whatever the hell he wanted, and it would not include kissing me again, that was for sure. I was over my secret crush on Cotton, over reliving the moments he had his hands on me, and I would be fine.

Fine, I say. *Fine*.

The plan was for me to meet Vincent at Bella's, the only sort of fancy place in town, at seven. We had traded a few brief texts to ascertain the time and location of our date. No real phone calls, which I suspected were due to Alyssa letting it leak I had phone-phobia. I found myself almost wishing we'd talked, so that I could fall back on the sound of his voice, so that I could detect his level of enthusiasm for our date. Texting did leave a bit to be desired when it came to finding a connection.

I was ready to leave the house and head for the restaurant when two things happened at once. My mama arrived home from her day trip. And my phone lit up with a text from an unknown number - though the message indicated it was from Cotton and he had gotten my number from his brother.

"Hello, hello!" Came my mama's familiar voice as she came into the house.

I rushed to greet my mom at the front door and took a couple of her bags. My heart stopped beating for a second, while I processed what it might mean that Cotton had texted me. I tried to greet my mother without looking like I was having a heart attack. Distracted wasn't a strong enough word.

"Hi. Did you have fun?" I asked, willing myself to pay attention.

"I did." Her smile was more natural and relaxed than usual. The kind she only wore after having a break from her normal day-to-day life. "I'll tell you all about it over dinner."

111

"Oh. I made you dinner, so everything is ready, but I -"

"You are such a good kid." She pulled me in for a hug that was encumbered by all the bags. The woman had at least four tote bags, a soft cooler, several shopping bags, and her purse.

"Thanks. I'm going out. With Vincent Berry. Remember?"

"I forgot all about that. I was looking forward to seeing you tonight and talking with you." Her face fell, and her eyes accused me of awful things.

"I understand. We'll catch up tomorrow." It had occurred to me to remind her of my plans earlier before she came home, but unlike me she hated to text. So I hadn't bothered to text her my exact plans. I was hoping to leave her a note with the dinner I'd prepared, and be gone before she got back. "In fact I have to leave now."

My heart was settling down to a regular and less painful rhythm, but wasn't allowed to fully calm because my phone kept buzzing as more texts came in. I tried to focus completely on my mama and getting myself out the door. It occurred to me that it was highly unlikely she had forgotten about my date, because she had already been counting on me going on one so that she could use it to her advantage and set me up. Her feigned ignorance of my date pissed me off. As per usual, I couldn't figure out if it was me being selfish or her, and I didn't like either outcome. Our relationship was a mess.

"What is wrong with your phone?" She demanded, the earlier traces of her relaxed mood slipping away.

"What?" I snapped out of my thoughts. It had been chiming and chirping and buzzing like crazy in my pocket. "Texts, that's all."

"That sound is intolerable. Respond or turn the thing on silent." Yep, her good mood and relaxed smile: gone. I sighed and pulled my phone out.

Unknown: *Hi Sweet Maggie. This is Cotton. I got your number from Dom.*

Unknown: *I am trying very hard to stay away from you.*

Oh lord. My eyes - and heart - bounced back and forth

between the first two messages. *Sweet Maggie.* Good gracious. *Trying to stay away.* I groaned, then regretted it with my mama in the room.

Unknown: *I want to apologize. For my behavior last night.*
Unknown: *And last week.*

He was sweet. He was annoyingly formal. I was going to be late for my date.

While my mama carted her bags fully into the house and began delivering them to the kitchen, her bedroom or bathroom, and wasn't standing over me, I added Cotton to my contacts.

Me: *No need.*
Me: *You were right. About hurting me, I just didn't listen.*

I sent the response in a rush. I didn't allow myself to think first. My chest ached with the pain of the interaction, his apologizing and my being a martyr about it. I allowed myself a brief lapse in time and judgment to accept that he regretted kissing me. That I was stupid stupid stupid. I switched my phone to silent, and slipped it into my purse rather than my pocket, to better ignore any further texts. Not that I expected him to say anything further. What else was there to say?

"I have to go, Mama. I don't want to be late."

"Fine. I'll talk to you tomorrow." She was upset and giving me the cold shoulder.

Damn it.

"I'm sorry I won't be here tonight. I didn't realize it was so important to you."

"It's fine, Magnolia."

When a woman, particularly an angry southern woman, says fine - nothing is fine. She was mad. No, she was hurt. I knew her well enough to know that she would consider my actions as abandoning her, or not caring about her. If I cared about her I would be home to hear all about her trip. I wouldn't be leaving her to an empty house.

More and more, the older I got, I could not give in to her demands of my time. I recognized her tone, the clipped words, the mix of shock and hurt on her face. My whole life, I avoided doing or saying anything that would cause her to be upset. Between single parenting and Lucian's antics, she didn't need more stress. I erred on the side of overly placating to keep from making things hard for her. As an adult, I grew tired of the pressure. I could never quite discern if I placed it on myself or if it came from her. More likely it was some combination of the two, and what she expected from me got hopelessly entangled with what I thought was the right thing. I couldn't do it anymore. I tried, and for the most part stayed the path, but I couldn't be made to feel guilty for having a life. As an adult, I was well within my rights to have plans and to keep them. She knew about the plans upfront, and I wasn't convinced she truly forgot about them. I schooled my features, steeled my gut from giving into guilt, and I stayed strong.

I gave her a quick hug and left.

***

Bella's was downtown off Elm Street. I could have walked the few blocks over, and that had been my original plan. After getting held up for a few minutes more than I expected, if I walked I would be late.

I took the car.

It was technically my car. My name had been put on the title after Lucian died, making it mine. I only drove it when absolutely necessary. After four years, it wasn't possible that it held any of my brother. When I pushed myself into the driver's seat, I must have imagined the way it smelled like him. No amount of telling myself it wasn't real made it any less real. That nineties something Honda Civic hatchback would always be Luke's car, would always bring him to the forefront of my mind, and would continue to taunt me with his cigarette and Ralph Lauren Polo cologne scent. What would have taken me twenty minutes to walk, took all of five to drive.

Vincent waited for me out front.

He was cute. Impossibly intriguing. Tall and thin, bordering on lanky, with long honey brown hair pulled back into a messy man bun. Tattoos covered all exposed skin, except his face, in splashes of indiscernible shapes and colors. You couldn't not look at him. He stood near the entrance, hands stuffed into the pockets of his green chino pants. He would never fit in. I liked him, without actually knowing him, based on his ability to be himself. People stared. As I walked from my car to the glass door of Bella's, I saw people point and whisper, not bothering to hide that they were talking about him. People were rude.

"Hi."

"Hi." His lips were in an almost smile and his eyes roamed over me.

I found it easy to focus on him, our date, and not the drama I had walked away from.

At that he opened the door for me, and we went inside. The hostess was not immune to Vincent, and looked torn between finding him hot and finding him appalling. She was too young for him at any rate, not out of high school. Her candy apple red lips smiled at us as her focus stayed on Vin, and she showed us to a booth.

"How are you?"

"You look nice tonight."

He spoke at the same time I spoke, our words falling all over each other. We shared awkward smiles, and it helped. I looked at him, and he seemed a bit nervous, though his smile seemed natural, and it helped. I took a breath and tried to relax, including making myself stop fidgeting with the silver ring on my left thumb.

"I'm good."

"Thank you."

We did it again. Maybe on purpose. His shoulders marginally relaxed and he leaned against the booth back. I took an incomplete inventory of his visible tattoos while he openly appraised me. A cardinal on his neck with Dogwood flowers. A gypsy lady head on his forearm. An open rose on his hand. Symbols across his knuckles. All were artistic, with rich beautiful colors, good shadowing, and flowing clean lines.

Vincent Berry was a walking piece of art, and his tattoo artists were mega talented. I looked back up to his face, determined not to stare at his ink all night, and found him waiting for my gaze to lift.

"I'm sorry."

"Don't be."

"You must get sick of people staring at you."

He shrugged. His eyes never leaving my face, specifically my lips. Outwardly, he was relaxed, and he kept up his end of the conversation. But there was something about the way he watched me, his eyes lingering on my features, that told me he wasn't immune to me. It was a sort of rush to think he found me attractive, or that he wanted this to go as well as I did.

"Nah. I'm used it. The first couple years, it sucked. I hated the attention." He cocked his head to one side, remembering back to that time. "I don't like the attention now. Usually. More like I'm used to it."

I didn't miss the way his voice lowered when he said the word usually. He was either a skilled flirt, in which case I could smile and not take it personally. Much as I would if I was with Dominic. Or he was into me, and he was letting me know, and in that case my hands went clammy and my tongue went numb.

Our waitress, a girl I recognized from school and by proxy of living in our small town, but that I did not know personally, paused at the edge of our table. She did a double take, her eyes skipping from Vin to me and back again. The few seconds it took her to recover spoke volumes. Only, I wasn't sure what they said. She found it strange Vincent was out with me, or that I was out with him. Or maybe she had heard about my "dating" Dominic MacKenna, and she was disapproving about my being out with another guy. Hell, maybe she was having a bad day with a long shift working on her feet and she dazed out for a sec.

Moving on, Maggie, moving on.

"Hi, my name is Emily. I will be your server this evening. Do you know what you want to drink?" Her southern twang was more pronounced than most people in town. Her words came carefully, and I shoved away thoughts that she was being weird and that it had something to do with me.

Emily Tanner. That's right. She was a grade behind me. Band geek. Excellent softball player. No connection to me as far as I knew. No telling if she dated Dominic at some point. Vincent didn't look at her with a speck of weirdness, so I didn't figure he had dated her in the past. Actually, Vin was pretty well known for not dating since he'd been back in town. Huh.

He ordered a dark malty beer. I ordered a red blend wine. Emily walked away with her fake smile still in place.

"That was weird. Right?" I asked to confirm my assessment of the girl.

"I don't know her; I was hoping you could shed some light on what that was about."

"She looked like she'd seen a ghost."

"She looked like she wanted to claw your eyes out." Vincent's words were slow and sure, with a hint of a smile playing on his lips.

"What?" I sat back, surprised by his assessment. "She did not."

"That girl had a definite woman scorned air about her. You didn't steal her boyfriend?"

"Um, unless you are her boyfriend, no." Did he not know anything about me? I had zero boyfriends, zero potential boyfriends. I wasn't counting kissing Cotton because no one knew about that. "Oh, or Dominic."

"Are you saying you both dated Dominic?"

"No. I don't know." I was not being clear. Darn it. "I mean, I don't know if she has ever dated Dominic. I am not dating him, but we are friends, and she could have thought we were more."

"Interesting." He sat back again, cocked his head again, and studied me.

It was not interesting. It was disturbing. Emily. Not the thing with Dominic. Maybe a little bit Vin's reaction. Oh lord, think of something to say and change the subject. Something. Anything.

"So, you work with Alyssa."

117

"Yes." His smile was sly. I got the feeling he knew I blurted out random words because I was a crazy person and couldn't carry on a conversation.

When he didn't expand upon the topic I had presented, I searched for another.

"How's your sister?"

"Lu's good."

He continued to tell me about Louisa's struggles and successes at school, what she was up to at home, and more than I actually needed to know. It was an improvement over the stuttered conversation leading up to it, and I'd take it.

Our waitress dropped off drinks, took our order, and got away from us as soon as possible. With Vin's idea in my head, when I looked at her, I could see that she was aiming her desperate angry eyes my way. I chalked it up to a history with or crush on Dominic. I found it easy to ignore her with Vincent sitting across from me.

Every few minutes, my mind forced me to think of Cotton. The way he looked at me, the words he said to me, the searing of his lips on mine. It was impossible to put him completely out of my head. Which pissed me off. I wanted to forget about him and only have beautiful intriguing Vincent in my head.

We talked about mundane topics. It became easy and more comfortable as more time passed. The food was good, the wine warmed my belly and helped relax me, and I noticed Vincent's eyes were beautiful. A caramel brown with shots of gold that fanned out from his pupils. I picked my favorite of the tattoos that were visible to me, a black and gray cat in a swanky suit doing a little curtsy. It was small and on the underside of his forearm, tucked away so that I didn't see it unless he turned his arm a certain way. I enjoyed watching Vincent, the way his hands moved as he ate and talked, the small movements of his lips that made his smile seem like a well-guarded secret.

He paid for dinner, though I offered to cover my half. He walked me to my car, with a hand on my elbow, which was such a strangely gentle gesture. There was that moment, before I got in my car, before he walked away to his own vehicle, that moment filled with anticipation of the good night kiss. I had always hated when I got to that point of a date, when I was ready to escape, and I was freaking out hoping for or hoping against a kiss. Truthfully, it could go either way. Most of the guys my mama had set me up with weren't my type, and after a couple hours in their presence I liked them less, and I wanted to slip away without the kiss. A few times I was curious and wanted to rack up a little more experience. Even when I wanted the small peck on the lips, I wanted to get it over with and move on. These were guys that I had no intention of seeing again.

It was different with Vincent. I looked up at him and my eyes fell on his lips that curved ever so slightly into a smile. A hint of a smile. I wanted him to kiss me, and I wanted him to do it because I wanted to feel his lips on mine.

"Can we do this again?" Vincent edged closer, the toes of his skater shoes bumping into the toes of my ballet flats.

I nodded. There wasn't enough air in my lungs to respond properly, the anticipation burning it off. He slipped one hand behind my back and put a gentle pressure there, while he lowered his head. I lifted on my toes to meet him. Vin's lips were full and soft, he tasted like dark beer and marinara sauce, and after a brief lip-to-lip encounter he pressed in again to extend the kiss. I kissed him right back. I felt when his lips moved into that little smile right against my lips before he pulled away.

All the way home I replayed the kiss in my head. It was sweet. Vincent was sweet. He was smart and interesting, and I liked the way he looked at me. I would go out with him again - which would make Alyssa extremely happy - and I had no reason to think it wouldn't go well.

I climbed in bed, played screaming music through my headphones, and I cursed myself for being a terrible bad no good person. Because no matter how I tried not to think about it, the fact was I kept comparing my most recent kisses, and kept firmly landing in Team Cotton. He was bad for me, he wasn't even interested in going out with me, he was a big stupid boy that I wanted to hate. The feel of his hands on my body, his lips on my lips, his breath stealing mine, it consumed me. I silently screamed out my frustration and willed those memories to vanish from my mind. The problem was his touch had become known to my body, and it wasn't only my mind that wanted him. In fact, that was the problem, after having tasted him, my body definitely wanted him. My mind, it knew better. All the smart rational thinking parts of me were excited about going out with Vincent again. I would just have to show my body that it was wrong, and that it didn't need Cotton MacKenna, that he wasn't the only boy around. A little making out and heavy petting with Vincent, and all of me would be on Team Vincent.

Chapter Fifteen

Cotton

Denver had read me the riot act. Which was odd coming from him. Five years older than me was just enough that we weren't in the same circles. He was gone all the time doing little tours or going to teach fiddle workshops. We got along peaceably because we were both too quiet to bother with unnecessary conversation, and too much inside our own heads to worry what anyone else was doing. Except with him, it wasn't that he didn't care, it was more that he didn't know how to show it. We all knew - and discussed it behind his back - that once he fell for someone, it would be life altering. He did nothing half way. He did nothing even ninety percent. Whatever he was into, it was a total fixation. After he had told me off for being an asshole to Maggie, I asked him how to get over her. He was useless, had no advice, and told me if I insisted on being awful to her again he'd kick my ass.

I was beating myself up enough for both of us, thanks. Knowing Denver was disappointed in me hurt more than I would've thought. I hadn't come face to face with my oldest brother that way in a whole lot of years. Not since I used to pick fights, get suspended, and make our mama worry. Denver was the first one to pull me aside and tell me knock it off back in the day. He didn't like to get physical, and he hated confrontation, but he had taken me out a few times and punched some sense into me.

Thankfully the next brother in line, Joseph, had his head too far up his own ass to know what was going on. I loved all my brothers, and if it came down to it I would do anything for them, including Joe. But he had taken it on himself at an early age to try and be our dad. His sense of right and wrong was infallible, and his sense of duty to our family was his guiding light. For years we all ganged up on him and made it hard for him to try and point us in the right direction. We weren't interested in a big brother playing daddy and bossing us around. He met Missy and they got married right away, they had children, and he had an outlet for all his bossy father figure tendencies. I got along with him a helluva lot better after he moved out and stopped telling me what a screw up I was, and how much I embarrassed the family. If he had known how I treated Magnolia Porter, he wouldn't have taken it easy on me.

Beau and Elliot didn't say a damn word to me. Not after I trudged back to the house, looking like the puppy Denver had kicked and drug up the lawn. Not after we went inside and helped Dominic clean up from dinner. Only when they took off for Elliot's place and left with a parting reminder that I was house sitting the next few days. I answered with a curt nod. Their silence was worse than if they'd yelled at me.

"What the fuck is wrong with you?" Dominic rounded on me as soon as our brother and his boyfriend closed the front door.

"I don't want to talk."

"I'm sorry, did you think I was giving you a choice?" Dom's eyes flashed with anger like I had never seen directed at me; not from him.

"What I meant to say is, I will not fight with you over a girl." I clarified it for him. It wasn't an argument that would hold up, seeing as how we had gotten into a fight over her just a week prior.

The kitchen was clean. The house was still. We faced off in the front room, Dom with a towel still in his hands, and me shaking with the need to let him hit me. I wanted the release of fighting him, but more than that I wanted the punishment he would rain down on me.

"What the hell ever, Cotton. We are too far past that. I will not stand by and let you toy with her."

"I'm not toying with her." I ground out the words, and he

gave me a wide-eyed stare. I shoved my hands in my pockets. "Or, that's not my intention."

"I didn't say you were doing it on purpose. I know that you aren't trying to hurt her. But the thing is, you are." The fight hadn't drained out of him exactly, but it was taking a backseat to his need to move in close and lay it on the line. "If she comes to me crying over you again, I will not show restraint."

I chuckled, a dark sound that bubbled up from deep in my chest. The laugh was for his threat. The laugh was to cover the stabbing pain at hearing him say that Maggie had been crying. She went to him, my brother, when she was sad. Worse still, I had caused her tears.

I wanted to protect her, and instead I'd hurt her. I wanted to be the reason for her smiles, not her tears. Only how would she know how much I wanted to make her happy, when all I'd ever done was hold up my end of the bargain to hurt her?

"You will apologize." Dominic laid the order out before me. His face stony, resolute. "Then you will go back to avoiding her. No kissing that girl unless you are ready and willing to be with her."

"What, like that's an option?" He wasn't going to hit me. I relaxed my stance and moved to lean on the back of a fancy wingback chair our mama had liked and we had kept because none of us could bear to get rid of it.

"She likes you, Cotton." His admission was barely audible.

I watched him not know what to do with his hands as he told me something he maybe shouldn't have. His eyes moved around the room, and his voice dipped. I tried to swallow and found my throat unwilling.

"Maybe more than like," he continued. My heart sped, the flapping of wings in my chest. "If you want to be with her, yeah, it's an option."

"I'll apologize." I was not sure I could be near her and not pull her body into mine, not claim her mouth and body as mine. She would never be mine, and I severely lacked self-control when it came to Maggie, therefore I couldn't be near her again. "Give me her number. I'll text her."

"That's a good idea. I don't trust you to do it in person.

You'd just kiss her again."

"Shut up."

He laughed, and I knew we would be okay. For now. If I followed through. I tried out a laugh but it lodged in my throat, so that I sounded like I was choking.

I worked a few hours before I went to Elliot's place and checked on the plants and Jango. The upside was Elliot's house itself. It was gracefully old and tucked behind a mass of hickory trees boasting a three acre fenced back yard. The down side was Elliot's house. It was my big brother's boyfriend's house, and as such not ideal for complete abandon. Everywhere I looked I thought of Beau and Elliot, and while I loved them both, I was in no mood for their love and devotion.

I brought work with me, to occupy my errant mind, and to keep from falling farther behind. I bumped a couple other shoots to edit a newborn shoot first. The idea had been to give it priority in order to bring joy to the family. Babies grow and change so fast I didn't want a month to go by before they had their pictures. It was a mistake because when I looked at the parents and the images of the sleeping peaceful baby, it was with a pang low in my gut that couldn't be explained away. Not unless I was willing to look at my life choices which did not include getting married or having babies, and why my gut wanted me to make changes.

Elliot had orchids and African violets, he had a dozen green plants with names I didn't know off hand. I wandered through the meticulous and eccentric house and took care of each one. If nothing else, I could follow the simple instructions, and tend to his thriving plant life. Jango, the monstrous orange cat, was too big in a way that made me think he was part something other than house cat. He followed me when I moved from one room to another, he sat at my feet when I worked on my laptop, and he kept me company when I came around to doing the task I'd put off long enough.

Maggie's number programmed into my phone was a drug. A dangerous and compelling temptation. I carried her number with me, as if it equaled a real connection to her, and postponed the inevitable. If I waited too long, it would get back to Dominic I hadn't apologized.

I held out until Friday evening. Then I could no longer stand knowing that I could text her but that I hadn't. I could no longer pretend that I shouldn't have apologized already. I wasn't sorry I had kissed her. Regret for tasting her mouth and letting my hands memorize her curves didn't exist in me. The only thing I could regret was that I was wrong for her, and that I had hurt her feelings. Her shedding tears over me was powerful as much as it was devastating.

I meant to say, *This is Cotton. Sorry I'm an asshole.* That wasn't what came out when given the chance to communicate with her.

I tapped out a message. Then another. She didn't respond. There were no blinking dots indicating she was currently responding. I sent another.

Me: *Hi Sweet Maggie. This is Cotton. I got your number from Dom.*

Because she's the sweetest thing, and it was one of the reasons I craved her. Because she wouldn't know who I was. And likely she'd be alarmed that I had her number if I didn't say that her super amazing best friend Dominic passed it along to me.

I was angry. I was hopeful, for what I couldn't say, except that it had something to do with waiting for her response.

Me: *I am trying very hard to stay away from you.*
Me: *I want to apologize. For my behavior last night.*

Couldn't say, *I'm sorry.* Instead, *I want to apologize.* God, I didn't even apologize correctly. It wasn't just the night before either; there had been the first kiss outside Prissy Polly's.

Me: *And last week.*

Finally, she texted me back. Not a lot of time had passed,

but enough that it seemed likely she'd put some thought into her answer.

Maggie: *No need.*
Maggie: *You were right. About hurting me. I just didn't listen.*

And just like that I was wrecked. The first message, her blowing off my need to apologize, came as no surprise. It would be like her to tell me I didn't need to say sorry. I had certainly told her not to say it to me. Then the next blurb came and I squeezed my eyes shut against her words. I threw my phone across the room, only aware enough to aim for the floor so I didn't break anything in Elliot's house. I couldn't erase her response from my memory, the words etched on the backs of my eyelids.

I should be glad. That she was finally listening to me, believing me, and telling me to fuck off. It was the right thing.

The pain that expanded outward inside me until I was consumed, quickly turned to anger. Proof that I had been right, that all my warnings to myself as well as to Maggie were warranted, blazed a trail of fury through my system. I had hurt her. Not that I hadn't already known it, but seeing it come from her made it so much worse. She didn't want my apology because she was writing me off and accepting that I could do nothing other than hurt her.

When I could see something other than red that pulsed in time to my hammering heart, I gathered up my phone. The case had split and come away in pieces. The phone was perfectly fine.

Me: *Where is she?*

Dom: *I assume you mean Maggie.*

Me: *Obviously.*

Dom: *I don't know.*

126

Me: *Liar.*

Dom: *Come to the jam. We can talk then.*
Dom: *She won't be there.*

What was I doing?
I needed to see her.
I had to stay away from her.
God damn it, I was going to destroy this phone before the night was through. Or else text her again, track her down, and take her. The want for her had transformed into need. It was so much more than kissing her, than holding her body in my hands - it was knowing her and falling for the depth in her eyes, the sweetness in her smile, the hidden secrets behind her mask. Maggie was a fragile thing with a spine of steel; only she didn't seem to know she had that strength deep within her. I wanted to show her, to be there when she finally saw her own worth and took a stand. I wanted nothing more than to feel the wind from her wings when she learned she could fly.

You were right. About hurting me. All the fantasies that played out in my mind were dashed by the truth. Her words obliterating any possibilities.

The jam. I wasn't in the right headspace to play music. It would be a good distraction. I would surround myself with people, I would go someplace Maggie was guaranteed not to be, and I would resist finding her. Gathering up my banjo, I made sure Jango had food and water, then headed to the weekly bluegrass jam.

***

It was hot, which matched my foul mood. Within ten minutes I was sweating through my t-shirt. Denver didn't speak to me, but he shot a hostile glare my way more than once. I flipped him the bird, then intercepted a severe frown from Mr. Wakefield. I was clearly determined to fuck up no matter what. Rather than make things worse, I stolidly ignored my eldest brother while he fiddled and unassumingly led the jam circle.

"What's your deal?" Dominic demanded in a low voice between songs.

"No deal." I claimed, the falsehood a stupid attempt at ignoring my problems.

"I thought we were talking about this."

"I changed my mind." Talking was the last thing I wanted to do now faced with the prospect.

"Liar."

Dominic had traded seats with Grover Abbot, pretending that I hadn't sat far away from him on purpose, with the intent to interrogate me. Grover was happy enough to put distance between us because I was being a jerk to anyone within a ten-mile radius. Add him to the list of people needing an apology from me.

"You texted me, brother." Dom chopped on his mandolin, as *Red Wing* made its way around the circle. He wasn't paying any attention to the song, but he didn't need to. We'd been playing that song since we were about eight and ten years old. "What would you have done if I'd told you where she was?"

I would have gone to her. I would've done more stupid things. It was better I stay firmly seated at the jam.

"Do you know where she is?" Yet, I couldn't resist asking. The need to know coursed through me.

"Yes." His smile was unmistakable and unashamed.

I'd known he was lying when he'd claimed to not know her whereabouts. I also recognized the lie had been for my own good.

Knowing he knew; I wanted to know. That clawing need resurfaced and demanded I go to her. I turned away from my brother and focused on the song. I played it with too many notes, coming up with complicated improvs as I went, and garnering a few odd looks from the group. I could hear Dom's laughter thread through the sound of my banjo, weaving maniacally into the melody.

At the end of the night, Dominic caught up to me at my truck and stopped me before I could escape. He was as damp with sweat as me, sticky from the late June heat. It wasn't even the hottest part of summer yet, and the remainder of the season promised to be brutal.

"I've gone back and forth about what to tell you." He admitted, his smile wavering, and his eyes piercing.

I stared at him and waited him out. I was tired of games, especially with myself. I didn't want to guess what he was talking about or whether he'd tell me.

"Hell, I can't even decide what I hope you'll do when I tell you." When, not if. There was that. But his words hinted at something I would find unpleasant and my pulse spiked.

"Spill it already. I'm tired." It was nine o'clock on a Friday night and all I wanted to do was go back to Elliot's and sleep on his guest bed. Maybe a beer first. I kept myself from making guesses as to Dominic's hints by considering the beer I would drink and the bad TV I could watch.

"She's out on a date." Dominic put a hand up palm out, fast and firm, knowing I would potentially lose it. "You can leave her alone, and let her be with ... this guy."

This guy. He purposely withheld the name of her date. A date. Assuming Alyssa had her way in setting Maggie up, she was out with Vincent Berry. My mind was a string of swear words, they tangled together into a complicated mass.

"Or you can go to her and the both of you can stop pretending you don't want to be together." He shrugged, like it was simple. "Either way is fine by me. So long as you pick one and see it through."

Smart boy that he was, walked away before I could react.

What the hell? Leave her alone? Leave her to date some guy? So that he could kiss her, he could lay hands on her? No effing way.

Go to her? Ruin her date for what purpose? So I could come to my senses and walk away again? No.

I got in my truck and I drove. I drove until I was out of Fox River. Dominic had said, either or, handing me two options, and fully aware neither was an option. I was torn apart. Torn between my jealousy of her with another guy, and a lifetime of telling myself I wasn't good enough for Maggie Porter.

Well into the night, darkness pressing in on all sides, I turned the truck around and drove back to town. I played a Joe

Purdy album I had bought years ago, after overhearing Maggie tell Alyssa it was her favorite. His troubadour style of songwriting, and his lone acoustic guitar, wove into my warring emotions. This was a turning point, and I knew it. Dominic was right, that I had to make a choice and see it through. After hours driving away, I realized it was pointless to try and escape my own thoughts. Re-entering our town, asleep and peaceful excepting the loud rumble of my truck, I looked through the exhaustion and saw what I had to do. It came down to which outcome I could live with, and which would slowly kill me. I had spent the better part of a lifetime staying away from Maggie and resisting the pull to her. That brand of torture was no longer appealing. I wasn't sure how to make it up to her, to heal the pain I had caused her, but I was well beyond being able to keep my distance.

Chapter Sixteen

Magnolia

Sunday had been the longest day in the history of long days. Waiting for Alyssa to get home from her trip was testing my patience, stretching my ability to wait thin to the point of cracking. We shared frantic texts when she regained phone service, but there was no way I could tell her everything over text. It needed to be in person. We both had to work on Monday, and I had to bide my time. I had to sit tight, that was all there was for it.

Work ticked by in a slow painful droll of time, made worse by my incessant clock checking. By the time five thirty rolled around and I could show up on Alyssa's doorstep, I was antsy, half crazed from the need to hear her take on things.

As promised I showed up with ice cream.

"I ordered pizza. We are not starting with the ice cream." She yanked me through her back door and snatched the carton from my hands.

"Okay, yeah, that's fine." I was swept into her fast pace and followed her through the mudroom into the kitchen.

"Do not start talking yet!" She screamed at me and I laughed. "I'm pouring wine. Don't tell me you aren't drinking tonight. We're going to sit in the sun room and you are not skipping a single detail."

I agreed. We drank glasses of fizzy sweet Moscato sitting in the room made of glass. Like being outside but with her a/c pumping cool air on us.

"Go." She settled into a wide comfy chair, her feet tucked under her. Her face was expectant, and her fingers tapped out a rhythm that begged for me to spill the news.

"Oh my God, Lyss, I don't know where to start. I guess the beginning. Dinner at the MacKenna's." I took a gulp of my wine and cringed when it hit the back of my throat, syrupy sweet with the shock of alcohol. "They were all there. Not Joe, but you know what I mean. Five of them, if you count Elliot. Why are they all so big? Talk about intimidating!"

I told her about Dom cooking, about how sweet and friendly Beau and Elliot were. I told her how Denver had dragged Cotton into the kitchen, and it was obvious he didn't want to be there. I told her how I followed him into the darkening yard and he kissed me again. We paused only so that Alyssa could answer the door, pay for the pizza, and grab a couple plates. We went right back to our seats, with plates on our laps, and picked up where we left off.

"It was amazing. Perfect. I can't begin to think of a better kiss happening ever in all of time."

"But?"

"But he didn't mean to." I clutched my glass, steadied my plate, and stared out the window into her little fenced in yard. I thought back to that night and I was there all over again. "Clearly he's attracted to me. But he stops himself, says some bull like being no good for me, then leaves."

"He left you there?"

"He walked me back to the house first. But, yeah, he left me."

I told her how I cried into Dominic's chest. I skipped my conflicted feelings about running into his arms while I was still so upset about another boy's embrace. It was too complicated.

"What an asshole." Alyssa looked miffed, and a little like she pitied me. I couldn't blame her. "Sorry, Magpie."

"He apologized." I shrugged and finished my wine. "Via text."

"That doesn't even count. Puh-lease."

"Right?" I had gone back and re-read the brief text exchange too many times to count. I wanted to go back and say something else in response. Something less hurtful. I hated the way I had ended things in that bit of contact between us.

132

After everything, with all the fear and hurt he caused, I cared for him.

"Enough about him. Tell me about your date!"

Just like that she was excited, bouncing in her seat, and filled with hope. It made it easier for me to transition from the sadness that came with my memories of Cotton, and to focus on the good time I had with Vincent. I allowed myself to be swept up in her mood rather than dwell on the way I wanted to fall apart when I thought about Cotton.

She peppered me with questions about the date with Vin. We dissected little things he said and what I thought about every part of him. When it came to Emily Tanner acting weird, she agreed it was about Dominic. Apparently Emily had a big thing for Dom, but he'd never asked her out in all these years.

"How was *that* kiss?" We were on our second glasses of wine, stuffed with pizza, and heavy in our chairs. My friend tipped her head to one side, and her voice was threaded through with all her optimism. She wanted it to have been spectacular.

It was great, right? It was a first date kiss, not a make out session. It wasn't Vin's fault I compared all lip-to-lip contact with Cotton's assault on my sensibilities.

"It was sweet. Vin is sweet."

"Aww! Yay! When are you going out again?" She clapped her hands then laughed when she sloshed wine down the hand still holding her glass.

"Saturday." It was good to put thoughts of Cotton out of my head. I redoubled my efforts to think about Vincent, and our upcoming second date. "He asked me to go to the stupid Slip'n Slide thing with him."

"No freaking way! And you're going?" She jumped up and placed her glass on a side table. She stood over me and radiated her excited approval.

I nodded and fought my smile.

"You never go! Every year I beg and beg and you refuse. This is going to be so much fun!"

Alyssa pulled me up and still holding my hands bounced on her feet. I borrowed from her joy and let it become my own.

Vincent was a possibility, or at least he wanted to go out with me again, and there wasn't a negative thing about that. Possibilities were exciting, open ended, filled with risk and anticipation. In the case of Vin the risk appeared null, which made it easier to focus on the anticipation part.

All week Alyssa texted me about Vincent and about the silly town event. She and Jacob had plans to pass out water guns and up the ante on the wet fun. She all out refused to listen when I warned that she'd get thrown out and banned from coming back. It was a halfhearted warning at best. Everyone loved her and her goofy husband. Their antics were welcomed.

We made plans for her to come to my house on Thursday. Alyssa insisted at looking through my swimsuit collection and weighing in on which one I should wear on Saturday. Bearing in mind not just the town would be seeing me in it, but Vincent Berry would be ogling my body on our second date. I was having reservations about going to the event when she put it that way.

"I haven't told my mama yet." I was wearing a solid black one piece. Simple, with a classic neckline and skimpy enough down below I pulled a polka dot swim skirt over top.

"She'll lose her ever loving mind." Alyssa grumbled and shook her head at my swimsuit. "Maybe don't tell her until it's too late. Like on your way out the door, or the day after."

Her voice was dark as she joked, and her eyes critiqued my body and swimwear options. I owned all of three swimsuits. It wouldn't take long to narrow it down to the right one for the occasion.

"I keep hoping she won't care. You know? It's been so many years since Lucian was around to make trouble. It's not like when I show up that's all people will talk about."

"Of course not, hon." She knew I needed her to say it. Plus it was probably true. She waved a hand at me, and I knew she didn't want to go down that road. The one-way highway into awkward, resentment, and trouble that came from discussing my brother.

I pulled on a hot pink one piece with panels missing from

the sides. At least it covered my entire butt.

"This one has potential. Look at your hot little bod." She viewed me from all sides and smacked my butt as she came back around.

The last suit was my only two-piece. I'd only worn it trying to get sun in my backyard. It wasn't skimpy, and maybe didn't show any more skin than the one piece with the cut outs, but it still seemed like I was closer to being naked when I wore it. The bottom was yellow with coral stripes, a full seat, and a high waist. The top was coral with yellow straps and bow, fit like a bra with underwire and a little push up action.

"What the hell? This is the ugliest swimsuit I have ever seen." Alyssa screamed at me, her pleased level of surprise too big for my bedroom. "Then you put it on and holy hell. It shows how tiny your waist is and pushes your boobs out all over the place. Definitely that one."

The cut did accentuate my waist, but also that my hips were so much wider than my waist. Boobs all over the place didn't sound like a good thing, but I liked the support offered by cups.

"Wear your high-waisted cut off shorts as a cover up."

"That barely constitutes a cover up!" I smacked her and began changing back into real clothes. I could see her point, and they'd pair well with the suit. I could bring a long sleeve white button up as well, roll the sleeves up and tie it off just above my waist. I'd be covered, but it would still be cute.

"Vincent Berry is going to shit himself."

"I hope not, Alyssa." She fell into a fit of giggles and I couldn't help joining her.

All that remained was informing my mama that I planned to attend the silly Slip'n Slide shindig. I had several opportunities to mention my plans. They came and went, and I said nothing. I chickened out every time; my mouth refusing to utter the words. Mostly because conversation with my mama that week teetered between her working Friday night, and her friend's son whom she intended to set me up with. It might seem as if that was the perfect opportunity to inform her I was in fact

135

going out with Vincent again, and therefore did not require her to find me a man to date. I knew better. I knew as soon as I said my next date was to take part in a big deal all out town festivity, she would double her efforts at finding me an appropriate date. Instead of facing the dating issue, I turned the topic to her work schedule and the damn hot weather and anything not to do with me.

Dom: *Tell me you're breaking tradition and planning to spend time throwing yourself down sheets of wet plastic.*
Dom: *Next tell me when I can see you again. I'm hankering for another "date" with my best girl.*

Me: *As it happens I am going to the stupid thing on Saturday. I do not intend to slip nor slide.*
Me: *Come over Friday night. My mom will be out all night.*

I realized too late how that sounded. I cringed as I waited for his response.

Dom: *Magnolia Peach!*
Dom: *I would love to come to your house when you are home alone and assist in debauchery.*

Me: *OMG I said nothing of debauchery. You're ridiculous!*

Dom: *Yeah, yeah, you know you love me. Jam first, then corruption of sweet innocent Maggie.*

Knowing I had plans to see Dominic soothed my frayed nerves. The anxiety that came from not thinking about his stupid brother and how much my heart ached for him despite the pain that lingered there as a reminder why that was a bad idea. The overwhelming apprehension that came with plans to be in next to no clothes all day with a boy I potentially liked while wondering if I was betraying my mama. I was a mess, and I needed that night with Dominic.

Chapter Seventeen

Magnolia

For the last six years, my mama worked as a home health nurse, visiting patients in their homes. Fox River wasn't big enough to need much in the way of home health, and for years she worked all over, driving for hours from one small mountain town to another. It was a relief when she was finally able to secure the job with the agency that put her as the head nurse for Fox River. The hours were magnitudes better seeing all her patients in one area and not so spread out. Since she'd gotten her nursing degree, she'd been able to work one job instead of several. The pay was enough to keep normal hours. My mama worked hard, still, never able to feel secure financially. After knowing what it was like to be left jobless with two children, having to work three jobs and still struggle to get by, to put herself through school and come out on the other side, she never forgot those days. I knew each week, when her paycheck was automatically deposited into her bank account, she breathed a sigh of relief. Pennies were pinched more than strictly necessary, just in case, to appease that ever present background of fear. It was that residual fear that led her to occasionally take on extra work. Her name was on the list of nurses available to stay overnight with a patient, to give the family a break or fill in for a nurse that needed a shift off. It was rare she took one of those night shifts.

"I'll be in Deep Gap all night. It should be easy. Truthfully, the patient is low needs, will sleep all night, and I won't have much to do. They only need an RN there to give the meds in the morning."

I sat at the bar snacking on pretzels and watched my mama

pack a bag of snacks for her time at the patient's house. She'd already eaten dinner. I was waiting until after the jam. It would likely be nine before Dominic and I pulled off making dinner, and I'd be starved by that time if I didn't snack before heading out.

She didn't like night shifts. It messed her up for days after. I was half tempted to tell her to stop doing them altogether. Especially since I'd finished college and pulled in my own steady income, she didn't need as much money coming in herself. She barely let me help out with bills, claiming I was still her little girl and she was well within her rights to take care of me. It allowed me to sock money away for when I eventually moved out and had my own place.

"Hug your mother."

I dutifully hopped up and fell into her embrace. She was soft and comfortable and familiar in a way that felt like home. Her sweet cloying jasmine scent was caught in my nose, one more thing that was familiar as she was to me.

"Be good!" She called out those last words as she left me alone.

Be good. Right, as if I'd be anything other than good.

She didn't ask if I had invited a boy over. She didn't ask about my plans at all. I swam in a dark mix of guilt for not having volunteered the information, and shame that I was somewhat pleased to be getting away with something. Mm hmm, being good, as usual. Or not. But I was able to let go of the back and forth of my worries, because the more I thought about it, the more I didn't care. What I had planned wasn't all that bad, in fact was so innocent as to mock my initial guilt at not sharing the plans.

I scheduled my arrival at the jam so that it wouldn't risk my having to interact with the participants. Jam started at six. I walked into the city park at 6:15. It was a shitty thing to do to Dominic, who had texted me a quarter till six asking where I was. I told him I was running late. I was bad person and a liar, but I convinced myself it was barely a mis-truth and that it was for the greater good. I heard the music before I saw the group of players.

Half way across the park, making a beeline for my Dogwood tree, I was intercepted by an angry boy.

"I was worried." His face was etched with it, and his chest heaved with the quick sprint he'd made to me.

"Sorry, D." Re-enter guilt. I was a bad friend.

He hugged me. Pulled me right in there, with his mandolin gripped around the neck in one hand, and me suddenly gripped by the other.

"I'm like a half hour late." I mumbled into his shoulder and he released me. "I texted, you know, so you wouldn't worry."

"You're right." He shook his head; his face told me he couldn't shake off his feelings.

"Go." I shoved him, and he finally smiled at me. "I came here for the music, and it's not music without you."

"Ha. You are a shameless flirt when you wanna be, Maggie Bee."

Was I flirting? With Dominic? I was so wretched at flirting; I didn't even recognize it when I did it. He went to the uneven circle of musicians and I went to my shady spot. I hadn't bothered with the chair and cooler, instead opting to sit on the ground and sweat it out. My fingers tangled in the thick grass at the roots of the little tree, and I gave up worrying that my butt would be a mess of dirt and grass when I stood at the end of the jam.

Cotton sat on the far side of the circle from where I sat to watch. It was his usual spot, unlike a couple weeks before when he'd put his back to me. My eyes were drawn to him. As a general rule, I didn't mind looking in his direction. Cotton MacKenna was nice to look at. His bright red hair was especially pretty in the sunlight. The problem was every time I looked his way, he caught me. I was fascinated by how often he looked at me, his heated gaze combing over me before bouncing away. His expression as intense as always. Not being a normal person, I didn't find it off-putting in the least. I was curious what he was thinking about, what was going on that he didn't speak up about, what made him cut his eyes to me so frequently. I wondered if he thought about the kiss.

I wondered if he wanted a repeat or if he had regrets.

Despite the way he'd torn himself away from me, I wasn't convinced it was what he wanted. The more I'd thought about it, the more I'd seen he was just doing what he thought was right. Not what he wanted.

Dominic came over as soon as the jam wrapped up. Cotton packed up and lingered at the park, but didn't join us or say hi. Dom led me to his car, guiding me with a hand behind my back, warm and steady. He stopped a few times to talk with people, and I stood at his side wishing I knew how to respond. I never knew what to say other than muttering a *hi* or *bye*. A halfhearted *how are you?*, *I'm fine thank you*, thrown in because it was automatic. I paid attention to Dominic, the way he playfully teased folks, dropped easy compliments, and made it look so easy. He had told me that up front it came easy to him. I wasn't convinced I could learn to be so friendly or outgoing. I was getting better at one on one, at least with him, and that was enough progress.

***

Dominic MacKenna was a sneaky guy. Without a hint of what he had planned, when we got back to my house, he unpacked coolers with everything we needed for dinner and drinks. He wouldn't tell me what he planned. He wouldn't let me help carry a thing. I pulled open the front door, happy to see him in without interference from a parent, and there he stood all glorious mischievous smile and laden with supplies.

"Enough with the suspense. What did you bring me?"

"Us." He slid past me and fully into the house. "I brought us tacos and margaritas, in their raw form."

"Raw form?"

"We have to make them."

"Right. Cool."

We went to the kitchen. I had never cooked with anyone other than my mama or Alyssa. My mama on a regular basis, mostly out of necessity on account of sharing a house and kitchen, but also because she liked to bake and I liked to help. Alyssa because she was into making cookies and a couple times a month we met in my kitchen to do so. Dominic in my house and in my kitchen was a wholly different experience. I was unprepared for how to handle such a situation. Nerves ratcheted up my spine and left me more unsure than usual how to proceed. I unpacked his reusable shopping bags, spreading ingredients across the laminate counters, and took stock, for lack of other ideas what to do.

"Blender? Tell me you have a blender."

"I do. Bottom cabinet to the left of the fridge." I pointed and watched as he located the appliance and placed it on the counter top. His priorities were clear. "I see you're starting with the drinks."

"Correct." His laugh was a low rumble. It served to remind me there hadn't been a man in this kitchen in ... many years.

We blended tequila into icy slightly syrupy drinks. Then we began preparations for tacos. The longer we spent working together in the kitchen, the more fun I had. I was still on edge, jumpy, unable to drop off that feeling of weird that came with him being in the house. But I found I could ignore it for longer and longer stretches of time.

"Hey, you okay?" Dominic placed a hand on my low back and looked down at me. He had pulled me out of my thoughts, and I looked up at his pretty soft blue eyes.

"Uh huh." I said with no conviction. "Sorry."

"Dating tip number 47: don't apologize for spacing out."

I leaned in so that I nudged his chest with my shoulder, then continued stirring the pan of beans and peppers and taco makings.

"Next level dating tip number, hmm, 13: share your thoughts."

"Next level?"

"You heard me." He paused, looked at me closely, then explained himself. "First date, not sure about the guy: you don't have to tell him everything. Boyfriend type, you're connecting with the guy and taking it to the next level: he wants to know. It's good to share, Maggie."

Dom didn't precisely fall under the boyfriend type. But we were getting closer and he obviously cared enough to want to know what was going on in my head.

"I was thinking about my brother. Not exactly about him, more like the lack of him."

Dominic stilled. I was aware of the air in the room, and how it altered to be more still too, and thicker.

"Not like that." My words tumbled out in a rush to make it better. "God, I can't get my thoughts out."

"Try again, Peach."

I rolled my eyes at the pet name. He was somber and listening. My chest warmed, filling full. I wasn't used to this, a connection with someone so real and easy that I could say anything. Not even with Alyssa who was my best friend in the world. She got weird when I brought up family stuff.

"You, being here, it made me think that there hasn't been a man in our house in a long time. It feels ... weird. But not bad."

"Yeah. Okay. I can see that."

He was too quiet. Thoughtful. I didn't know what to do with that. Dom was normally joking, doing more than his fair share of the talking. I left him to it and turned the heat off on the pan of food.

"Your mom doesn't date?" He asked, still quiet and thoughtful.

"Yes. No. Well, not really. She has over the years, but not in a long time."

"You haven't dated much. Until Berry."

That one was a statement rather than a question. I sighed. We had sort of talked about this up front, which led to our fake dating in the first place. Rather than get into my confused feelings where Vincent Berry was concerned, I brought up the past.

"I went out with Tiny Douglas in high school." I didn't mention the guy I had briefly dated during college. It had been an epic disaster, and he hadn't been a Fox River boy so chances were Dom didn't know anything about it. I didn't bother with the string of first dates that had stemmed from my mama's best intentions gone awry.

"Oh my God, I forgot about that." He offered me a smile,

and I focused on that to get me through.

Tiny had been a large guy, tall and broad and proud of his spot on the football team. One grade ahead of us, and the sweetest guy around by a long shot. His name was James, and his mama called him Jamie, and he had been nervous to hold my hand. We progressed to kissing, which never failed to leave him without a deep scarlet blush on his cheeks. I hadn't thought about him in a long time either.

"He's in Montgomery, Alabama now. Married with like three little girls."

"Dang. He has three kids? He's like twenty five." I was only sort of surprised that Dom didn't know the details. Seeing as his brother was married to Tiny's sister, but they'd been estranged for a number of years. And of all the MacKenna brothers, Joseph was the one that lifted out. The one least likely to be around.

"Yep. He met his wife freshman year of college. They were married and had the first baby before they graduated."

"How do you know all of this?"

"Social media. You aren't friends with him?"

"Guess not." He shrugged. They hadn't been friends in real life. Plus family drama.

"I'm not actually friends with him. His wife said no." It had hurt my feelings at the time, when he unfriended me. But he was happy, and I saw updates occasionally through other friends. Social media was a complicated web.

"Hey, promise me something." Dominic said in a sudden urgent tone.

I paused arranging tacos on plates and looked him in the eye at his urgent tone. I nodded.

"Whoever you end up dating, and eventually marrying, don't let them make you unfriend me."

"I'm not sure you and I are friends." In my mind, I flicked through my Facebook friends.

He looked hurt, severely hurt, for a second. I was hit was a fat tree limb across the gut of guilt. What had I said? But then his face cleared, and he found a small smile.

"Clarify: online or in real life?"

"Oh! Oh God, D. Online. We aren't friends online." I was relieved that he had misunderstood my statement, and that I hadn't actually caused him too much grief. But I was also oddly confused by his devotion to me; surprised that it would hurt him when I suggested we weren't friends. "I didn't mean it the way it sounded."

"Good. We came close to needing a pinky swear friends forever moment." His relief colored his words, along with his wide-open feelings for me. I had never had someone so quickly and resolutely faithful to me.

"I'll pinky swear if you want."

He hooked his pinky in mine, as our hands hung down at our sides. Just for a second. It was sweet, so incredibly sweet I ached from it. How had we become so close so fast?

We took our tacos, messy as they promised to be, to the couch and set up camp in front of the not flat screen television. He made a fresh blender full of margaritas for refills. I let him flip through our DVDs. His eyebrows had risen high on his forehead when I told him no Netflix, no streaming of any sort to the TV. I explained my mom was old school, if old school meant afraid of technology. After a few minutes of vetoing ideas, he stuck in a movie and gave me no choice.

"*Back to the Future*? Good call."

"Classic."

"I haven't seen it in a long time. I kind of forgot it was in there."

"Was it Luke's?" His voice was quiet when he asked, like he wasn't sure if it was okay to bring him up.

"Um, yeah." I shifted and rearranged my feet under my body, balancing my plate on my knees. "But it's one of the few movies we all liked."

Growing up there had been a divide, a canyon sized divide, between what my brother liked and what I liked. Our choices were so stereotypical "boy" and "girl" it was funny when I looked back on it. He was all action movies, fast cars, and westerns. I was all rom coms, teeny bopper, and tear jerkers. Somewhere in the magical middle ground we had things like *Back to the Future*, anything with Robin Williams, and the original *Jurassic Park*. That divide carried over to all areas of our life. We never shared the same interests in clothes or food, activities and hobbies, morals or anything. I had lived with my brother the majority of my life, and I felt a hollowness when I thought about how little we knew each other.

The opening scene played out. We munched on tacos and slurped margaritas. It was easy. The ease of it freaked me out. Again. Tiny fizzy bubbles of anxiety beginning to rise.

"The clothes are so so bad." I blurted to break the silence.

Dom's laugh was a rumble while he chewed his food.

"It bugs me every time that it's not the same Jennifer in this one and the next one." He admitted between bites of food.

"The new Jennifer is better. Elizabeth Shue is better."

"She ended up more famous, that's for sure."

We swapped off quoting the movie as we watched it. Plates were discarded to my mama's antique phone table turned end table, and glasses were refilled. I drank more than my norm, allowing myself to fall into the warmth and relaxation of it. I slid down and sat on the floor, with my back against the couch. I sat close enough to Dominic, or he sat close enough to me, that my shoulder pressed against his knee.

"I hate this part!" I wanted to throw a hand over my eyes.

Biff was having his way with Lorraine in the car. Her skirts pushed up, panic racing across her face as she scrambled for freedom. Seconds ticking by as I waited for her to be saved.

"Hey." Dom's voice beckoned to me.

I turned my head and tipped it back to look up at him. He was at home on my mama's pink and white sofa that matched nothing but somehow worked in the room, with one arm casually across the back and his knees spread wide.

"What?" I asked, thankful for the diversion.

"You remember when Wesley Donovan showed up at the bluegrass jam dressed like Doc Brown?"

I cracked up laughing at the memory before I could even respond. Dominic was sensitive enough to know when I needed distracting. I wouldn't have predicted he would be so in tune with me.

"He was brilliant!" I got up on my knees, so I could face

Dom better without craning my neck. "Had the mannerisms down and everything. Too bad he doesn't drive a De Lorean."

"Can you imagine the business he'd drum up?"

Our voices had risen, the movie forgotten in the background. Wes and his designated driver service became hilarious as we envisioned his driving the infamous car in the movie.

"People would need a ride everywhere they went. Hey, Wes, could you bring me to work, and pick me up, and take me grocery shopping after? Times like a million." I said it all in a snooty weird voice, not my own, and made a funny face while I did it.

"Oh, that we had a million residents in Fox River."

We laughed again. I thought through the ramifications. It was unforeseeable because Fox River was Fox River largely because it was a small tight knit community.

"Oh, that we didn't. I can get grouchy about the small town thing, but I think I prefer it."

"Me too." He admitted. "We should have a Back to the Future marathon for the next movie series in the park. And have Wes reprise his role. His brother Seth can be Marty McFly. But who will be Jennifer?"

"It doesn't matter. She's interchangeable." I reminded him.

"That would be awesome." He was laughing, then he wasn't laughing, and his face had lost some of the hilarity of the moment and I was left with just his smile. "I had no idea you were so ..."

"What?" I blanched. I felt it happen, the blood drain out of my face. Despite all the progress we'd made as friends, my first thought was that he'd tell me I was lame, too sweet, or some other form of not cool enough. When he didn't answer immediately, I asked again. "What's wrong?"

"Nothing, it's just, you're so fun. Different than I thought." He shook his head and I could tell he wasn't finished, so I let him keep going. "That sounded bad, but it's not how I meant it. You're so quiet all the time. I've never seen you like this, being silly."

"Oh." I had to sit with that for a minute. Or several. I had to

146

sort out of this was a compliment or an insult.

"Does Cotton know? He'd love it."

"Does Cotton know what?" It was weird how separate each word was, how hard it was to say them in a neat row. "What do you mean?"

I had managed to live through several Cotton Free hours in my head, since arriving back at my house with Dominic. I had been lost in the movie and our dinner and not thinking of Cotton MacKenna one bit. The kissing montage had ceased to be playing in the background of my head. I should have been glad for the reprieve. Instead I missed him. I missed the constant thoughts of him, the longing that came with remembering his lips and hands on me, and the imaginary way he stayed after the kiss rather than the reality of his leaving. It all came rolling back over me, smashing me with a renewed intensity.

"You don't know." A statement. Not a question. Dominic's face was pained, that was the only word for it. The shift was heavy and tasted a little like pennies. His change of topic from me to his brother had me scrambling to keep up. His change in mood was hefty and I lagged behind.

"Know what? Dom, you're freaking me out."

"Nothing, I thought you knew." He went to wave it away, like whatever bomb he was inadvertently dropping could waft away with the air between us. My eyes were bugging out of my head. I reached a hand out and grabbed his wrist because I couldn't help it. "You should talk to him. Maggie, it should be him taking you out. I mean, for real out. Not me."

"I still don't know what you're talking about." I sank back down, sitting on my heels on the floor. My hand still on Dom's wrist.

His phone chirped and buzzed, and I flinched in surprise. I let go of him and turned back to face the movie. It was near the end, with the clock tower debacle. His phone chirped again.

"You can get that. I don't mind."

"It's probably Cotton."

I wasn't sure whether that meant he would or would not

check his texts. Dominic had told me on our first fake date that texting during a date was a faux pas. I had agreed. It was dating rule number 47 or 13 - they were almost all either 47 or 13 which I never stopped finding funny.

He shifted, his knee moving against my shoulder, and I knew he pulled his phone from his pocket. I sat very still and didn't turn away from the tv. Dom silenced his phone so his tick tack typing sound wasn't disrupting the climax of the movie. He was thoughtful and polite, and I was pretty sure not everyone knew that about him. I thought about the girls he took out, the casual easy way he dated his way through the eligible girls in our town. Did they all know? Or did they not get this version of him? I got the feeling he kept the charming persona fully intact when he for real dated, and those girls weren't privy to the real softer sweeter albeit still charming Dominic MacKenna.

The end of the movie came and went, and Dom became furious at his phone.

"Maybe I was wrong and you shouldn't have checked your messages." My brain was on a loop of Cotton, Cotton, Cotton. Damn him.

"Look, I have to go." The strained tone of Dom's voice was disconcerting to say the least.

"What?"

I stood, in alarm, and looked around me. Which made no sense, but I hadn't been thinking about it when I did it. I needed a reason. His abrupt departure was blatantly wrong. My fingers curled and flexed, longing for something to hold, something solid.

"Everything is okay." Dominic's voice was serious but laced with something else. I stared up into his face when he stood too, and tried to figure out what I saw there. "I'm going to go. You're going to stay."

"What?" I had already asked that. It was still the only thing that made sense to ask. I blinked up at him, my hands moved to my hips. I felt anger rise, snaking up my spine, as I faced the fact he was cryptically abandoning me.

Oh. Maybe it wasn't Cotton on the phone. Maybe he was

going to hook up with some girl. That made sense. The sting of rejection was minor, but still existed, and I was madder on account of my feelings being hurt. I had no leg to stand on with him, and I knew it. Not when it came to going out with a girl that would sleep with him. Not that he expected that of me, or even wanted it, because we were happily friends. I thought back to his making me promise not to unfriend him if a future boyfriend asked me to, and it would be hypocritical of him to drop me for a date. I seethed with anxiety and anger and embarrassment.

"Don't be mad at me!" He put up both hands, like he was surrendering and his face was slowly becoming more and more playful. He was up to something. He backed toward the door. "I told Cotton that you were home alone, and you got scared so you called me. I told him I was going to come over to check on things, and he got all crazy about that ... so I was never here. Cotton's on his way."

"What the heck are you talking about Dominic MacKenna?" I yelled at him. He smiled, with dancing eyes and wider smile. My riled-up emotions had nowhere to go.

"Trust me, Peach."

He let himself out the front door and left me standing there confused as ever. Cotton was coming over? Because I was pretend scared to be home alone? Say what?

Chapter Eighteen

Cotton

I was more than a glutton for punishment. I was a self-sabotaging masochist.

Years had gone by with Magnolia Porter steadily on my radar, yet I had successfully not fixated on her. Out of sight, out of mind. Marginally in sight, marginally in mind. Then I kissed her. Then I had fucking kissed her again. What the hell I had been thinking, I had yet to reckon. My brain had taken a back burner along with my impulse control. Whatever led to the kissing didn't so much matter as much as the kisses themselves. No matter what I did, I could not stop wishing for her lips on mine, her body in my hands. Her sweet attention given freely to me. I was driven to distraction.

Knowing she had gone on a date made it worse. So much worse. My mind couldn't shut down the images of her with another guy. I tried not to think about it, though it festered. Then on Wednesday grabbing coffee at Darlene's, I overheard Olivia Hamilton tell Haley Jenkins that she heard from Emily Tanner that Vincent Berry had taken Maggie Porter out. I wanted to stab myself in the eye listening to gossip between those catty girls. I couldn't stop myself from eavesdropping when they mentioned Maggie. Dropping the details I so badly wanted to know - that I needed to know despite all the work to convince myself otherwise. Apparently Vincent and Maggie had gone to Bella's on Friday, and Emily had waited on them. She was hung up on Dominic, and from what Olivia was saying to Haley, she was very much not over him. It was her opinion that Maggie was cheating on Dominic when she was out with Vincent. God, it was a mess.

Clutching my paper cup of hot black coffee, I tore myself away from the front counter and left the gossiping girls behind. Haley and I had dated the last two years of high school, and only broke up after I'd lost my shit and punched a wall with her in the room with me. That event was the reason I didn't get involved with women. It wasn't worth the risk. Especially with Maggie.

I kept myself busy editing a shoot for a foodie magazine. Unemotional work. Still, my unease festered and grew the more I thought about Maggie's name dragged through the mud. I knew she wasn't dating Dominic, but I also knew Dom wanted to cultivate that image. He was happy to let people think they were dating in order to give himself a reprieve from dating other girls.

Vincent Berry. God damn it. Meddling Alyssa had actually set them up. He was my age, and I'd known him in school. As much as I wished I could bad mouth him and have good reason to warn Maggie away from him, it wouldn't be true. Vin was a good guy. He took a lot of slack for the tattoos and hipster thing he had going on. But when it came down to it, he was loyal to his family, and he was a stand-up guy. I'd never had a problem with him before; until I pictured his slim hands on Maggie. My hatred for him bloomed fast in a flurry of jealousy.

The jam had been torturous. Dominic had paced around unable to settle down with the rest of us, and I knew he was waiting for Maggie. The more worked up he became, the more tormented I became. I watched him watching for her. I didn't relax until he pulled her into a fierce hug and I knew she was safe and sound.

Damn if she didn't look my way every few minutes the entirety of the jam. Two and half hours or so of intercepting her intense gaze, for it to skate immediately away, then drift back once again. I didn't have it in me to pretend I was immune to her attention. The muscles in my jaw were sore from the way I clenched my teeth together. I'd broken another string from playing too hard. My hands wanted to find release, and my banjo wasn't doing it for me.

Dominic had taken Maggie home, and it had taken a great deal of practiced restraint for me to let that happen. I knew she was unquestionably all right with him. It was a good thing he took her rather than her walking back alone. I should have been happy because I could trust that she was safe. Instead, all I could focus on was watching them walk away. Their backs to me, my brother placing a hand on her hip to guide her along, and her leaning into him slightly. She liked him and trusted him.

Him. Not me.

I went home alone, shut myself in my bedroom, and wished I could get that girl out of my damn head. I channel surfed and opened another beer and did not wallow in self-pity.

Boredom was to blame for my stupidity. A nineties sitcom was not enough to engage my errant mind, so I texted Dominic. As a general rule, I wasn't fond of texting. Hell, I wasn't fond of cell phones much less the expectation to read and respond to arbitrary messages. I scrolled through my inbox - of calls, emails, and texts - once a day maximum. If anyone required a response, I sent it out then and put the phone away to charge someplace out of earshot. I told myself I was texting Dom to ask him about the mix up regarding Maggie dating both him and Vincent. It was a lie I told to myself, which is the worst sort, and I knew it had considerably more to do with my not wanting her to date at all. Unless it was me. Which was not an option.

Me: *Hey man. I heard some gossip today.*
Me: *About Maggie cheating on you.*

Dom: *Good lord. People have nothing better to do than make shit up.*

Me: *Come on. You know you've let people think you two are together.*

Dom: *Are you pissed that people think she's with me?*

152

Me: *I'm pissed that people think she's cheating on her boyfriend.*

Dom: *Damn. I'll clear it up - spread the word she isn't with me.*
Dom: *Is this about her rep? Or about her date?*

Me: *I'm pretending I don't know about that in order to not kill Vincent Berry.*

Dom: *Ah. So you know. Sorry, man.*
Dom: *For what it's worth, I still think she's into you.*

Me: *Not happening.*
Me: *Where the hell are you anyway?*

Dom: *Maggie's.*

Me: *Maggie's? What the fuck?*

The phone screen blurred, and I blinked with no success at clearing the mist of jealous indignation that swelled and took over my senses.

Dom: *Actually just heading over there.*

My hand shook. My lack of control pissed me off more than anything else. It gave me a direction for my disproportional anger.

Heading to Maggie's? As in on his way to her house? It was almost midnight. I didn't care if he said it was a non-date, a fake date, that they were friends, whatever the hell. All I could think about was my brother at her house, alone with her, in the middle of the night. My brother that dated more girls in a year than most did in their lifetime, that slept with most of those girls and convinced them they didn't want anything serious from him. With Maggie. My Maggie.

Dom: *Chill. I brought her home. But she called me back over.*

Dom: *She's home alone and got scared. She called me to come check things out.*

Scared? I stood up and dug in my front pocket for my keys. Scared? She was scared? Of what? My heart jack hammered in my chest and shook me to my core. The idea of her in danger sent me to my truck before I could think through my actions.

Me: *Don't. I'll go. I can be there in 10.*

Dom: *You're closer than me. You go. I'll let her know it won't be me.*

Shit. Shit. Shit.

The adrenaline that pumped through my body kept me in motion. I drove toward Maggie's house, reckless in my need to get to her. I knew where it was, but I had never been. There had never been cause for me to visit her house.

Was there legitimate cause now?

The doubting voice in my head, the one that pounded harsh along with my heart, told me this was a bad idea. That Maggie didn't want to see me. That she called Dominic and was expecting her safe friend to show up in the middle of the night. Not the asshole that kissed with no warning then took off with no explanation.

Not me.

I was able to dismiss that voice because there was no way I was leaving her to sit in an empty house feeling afraid. Not happening. I physically could not sit by and let Dom handle the situation. Whatever happened, it had to be me; I had to be there with her.

The front porch light spilled a puddle of yellow across the entry, and the windows along the front of the house glowed golden around lightweight curtains. A typical ranch style house in a row of cookie cutter houses. Completely suburban. Old enough to need new shutters, new enough to not be considered

154

old. The gutters needed cleaning. I calmed my blazing mind by making a list of things I would do to help her mama take care of this house.

My fist pounded on her door twice. I was fully prepared to rip the door open to get inside to her, but I didn't want to scare her.

As the door drifted slowly open, Maggie's small form appeared in the space.

My eyes raked over what I could see of her as I stepped into the house. Her dark brown eyes, normally full of warmth, were wide and cautious. She chewed her lips, the bottom then the top then the bottom, raking the skin through her teeth and leaving her lips red and swollen. She was beautiful with her hair in curls around her face and down over her shoulders, in only a simple camisole and cotton sleep pants.

"Maggie. Are you okay? What happened?"

"I'm fine, Cotton."

My breath caught, as it always did, when she said my name. It went back to some deeper carnal desire to hear her calling out my name as I wrecked her sweet body with pleasure. It drove into my heart, begging that she trust me and whisper my name as a promise. I still looked over her, determined not to miss some sign that she was in danger, while my heart continued to crash into my ribs.

"Dominic told me you were home alone and something scared you."

"Yeah ..." She tucked her head down, her hair shielding part of her face, and let the word out with a sigh. "I heard a sound?"

Did she think she could hide away from me? I kept my hands strictly to myself, rather than adjusting her curtain of hair and revealing her face.

"Is that a question?" Clarification was the first step, and it was a slow tangled process that I didn't have the patience for.

"Yes?"

I stepped fully into the house, and closed the door behind me. I moved closer and closer to Magnolia Porter, a magnet drawn to its opposite. My fingers tucked under her chin, gently tipping her head back so that I could see her face. Porcelain skin sprinkled with a light dusting of freckles, long lashes fluttering over wide eyes, she was a gorgeous girl. True, she appeared startled, and she was covered with chill bumps. But not afraid so much as rattled or nervous. I left my hand to linger on the skin under her jaw, soaking up her warmth and trust.

"Tell me what happened, Maggie." With effort I kept my voice pitched low and soft. As gentle as I could pull off while my heart began its deceleration. Finding her whole did its job in calming my system, while part of me stayed on guard, skeptical of what would come next.

"I don't want to lie to you."

"Then don't." Doubt and suspicion took the place of concern, a slithering of ice up and up until it wrapped around my throat. Why would she lie to me? The idea of her lying to me caused all sorts of bad feelings to spiral.

"Dominic wasn't telling the truth." She said in a skittish whisper.

"Which part?" I ground my teeth together. My brother had lied to me? What game was he playing?

"Um," She licked her lips and I watched the flick of her tongue. I salivated over her pink lips and only just managed not to kiss her again. She blinked at me but seemed resolved to get the story out. "Dominic was over here. We were hanging out."

"So you weren't here alone?"

"My mama is out of town for the night." She explained. Her small voice sounded a touch more southern when she said *Mama*. It was distractingly cute.

"But Dom was here with you?"

"Yes. We made tacos." She looked around and I noticed two abandoned plates as well as an empty pitcher. "And margaritas."

He was there with her. In the house alone with her. Drinking goddamn margaritas. Maggie rarely drank, as far as I knew. Was she tipsy or even drunk now? I finally moved my hand from beneath her chin because fisting my hands was delaying my expulsion of anger and my immediate desire to track down my baby brother. Now that I thought back on his texts - without panic skewing my reactions - they were off. His story had shifted.

"He just jumped up and left." Maggie was clearly in the dark as to Dom's reasons for abandoning her, but she was intuitive enough to have figured it out by now.

"This was a set up." I voiced my guess and watched to see her confirm.

She still looked up at me of her own accord. Memorizing her smile gave me a good outlet for my crazy wild emotions, I focused on how sweet and trusting this girl was, and how much I wanted to protect her. She nodded. Her cheeks went pink, which did frantic things to my insides.

"Before he left, he mentioned that it should be you taking me out." She spoke so softly, I completely stilled to hear her. "Not practicing or pretending, but for real."

I looked around the room and assessed places I could sit. Holy hell. I sank onto a chair that was bamboo and twisted wood with a bright pink cushion. It creaked as it supported my weight.

"He shouldn't have said that to you." I wasn't angry. All that rage from a minute before drained out. It pooled at my feet and left me a mess. All that remained was hopelessness. An empty hollow place in my chest that expanded outward until it hurt to breathe.

"Because it isn't true?" She sounded sad.

Because her new obviously trusted friend Dom possibly lied to her? Because I was here instead of him and I was screwing it up? Because I implied that it should not in fact be me taking her out? I was determined to leave Berry out of the equation. If he came up I would surely lose it. I wanted to know what she was feeling and why, and I wanted to fix it, even though it wasn't my place. Or was it? I had shown up and inserted myself into the equation after all.

"Because it's not his place to say," was the only answer I could offer.

Maggie walked, her bare feet padding softly on the generic

blue gray carpet, to stand before me. Then she dropped down to kneel in front of me. She leaned forward, hands on her knees, sitting on her feet and peering up at me.

"Why are you here, Cotton?"

"I was worried about you."

"Why? I mean, I know your terrible no good trickster brother lied." An indulgent smile snuck its way into her words. "But besides that, why do you care so much?"

I sighed and looked past her. The house was ... different. The base layer was generic, like the carpet, with white paint on the walls and a typical floor plan. The furniture was all mismatched, in style, color, size, age. I wasn't sure how it all worked together. But it did, and well. Stella Porter clearly had an eye for lines, color, style, and art. Her collection of art was layer upon layer deep; more than I could take in at a glance. She should be an artist, or an interior decorator. Nursing didn't seem to suite her, outside of her well-known tendency to want to take care of people. The woman was at odds with herself at every turn.

How could I answer Maggie's question? Why did I drop everything and rush to her house? I had no logical explanation. I sifted through possible stories to tell her, so that I could excuse myself and be on with my night. Then I looked back into her face, waiting and a touch too eager, and I couldn't lie to her. That same crawling of icy alarm that strangled me when I thought of her lying to me, it came back in full force when I considered lying to her. I could not betray her trust in me.

"Maggie, I ..." I drew in a long breath, then let it out in a rush. It was hard to think straight with her perched there in front of me. Her smell in my nose, the heat from her skin close enough I could feel it, and her looking at me like she cared what my answer might be. It was intoxicating. "I used to watch out for you, trying to stop Luke from hurting you before he could, and I think it became habit."

Her smile was slow and small. I saw nothing else. I locked my fingers onto my kneecaps to keep from grabbing her and pulling her into me.

"You came here tonight out of habit?" Her disbelief was

colored with something else, and it looked an awful lot like pleasure.

"I came here tonight because I couldn't stand the idea of you being alone and afraid."

"Oh." Her amused smile slipped and her word was a sound on a breath. It was too much for me to drop on her. I was being unfair. I was a jerk no matter what I did. There was no chance of us coming away from this unscathed, because if I stayed I'd make inappropriate confessions and likely kiss her again. That might well be good for me, but it wasn't likely good for her. I wasn't good for her. It always came back to that. But if I left? That option wasn't without its consequences either.

"I should go."

"Please don't." She reached forward with her hands, placing them on top of mine on my knees, small fingers gripping larger ones. Her whole body pitched forward, toward me.

"He's right." I watched her absorb my presence and my voice and my words. Maggie hung on each word and studied it, turning it over in her mind, testing it. I had to be careful with her. "And he's wrong. I want to be the one here with you, taking you out and making you smile and ..."

I looked to her lips.

As if she suspected the direction of my thoughts, color rose again in her cheeks. God, she was beautiful. So in tune with her feelings but hiding behind them. I wanted her more for it.

"But it shouldn't be me." I had to make her understand once and for all. "It's better that it's ... someone else. Someone that won't hurt you."

"You would?" She shifted closer to me, which was the opposite of the direction she should be moving. "You would hurt me?"

"Not on purpose."

"Then how do you know?" I watched her head move, tip to one side as she studied me. A fragile little bird curious about the world, and the wolf that had settled down at her feet. She looked at me like she might be able to see the answers written across my skin. I aimed to rub the words off, but knew they weren't really there. "If you hurt someone on accident, it's not the same, you know."

"I'm not the good guy, Maggie. If I had you, I wouldn't know how to share you." I hadn't meant for those to be the words I said to her. I was intoxicated by her close proximity that she damningly increased ever so steadily. Closer and closer. "I can't trust that I wouldn't lose my temper at some point. Not at you, never at you. But near enough to you that you'd ... It's not a risk I'm willing to take."

"I trust you, Cotton."

Jesus. I was busted up. Four words and I was done for. Resolve went out the damn window. Will power shifted from keeping myself from her, to holding her as close as possible without crushing her. Why the hell would she trust me? I hadn't done anything to prove myself trustworthy. It was a gift that she shouldn't hand out so thoughtlessly. I was already drawing her to me, hands around her ribs lifting her up to me, before I could stop and think. My lips were already well on their way to tasting her before I was willing to look at things and force myself to walk away from her. This, my lack of control, was the reason I had to walk away. But it was likewise the reason I couldn't. She was willing. Maggie leaned up and in, pressing herself to me. Her lips met mine with their own ferocity.

When I kissed her the first time, ambushed her outside Prissy Polly's, she had been surprised. She had given into the kiss, and she had clung to me desperately. But she had held back. Her movements were reserved.

When I'd kissed her again, standing in the tall grass under the stars behind the homestead, she had been responsive but still letting me lead.

Unlike the current kiss. She didn't just give in, she encouraged me to take it deeper, and she gave as good as she got. Her mouth was hungry and her hands greedy. She wanted me. Physically at least, Maggie wanted me. I wasn't as gentle as I always told myself I would be with her, spurred on by her advances. She moaned and it woke up the parts of me I had denied for so long when it came to this girl. I shifted my hands and her response was to swing her legs over mine and straddle my lap. There was no use holding back after that; she surely felt how much I wanted her. I was thorough in my caressing and exploration of her mouth. Only when I needed oxygen and sensed she needed the same did I leave her mouth. Her skin was divine.

Chapter Nineteen

Magnolia

I had been kissed before. More than once. I wasn't completely inexperienced.

Then there was kissing Cotton MacKenna, and it was something out of a whole different world. The intensity of physical longing and emotional exposure ripped me open and laid me bare. No, I had not been kissed like that before.

When Tiny Douglass had kissed me, my sixteen-year-old self had enjoyed the moments in the way you might enjoy walking through an art gallery versus painting the art yourself. I had been there, but I wasn't invested, more interested in it out of curiosity. I was willing and found it enjoyable. He was sweet and careful and nearly as shy as I was, which led to neither of us pushing past innocent exchanges that lacked heat.

When Mark Regents kissed my twenty-one-year-old self, it was sloppy and aggressive, and I had shied away from the contact with him. I knew right away I no longer wanted his lips on mine, his hands groping my body. I wanted space. He had inexplicably felt heat with me, and when I didn't reciprocate he called me frigid.

When I had been on the receiving end of first date good night kisses, never once did the parting act incite my blood to boil or my head to fog or my hands to reach out in order to lay claim. I had kissed and been kissed, but it had never been like this.

It had never been with Cotton.

His lips were soft, gentle when he tried too hard to hold himself back, firm when he gave into bouts of hunger for me. His hands followed suit, alternately tender or ferocious. I was sky high while on my knees before him. My hands moved up his thighs, then grabbed for his arms. He had magnificent arms, strong and firm with muscles. I gripped him tight and he pulled me ever closer. I shifted to his lap, with my knees on the outside of his legs in my mom's stupid rattan chair. My knees ached from the press of the wood on my skin, but I pressed harder into Cotton's lap. He stopped kissing me in favor of nibbling along my neck and suckling my earlobe. I gasped, for air after prolonged kissing, yet mostly because it was so good. One of his hands had fingers tangled into my mess of hair, and supporting the weight of my tipped head. His other hand skimmed up my ribcage, then back down, and found my bare skin beneath my camisole.

Some small part of my brain, that I wholeheartedly ignored, was shouting about how embarrassed I ought to be. Panting. Rocking my hips so that the hard length of him rubbed against me. My body took over and told my head to shut up. It was better to feel, to know the searing burn of Cotton's hand curved around my waist. His fingers pressing into the skin of my back and his thumb moving up and down and making me go crazy. How could such a simple thing bring forth such a riot of sensations in me?

A moan of some sort passed my lips. Cotton's mouth moved across my collarbone from one side to the other. His tongue was warm where it tasted my skin, then his breath cooling as he moved to a new spot. I was hot and cold at the same time, wanting to strip off my clothes and also to shiver, at impossible odds with myself.

He groaned. A strangled sound, like he was frustrated, and yanked my body closer to his. I couldn't actually get any closer, not in that chair, not sitting as we were. Not without removing clothes.

The shock of how much I wanted him was alarming. I gave into a convulsive shiver, and rocked again, craving the friction that came from pressing myself down onto him and relishing in how hard he was for me. Never had I been so turned on. I hadn't known it was possible to feel this way. I had experimented with masturbation over the years, tentative as I touched myself and learned what created a heat inside me that yearned for escape. That had been okay; it had been a good release. Cotton's firm grasp on me, along with his lips leaving a fiery trail along my skin, and his erection forcefully rubbed against my most sensitive parts, I was ready to come apart. I understood the phrase weak in the knees and was sure I would collapse if he let go of me.

He mumbled words into my neck and hair that I didn't catch. His hold on me was at once furious and tender, ever caught between wanting to have his way with me and wanting to do the right thing by me.

It was the realization that I would fall apart if he left that brought my higher faculties back into play. My brain knock knocked and let herself in to have a word. The cold shame that followed after he walked away before, kissing me to the brink of insanity then pulling away, came back in measures. He could do it again. He could turn away from me, leaving me to try and comprehend the residual longing within me. I couldn't turn it off like he had. I wanted him and let out soft mewling sounds at his touch on my body, hyper aware of him. I wanted him and shifted yet again to move his length down my center. I wanted him and it was an impossibility for me to change my mind.

Except, all the physical stuff wasn't enough.

I wanted more.

Fear slithered in, tiny tendrils that sought purchase in my head and my heart.

He could pull away. He could walk out. He could go so far as to have sex with me and still leave me alone in the end.

Cotton had told me he would hurt me. With simple honest words, he had warned me.

I shifted, not for our mutual pleasure, but to put space between us. My throbbing excited female parts away from his equally excited male part. An inch of space that spoke volumes. I lifted my head from his hand and twisted to release his fingers from my hair.

He held me tight. Unwilling to let me go.

"Cotton."

His answer was an animal sound, a low growl groan. He

bowed his head so that his forehead rested on mine. I worked on calming my frantic lungs that struggled to pull in enough air.

"Do you have any idea what you do to me?"

His harsh whispered tone wheedled into my ears and straight to my core. My fingers, not inclined to let go or to listen to my practical reasoning, clutched hard at his arms.

There was evidence enough that he was physically attracted to me. His hands had been worshipful and his mouth hungry. His nether regions had grown in response to my closeness, and I had felt first hand - albeit through layers of pajama pants and jeans - how much he desired me. I wasn't that girl. The physical would never be sufficient for me. I needed the emotional connection, the commitment, along with the physical gratification.

"I can't do this." My confession was barely audible.

He heard me, and he reacted. It was subtle, the way his shoulders stiffened and his breath staggered. The harder press of his fingertips on me, claiming me. I waited until he lifted his head and moved me farther back, onto his knees more than his lap. I slid my legs free of their cramped position, my toes meeting the ground.

I watched his head nod, just once. I saw the way he steeled himself, withdrawing all the parts of him he had been offering to me, and shutting down his emotions. His eyes were guarded and his lips pressed flat. I hated it. It caused me physical pain to watch him shut down, draw away, and prepare to leave me. I stood up, off his knees, and he let his hands fall away from me, the last bit of disconnection making it final. My hands were empty and useless without him in them, so I wrapped my arms around my chest.

Cotton stood, too. The burning pain in my chest seemed to be suspiciously located in the area of my heart. There was a burning behind me eyes as well, that told me I was on the verge of tears. I blinked frantically to keep them in check.

"I'm sorry." He was so damn tall, standing over me, uttering his useless words. In two steps he was at the front door and pulling it open. "I'll go."

165

"Don't be sorry." I called out to him, putting force behind my voice. I knew I sounded desperate and gave away my cards. "And don't go."

He spun around. I worried about the doorknob in his death grip. I faltered and moved a teeny step back from him. His eyes raked over me, missing nothing so that I was too exposed; he looked at me with steady eyes that called to mind a hawk.

"What do you want from me?"

"I don't know." I pulled in a breath and let all the words inside me tumble out. Cotton stood there all stony faced and intense. "Dominic hinted you maybe liked me, and then he left and you were here. You. Which is a lot to handle. I mean, after we kissed before, and now with the more kissing. Knowing that you can just walk away. I don't know what to do with that."

I was flustered. My cheeks burned and I lifted my hair up off my neck to cool myself down. I rambled and he let me, and I couldn't get a read on what he was thinking. I reminded myself that Dominic at least had my best interest at heart. He wouldn't have sent Cotton to me if he thought I'd end up in tears again.

"The thing is, Cotton, I can't just go around kissing you. I'm not that girl."

His teeth were clenched so tight I didn't think he could answer. His face was so darn handsome, even while he was unsure of me and visibly upset. His eyes were always his most amazing feature, the blue sharp and bright, with facets to catch the light. They were somehow both hot and cold. I wrapped my arms tighter around myself and hoped he would say something. After all my verbal vomit, I would take anything at all from him.

"Don't worry. It won't happen again."

He ground out the words. I flinched. The tears I'd been working so hard to keep at bay spilled over. I went cold, which was startling for my system after being so hot just seconds before.

I expected him to storm out, yank the door closed, and

avoid me for another decade. I braced myself as best I could, which was admittedly not well. Something inside me was breaking, and I knew that I would crumble at the first chance.

He surprised me. Cotton's face fell, his head bowed for a brief moment, and he let go his hold on the poor defenseless doorknob. I watched his chest expand as he took a breath. Then he came back to me.

Cotton's warm fingers swiped away the tears on my cheeks. His face wasn't stony, it wasn't guarded, it was open and filled with wonder as he looked at me. He placed one hand around me, barely there on my low back, and it sent shivers coursing through me. Such a simple gesture that touched me on a deeper level.

"First, let's clear a few things up." His voice was low, gravelly. If I didn't know better I'd think he'd been screaming until his throat was raw, instead I could only blame heightened emotions and close proximity. "I do like you. I've liked you for most of our whole lives. I am a lot to handle. I never do things halfway and I think that's the issue here now. I don't regret kissing you because there's no way in hell I would trade those moments. I am sorry about the way I'm going about this. You're right, you aren't that girl. Thing is, I like that about you."

I nodded. Not because I had come to terms with everything he had said, but because I was working on it and nodding seemed like the right answer. It was a lot to take in. Cotton MacKenna giving confessional in my living room with his hands on me. The Twilight Zone level strangeness made it hard to believe it was real. His breath on my face as he spoke grounded me. The scent of him, his woodsy soap along with a slight hint of beer, made him a solid entity before me that I could believe in. I focused on what my senses picked up because my brain had gone haywire.

"What did you mean about halfway being the issue?" I wasn't sure what the issue was, beyond ending our make out session and stirring us into turbulent waters. My hands once again found purchase on his arms, my fingers greedy to cling to him.

"Either I walk away and that's that. No more kissing. Nothing." He meant it, his words wrought with steel. I stilled and waited him out. If I held myself very still I could control my reaction to the hurt he might inflict. "Or I'm all in. You will be mine. Damn the consequences."

My heart thundered in my chest and my body felt the reverberations all the way to my fingers and toes. His words swam, in dizzying loops, around my mind as I tried to make sense of the last minute that had passed. I didn't know him well enough to make an all in commitment. Did I? I had known him virtually forever, and he was the guy that dropped everything to come check on me and ensure I wasn't afraid. He was the boy that had stood up for me to my brother countless times, though I hadn't understood the reason for their fighting at the time. I had harbored a crush on Cotton MacKenna most of my life, and he was laying it out before me. I didn't let a little thing like our barely knowing each other get in the way. There would be time for that. Right?

"If it was up to me, I'd choose the latter."

I looked up through my lashes to gauge his reaction. I knew my voice had lost all its power, coming out in a soft whisper. I tended to do that, to shrink when I was nervous.

"Would you now?" His eyes that I had thought were so cold and hard before, gleamed with light that was inviting, the hottest part of the fire. I pressed my lips together to keep from smiling too big too fast, as I watched the left side of his mouth curve up into a half smile.

My head moved up and down in a nod. His hands on me tightened, a giveaway of how much he wanted me to stay there, of how much he liked my answer. His grip on me was firm to the point of almost pain. I liked it, the way he held me, the way his hands told me the truth. That I was already his.

"All in."

"Uh huh." I fully gazed up at him, stunned by the turn of events, and unable to form complete words.

"Mine."

"As long as you're mine, too."

Hungry eyes, smiling lips, determined hands. Both of us

were breathing like we'd run a mile. Hesitation, as we held onto the sweet honesty of the conversation, kept us from mauling one another.

"Damn the consequences."

I agreed to that too, with a sound and a sort of nod. I wasn't sure what the consequences were or why they were damned. Or if we were damning them ourselves. All I knew was that Cotton was there, holding me in that way of his with careful restraint and wild abandon coming in turns, as he wrestled with his desires for me.

Chapter Twenty

Cotton

I was addled. I had a taste of Magnolia Porter, and the reality of it had addled my brain. There was no other explanation for what was happening.

After I had spent how many years avoiding this girl, for her own good mind you, I was rolling in and taking her? It was wrong, and I knew it was wrong. I was doing it anyway. Holding her in my hands, tasting her mouth and skin, giving in and going over the edge. That was it. I was done for. My hormones and my heart got tangled in the brambles of her and I made stupid proclamations. My brain had checked out, and refused to weigh in on the issue other than the buzzing reminder that I was going to hurt her. Eventually, I would hurt her.

I couldn't let her go. She was right there, in my hands, nodding her head at me. It would be like her to go along with whatever bullshit I spread.

The bullshit was more like manure, because it was useful and good for the growth of the garden. I couldn't be with her without my bullshit edicts. I was greedy. I was high on her presence and her answers to the positive.

If she had only climbed into my lap and then come to her senses, and if I had then been able to get out her door - I'd have stood a chance. As it was, hearing her voice wobble as she spilled her confession at my feet - chance gone. I was hers. Simple as that. I had been running from that truth for so many years it was my default. When it came down to it, I had devoted myself to her when we were kids, and I had never wanted another girl. She was it for me. My head was a mess, warring with itself to hold her tight while telling me to run.

She wiggled free from my embrace. I let her go, curious what she would do next. This girl that I knew, yet didn't know at all. She took my hand; her tiny hand slipped into mine and tugged. I followed her to the couch. Sitting in the center, poised as always, she tugged again to urge me to sit.

"Where's your mama?"

I did not want to talk about her mama. I opened my mouth, and that question fell out. There it sat, awkward as hell, between us. I focused on her amused smile.

"Work."

I nodded. I wasn't aware she worked nights. I didn't want to know more, so I didn't ask. Maggie didn't offer up any other information.

Promises made in moments of passion, in the stuttered calm that follows, become bigger. They grow with each passing second. With every minute that passed into normal, sitting on a couch and making small talk, what we'd said and done loomed larger and larger. The proverbial elephant in the room.

"What are you doing tomorrow?"

"I don't know." Her shoulders moved in a characteristic shrug as she answered. "I mean, I had plans, but ... I'll probably just stay home and do stuff around here. It's my turn to do the grocery shopping anyway. Maybe it will be a good day to run errands since everyone else will be at the Slip'n Slide thing in the park."

It was a trickle or a flood. She either said one word and left me guessing, or she dumped information at me. It was cute, and I was pathetic for thinking it was cute. She eyed my lips when I smiled at her. It was heady to have so much power, to know that if I smiled she was clued in and aware, that she would look to me and remember my mouth on hers.

I'd convince her to go to the Slip'n Slide event, if for no other reason than because it would be a way for her to make a stand. She had admitted before, during dinner at my house, that her reasons for not attending were wrapped up in her mama not wanting her to go. I didn't want to push her. But I thought Dom had mentioned her going with him, Beau, and

Elliot.

"What's the deal with you and Dominic?"

Damn it. I wasn't going to ask that either. I had lost control of the path between my brain and my tongue. Maggie moved back and away, tucking herself into the corner of the couch, and her eyebrows moved too close together.

"There's no deal. We're friends."

I knew she was being honest with me. Because I knew her well enough to know she would always be honest with me. Also because I knew from Dom's side that he wasn't into her. He adored her, and had devoted himself to her with puppy like infatuation. It was platonic. I knew the way it was for them, but knowing it didn't help. The fact of Dominic and Maggie rankled.

"It's ... unexpected."

"Right?" She bounced a little in her seat, happy and excited. Her evident happiness made me chill out on the jealousy front. "I've known him since absolutely forever, and we were never friends. Not even close. Now he's ..."

She paused, and I waited her out. Her brows knit together again.

"He's what?" I prompted her to continue and kept a casual tone, not betraying the way I wanted to scream. I had thoughts on what might happen if my brother hurt my girl. It was messed up and my loyalties were shifted away from my family, which in itself was weird for me, but then I had always put Maggie first.

"It's just he's become important to me in no time. It doesn't make sense." Her face was still pinched, and if I was reading her right, sad. But her words were happier than not.

"I thought you were going to the Slip'n Slide thing with him tomorrow."

"What?" There was an edge of panic to her voice, one she tried to keep subdued. "No. I mean, we talked about meeting up. I was thinking about going, but now I ... I don't think so."

I got the feeling she was keeping something from me. Whatever reason she had for bailing, she didn't want to fess up. She didn't want to lie either. I hated putting her in a hard spot. The longer we sat there, the more I wanted to know.

The question on my tongue was to ask what she wasn't telling me.

"Okay." I swallowed my worries and put faith in trusting her. I found we weren't to a point of mutual trust yet, and it required a leap of faith. "What about after? Don't you usually go down to the bonfire with the Hunters?"

"Yes?"

"Maggie. Why are you being weird about tomorrow? I would like it if you'd go with me, at least to the bonfire."

She chewed her lips again. I missed her dimples when she wasn't smiling. A thought struck me, and stoked the dying flames of anger back to life.

"Is it me? Don't want to parade about town with me?" I attempted to keep my voice level, to phrase my words as a joke.

"No." She moved closer to me. I liked that she did that, when she wanted to assure me, she got as close to me as she could. "No. It's not that at all. I just ..."

I watched her throat move as she swallowed. Her normally soft warm brown eyes were tight with caution. She was scared to tell me whatever it was, likely afraid of my reaction. What would be so bad that she wouldn't want to say it to me?

"You said you'd had plans. Then you backtracked." The truth dawned on me, all at once, in a wave of heated jealousy. "Tell me."

"I did have plans. I mean, technically I still do have plans. I haven't had the chance to cancel them. Yet."

"With Vincent?" How I kept myself seated, voice low, I will never know.

She nodded. I couldn't be angry about this; I had no right. She had made plans with him before I had shown up tonight, before I'd demanded she be mine and told her I didn't know how to share. It was hard enough for me to come to terms with her friendship with Dominic. It was impossible for me to consider her plans with this other guy.

"I see." It was a non-answer to buy me more time.

"Are you mad at me?" She sat on her hands, keeping them

173

off me, the opposite of what I wished she would do. Her worry was palpable. It was about more than me being mad at her; it spoke of a history of worrying about upsetting people. Her chronic need to never rock the boat.

"No, Maggie. No, I'm not mad at you." How could I be? "I do want you to cancel those plans."

"Of course." She nodded again. Her face was still too white, holding onto lingering anxiety. I tugged her hands free from their trap beneath her thighs and held them in mine. She softened at my touch.

"Do it now. Tell him you can't see him again."

"Right now? It's really late. Or really early."

"Right now." I needed him to know. I was a jealous prick, and if she couldn't manage to break things off with Vincent, I would have to find him and tell him myself. That couldn't end well.

She pulled free from my grasp and found her cell phone. I watched her quickly type a message, fingers light across the glass screen, to break things off with Vincent at a completely inappropriate time.

"Now that's settled, come with me tomorrow." I didn't ask, because it wasn't a question. She put her phone behind her back. I reclaimed her hands.

"Okay, Cotton." Her smile was small. A small victory I would try for again and again.

I could tell she was conflicted. It would be like her to worry about hurting his feelings by showing up with another guy after abruptly cancelling on him. As far as I knew they'd gone out once, and it wasn't serious. She didn't know it, but her showing up with me would cause drama because of her pretend thing with Dominic. We'd be a sight, all there at the same time. I would be sure to clear up perceptions and make it unmistakable she was mine.

"Good." I kissed her forehead and shifted her closer to me. "I'll pick you up at eleven."

"I'll pack our lunch." It was tradition to picnic for lunch, then later buy from the food trucks for dinner.

"What are you doing Sunday?"

174

"Something with you?"

Damn, her shy voice, and her attempt at sweet flirtation, reached right in and squeezed my heart.

"Of course. We could hike to Raven Falls."

"Can we run away and live there forever. It's my favorite spot." Her confession was in a rush. I knew she loved the spot; it's why I suggested that hike.

I nodded and watched her face light up. I found I loved making her smile. Her happiness made me happy. I was physically lighter, my heart less encumbered, when Maggie turned her smile my way. Truth was we didn't know one another well. What I knew I had gathered by observation. I was good at watching and learning, good at seeing people. It was part of what made me a good photographer. I had a keen eye, and the ability to pick up on undercurrents.

"Maybe we ought to hold off on living there until we can find the right place." I winked, and she let out a breathy soft giggle.

"What were you doing tonight? Dominic didn't interrupt anything, did he?" She was soft beside me, sleepy eyes on me as she asked after my night.

"No. I was at home."

Maggie alternately looked me in the eye, her face morphing into disbelieving happiness like she was lucky and I was the source of her joy, then ducking her head and peeking at me like she could possibly hide from me. I studied her openly, and it was when I looked at her with a steady gaze and held it that she tipped her head down. She didn't like my continued appraisal. I had no intention of stopping. I'd rather she get used to it and like it.

"Should I go? It's getting late."

"Not yet." She shrugged and took her hand back. She fiddled with her hair and I wondered what she was thinking.

"Hey?" I softened my eager eyes as much as I could when she lifted her face to me. "I know we started this all wrong. We can go slower."

"I don't want slow." I leaned in to catch her words. Her habit of barely there voice was somehow both endearing and

175

frustrating. "I want ... to kiss you again."

"Do you now?"

My ability to give her a throw away phrase and keep things light was to be marveled at. My blood ran too fast and too hot in my body. Sitting beside Maggie, hearing her whisper to me that she wanted me to kiss her, it tested my restraint. I was determined to go slow. Our progression had to be perfect for her. I wouldn't rush her, i.e. maul her as soon as I touched her. Practiced control was something I had perfected over the years. Initially to keep my temper in check. Then to stay away from Maggie. Now I would employ it to only touch her with the tenderness she deserved.

Chapter Twenty-One

Magnolia

I didn't know what was happening in my own head. I was either editing my words, trying desperately not to be awkward and crazy. Or I was drowning poor Cotton in a deluge of words. He sat there on my mama's sofa, too tall with legs too long, handsome in a casual rumpled way that came in the middle of the night. I stared at him until it occurred to me to be embarrassed by doing such a thing. But when I would finally pull my eyes away, Cotton would do something to encourage me to look at him again.

"I want ... to kiss you."

Those words actually came out of my mouth. My lips, craving his, my tongue restless to tangle with his, propelled my mouth into voicing what I wanted. Cotton wasn't averse. He wasted no time scooping me up from where I sat and moving me to his lap. I was more comfortable this time, with my legs both to one side and hanging free. I snuggled my body into his chest. No one was warm as him, and his heat fanned the flame building inside me. I tipped my head to look into his fire and ice blue eyes, and he captured my mouth with his. My eyelids drifted closed as I let myself free fall into kissing him. His lips were full and soft while the kiss escalated, and I tasted his hunger for me. It made no sense the way I kissed him back, eager to slip my tongue into his mouth, and nipping at his lips. I craved him in a way that shot zings through my body. All at once I was melting and lighting on fire. I was giving in and falling apart, letting him take lead. I was taking charge and twisting my body to better line up with his while lifting his shirt so that my hands had access to his skin. As my fingers raced across his bare stomach, he groaned into my mouth. There was a rhythm of give and take, or surrender and capture. I wanted to eat him; that thought actually crossed my mind.

Cotton worked a bit of magic maneuvering - he lifted me, shifted, and we were lying on the cramped sofa with him overtop me. He held his body just off mine. Close enough I felt the expansion of his ribcage with each breath he took, I felt the hammering of his heart against mine, I felt the hard length of him that pressed onto me and told me of his desire.

I laid my head back and sucked in air. Not missing a beat, Cotton moved his mouth along my jaw and down my neck. I took the opportunity to look at him, to see his handsome face as he put his mouth all over me. Mostly I could see his glorious hair, each strand a different color and still somehow all red. I ran my fingers through his hair, thick and glossy. My own was thick and wavy tending toward coarse and frizzy. I forgot about his hair when his hand slipped beneath the fabric of my top. I had already pulled his t-shirt up his chest to run my hands along his skin, to skim my fingers over his muscles, to feel him right there in reach. He took his turn, strong calloused fingertips caressing my skin, turning me inside out.

Thoughts were lost to me for as long as we lay together exploring. I would miss his mouth and pull him up to kiss until I was dizzy. I removed his shirt, but he refused to let me take off mine. My hips lifted, straining to be closer to him, to create a delirious friction between our bodies. The worn couch creaked in its strained support of our combined weight. Each time my back arched, Cotton slipped one hand under my back to hold me firmly against him, and he'd let out a sound like a low growl.

"I really should go."

"Mm hmm." I snared his mouth again with mine and got drunk on the taste of him.

He held himself in check, not letting things go too far, and moaning in frustration as I tried to press harder upward to get at him.

"Oh, Magnolia." He let out a long breath and pressed his face into my neck. He stayed there, unmoving, and slowed his breath and heart. My body mimicked his, slowing, coming back down from the ride up and up and up.

As sanity flooded back into my kiss drunk brain, I knew he was right. We should stop. He should go home. Reality, the things I had promised Cotton, facing my decision and the rippling reach of the consequences, stole my thoughts. Clutched me and sobered me fully.

I nodded. He sighed, and his eyelashes fluttered against the sensitive skin of my neck. When he lifted himself off me to standing, I flushed cold. The sounds I had made, and the urgency of my body, were embarrassing after the fact. Cotton's expression said otherwise.

He took my hand and pulled me up from the sofa. I trailed behind him to the door, not ready to say goodbye despite knowing it was time.

"Remind me to thank my meddling brother."

"He's a no-good liar." I pressed my lips together and didn't let out a laugh. He saw right through me and nodded at my joking assessment.

"I will see you tomorrow." He said each word with inflection, each one separate and given importance. He seemed to be seeking reassurance.

"Yes." My hand was still in his.

"Good night, Sweet Maggie."

Cotton kissed my forehead, in a move so gentle it was filled with more sentiment than all our previous making out. He gave away a depth of feeling in that move, the way he carefully held me and tenderly placed his lips to my head. I didn't come to my senses enough to respond until he had closed the front door. When I checked, I found it locked - Cotton always looking out for me. My lips were swollen and touch sore. My body was all exposed nerve endings, missing Cotton's touch and utterly too sensitive.

It wasn't until I was in bed, drifting to sleep, that I let myself imagine what it would be like when he showed up the next day to take me out and I introduced him to my mama as more than a friend. I wasn't sure what words I could use yet, which were the right ones for what we were to each other. I knew only that my mama would never approve of my being with Cotton. On top of that, going to a popular town event with him would send her right over the edge. I braced myself for an all-out tantrum on her part, and knew that it would involve pulling puppet strings still firmly attached to me. I slept poorly. Guilt at breaking things off with Vincent last minute, at an indecent hour, and then going out with a different guy immediately, was consuming in the way nausea refused to be ignored. Knowing that I would be put in an impossible place between Cotton and my mama wound tightly around me; I would have to choose between hurting one of them. Premature guilt wrapped me in a strait jacket while I wrestled with fleeting minutes of sleep.

Chapter Twenty-Two

Cotton

I wanted to ride the high for the few remaining hours until the sun rose, until I could go back to Maggie. There was nothing I wanted more than to relive the past few hours on repeat, zooming in on when she said, *as long as you're mine too.*

Mine.

It was a heady word, thick and full, with the ability to block out all reason.

The chance to drown in the sweet victory of claiming Maggie didn't come.

Dominic wanted to know what happened, with details, threatening to drive right back over to her house and get it from her if I didn't spill. I saw the fight in his eyes. The readiness to take me out if I had hurt her.

"You set me up, brother." I focused on the detail that allowed me to be pissed off at him, not that I rallied much in the way of anger. Also the detail that would in turn remind him he sent me over there in the first place, which led me to believe he didn't think I would in fact hurt her.

"Damn straight, I did. You two idiots couldn't get it together."

"It was risky. Don't pull shit like that again."

"Whatever, man. Just tell me what happened."

Knowing I wouldn't divulge times of our intimacy with him, that I wouldn't speak to him of her promises to me, I sifted through what was left to disclose.

"Against all logic, she wants to be with me."

"I told you!"

I simply gave him a nod. When I turned to head up the

stairs to my bedroom, he called me back.

"That's not good enough, Cotton. I already knew she wanted to be with you. What are you going to do about it?"

"It's already done. We are ... together."

Was together the right word? I wanted to simply say, she is mine. It was wrong on so many levels how I wanted to broadcast the fact that Maggie Porter now belonged to me. I knew it was wrong to view her that way, but I didn't care. I had told her what it meant, and she had agreed willingly. Absurd as it was, she wanted to be mine. More importantly she wanted me to be hers as well. My heart soared, which made it unfeasible to continue talking with Dominic.

"Fuck you!" He was gleeful. And too loud for whatever ungodly hour it was too near sunrise. "About damn time. Good. This is good."

"I'm taking her to the stupid Slip'n Slide thing tomorrow."

"Well hell, Cotton, you don't do anything halfway." His laughter was dark, and I focused on the soft gleam of his eyes in the dark house.

"What do you mean?" I had grown tired of this discussion before it began and my patience wore thin. "Be quick about it, I'm done with this."

"I happen to know she was planning to attend that little town function with Vincent Berry. Well now, I understand why she will no longer be seeing him, but ..." He was leading up to something, a playful and knowing lilt to his voice. I pulled in a long breath to wait him out. "Weren't you telling me that people in town are up in arms because they were under the impression our sweet Maggie was dating both Vincent and me?"

"If by people in town, you mean a gaggle of bored girls with nothing better to do than gossip, then yes."

"Obviously, yes, that is what I mean." I knew he had rolled his eyes as he pitched his voice to be droll. I released a sigh that told him he had four seconds left to get to his point before I left him standing there talking to the landing at the base of the front stairs. "How is it going to look when she shows up with you?"

"Like she is with me."

"Uh, no. Like she is with Vincent, me, and you."

He was right. Shit.

"We will make it clear she is only with me."

"How do you plan to do that? Don't tell me it involves pissing on her." His laughter grated on my nerves.

"God damn it, Dominic." He wasn't too far off base, at least not figuratively. I hadn't made specific plans, but as they came together in my mind there were many ways to show anyone looking that she was mine. Which of course was equivalent of pissing on the girl. "You spread the word that she is your friend, and has only ever been your friend. You were planning to do that anyway. Vincent will surely have his panties in a wad about being dropped, but he can get over it. They went out once; not like I stole his girlfriend."

Girlfriend.

A woefully inadequate word, yet fraught with enough meaning it would do well to drop it around town.

"True enough. I will see you tomorrow, brother."

He was entirely too pleased with himself. Rather than deck him, I let him go, so that I could finally make my way upstairs to dream about my girl.

***

I knew without a doubt that Stella Mae Porter hated me. She would not be indifferent to me, though she seemed to not care about Maggie's friendship with Dominic. She wasn't cautious of me based on rumors. No, that woman had been dealing with me as a pain in her ass for nearly twenty years. The first time we met was in the principal's office, after the first time I beat up her son. There were many such occasions to follow, all of which cemented her hatred for me. I saw it in her eyes each time she blamed me for the trouble Luke was in, and the relief that she could point the blame away from herself and her son. My mama was there for all those meetings too, and if there had been a chance of Stella Porter and Molly MacKenna being friends, their sons had dashed it. The difference between them, when we were all stuffed into an office and confessing our sins, was that my mama didn't blame me. I never said it to the principal or dean or police officer taking our accounts, but I always explained it to my mama after we left. I told her how Luke had picked on Maggie and I was protecting her. She wasn't proud of my tendency to solve my problems with my fists, but she understood I was doing it for the right reasons. That wasn't something that could be said for Maggie's mama. No, she hated me, and I was showing up at her house to take her daughter out.

More than that, I was showing up to introduce myself to her as Maggie's boyfriend. Meh, boyfriend for lack of a better word.

I was nervous. It had dawned on me that I wanted to get along with Mrs. Porter, I wanted her to like me and respect me, and I wanted her to be supportive of my being with her daughter. I didn't expect it up front. I would have to earn it. I was prepared to see this through, looking at the long range, and it had unleashed a flurry of nerves in me.

"Cotton MacKenna. Long time no see." Mrs. Porter pulled the door open before I knocked. She had been waiting for me, which meant Maggie had told her I was coming. In retrospect I should have talked with Maggie that morning and planned what we would say. Together.

Stella was a beautiful woman, and I could see what Maggie would look like in some twenty-odd years. They shared the same eyes and mouth, the same tumultuous hair, similar body shape and mannerisms. Stress and age had fanned lines around her eyes, softened her body, and hardened her spirit. She lacked the sweetness that Maggie had in spades.

"Good morning, Mrs. Porter. Nice to see you, too."

Her eyes squinted, pissed at my implication. I was holding it together and keeping it polite, she was on the verge of losing her shit. As soon as I was through the entryway, I sought Maggie. She hovered a few feet back, standing in the middle of the room, visibly upset. Ah, fuck. There was no way this was going well. I saw it playing out with my needing to protect her, needing to intervene when someone was hurting her, but fighting with her mama wasn't a good option. This felt suspiciously like a no win situation.

I moved immediately to her side and took her hand in mine. I had to touch her, hold her, forge a physical connection. All without kissing her because it was not the right time for that.

"How long have you been involved with my daughter?" She was wasting no time getting down to the nitty gritty. From her perspective, it was sudden. Hell, I could understand that along with her reservations.

"Officially? Since last night." I kept my tone conversational.

"Unofficially?" She wanted to catch me in a lie or trap me in a bad position; she wanted to tear me apart. And I would let her. To an extent.

"Since Maggie was six, and I was eight. That's when I fell in love with your daughter."

Maggie sucked in a breath, my revelation out of left field, and I wished I knew what she was thinking. I squeezed her hand, and left my attention on her mama.

"That's a bit overdramatic." Somehow my words had eased her mind rather than set off alarm bells. Like my divulging something she found utterly ridiculous made my feelings null and void. "Let's say I allow you to take my child out on a date. What is it you will be doing with her?"

Stella Porter's arms were crossed over her chest, her chin was lifted and jaw set firm, her eyes issued a challenge doused in a warning. She was being protective, even if she was also being unreasonable. So, Maggie hadn't told her our plans. I couldn't even blame her, not when she knew how her mama would likely react. But it occurred to me that she must not have told her of her original plan to go with Vincent to the town water fun day. Either way, I got stuck on her phrasing: if I allow you. As if she had some say in the matter.

Keep it together, Cotton. Just long enough to walk out of this house and spend the remaining hours of the day and night with Maggie.

"Stop with the inquisition, Mama. I'll be back sometime tonight. We can talk in the morning." Her voice was calm,

185

words even, and it sounded like what she meant to say was *I'm not a child*.

"Where are you going? Don't I deserve to know where my only child will be all day? Would you have me sit here alone and worried, knowing you're out with a dangerous man -"

"That's enough." I cut her off, and I did it with a roar. The one-way trip to drown in guilt wasn't on the agenda. "I am not dangerous, not to Magnolia. I understand your reservations where I am concerned, based on my past with Luke."

I didn't miss the way her eyes widened then narrowed when I brought up Luke. After all these years he was a source of pain for her. Would always be. It was the same for me with my own mama. I had lost a parent and knew the bone deep pain of it, and I couldn't imagine how much worse it must be to lose a child. I didn't want to make things worse. But no way was I standing there while she dragged Maggie into a pit of despair and demanded that she stay there and keep her company.

"You are not welcome in my house, young man. You are certainly not permitted to take my daughter out." She was making a bold stand. I pitied her because she was opening herself up to be defied. She had gone too far.

"Don't speak to him that way." Maggie stepped forward, closer to her mama, but I wouldn't release her hand and let her go.

"How dare you bring him in this house! How dare you bring me pain! I thought you were a good girl, Magnolia."

"You will not speak to her in that manner again." I shifted Maggie behind me. My new life mission: get Maggie out of that house, away from her mother's toxic influence, as soon as possible. Not for the day. Permanently.

"You will not date Magnolia." Her mother yelled back. I didn't care. I wasn't afraid of her. She had no power over me.

"There is nothing you can do or say that will change how I feel about Maggie. I am taking her to the Fox River City Park. She will be safe. With me and my family."

"No." Her eyes went around me to Maggie, searching and pleading. Panic rose with her voice and changed her face. "You can't go there. You remember what it's like. They'll all be

186

talking about us."

"Mama, it's not like that. Not anymore." Maggie's soft voice was barely audible.

"I don't want you to go." Enter last-ditch effort to guilt her into changing her mind.

"You don't have a say." I was yelling again. Damn it.

"Don't yell at my mama." Maggie pulled on my sleeve with her free hand, urging me to calm down.

"You're right. Sorry I raised my voice, Mrs. Porter. Excuse us for a second."

I pulled Maggie a few feet away from the desperate pleas of her mama. Both her hands in mine, I held her tight and looked her in the eye. I watched the war within her, struggling to keep the peace while finding her own footing.

"Don't let her decide. This is your life, sweetheart. What do you want to do?"

"I don't know what I want. But I don't want to upset her."

"She is a grown ass woman." I didn't say it unkindly, only as a blatant reminder. "Your mama is strong and smart, and she can handle whatever it is you choose to do."

This was a fact that would take some convincing over a number of months or years. When Maggie dipped her chin, I dropped one of her hands in favor of tipping her face back up. Her warm brown eyes were conflicted as they met mine.

"What do *you* want to do, Magnolia?" I asked the question softly, imploring her to think for herself and not base her decision on the outcome of her mama's emotional roller coaster. "If you want to hang out in a bathing suit with a few hundred of our closest neighbors and friends, then let's go. If not, I am okay with that. We can do our hike up to Raven Falls. We can have a Netflix marathon and not move all day. We can drive to Asheville and walk downtown until our feet hurt. What do *you* want to do?"

"I want to go to the stupid Slip'n Slide thing."

"Okay. Now let's go."

Her hand still firmly in mine, I led the way back to the center of the living room. Mrs. Porter was on the verge of tears. The woman was legitimately upset. I couldn't be sure if it had to do with me, or the town event, or simply Maggie defying her. Maybe the reality of her own life turning out so differently than she'd planned.

"Maggie would like to attend the town event." I kept my voice even. No yelling. No dark sarcasm or scathing words. Simple and honest and nothing else. "She would like for me to escort her. I will do what she wants me to do for as long as she'll let me, because her happiness is crucial to me. I'll ask you not to make this harder on her than you already have. I can assure you that she will be safe and well taken care of."

I tugged her right on out the front door, only pausing when Maggie reached for a tote bag and basket I hadn't noticed near the exit. I took the basket while she shouldered the bag, and I refused to let go of her hand. Ever.

Chapter Twenty-Three

Cotton

The weather was perfect for an outdoor watery event, if by perfect I meant blazing sun and incessant heat. No sooner were we off the front porch headed toward my truck was I sweating. I half dragged Maggie away from her house, determined to put space between her and the nay saying we left behind. I shoved her things inside the truck, then pushed her back against the vehicle. Kissing was inevitable. Not kissing her would have been a slow death. Only after thoroughly tasting every bit of her mouth and face, did I break away. I held her head between my hands, painfully aware how precious she was to me.

My heart beat out a warning: too fast, too fast, too fast. I was afraid my pace would frighten her.

She was wrapped up in a crisp white collared shirt, the sleeves rolled to her elbows, in shorts cut to show the full length of her legs.

"You look amazing. I will never get over being allowed to touch you when I want."

Touch her I did, sliding my hands down her body to clutch at her waist. She panted gently and smiled up at me. Her eyes were wide in amazement and her happiness was tempered with her awareness of our location.

I nodded and tucked her into the truck.

She changed the music on the radio, switching away from the local public radio to the classic rock station. I blamed Dominic's influence for her choice.

"What kind of music do you listen to?" All I knew was that it wasn't bluegrass, and it wasn't likely classic rock either.

"Everything." She shrugged and held her lower lip between

her teeth. "Mostly singer songwriter folk stuff."

She listed off names I hadn't heard and I made her promise to play me the songs sometime soon. Her smile was sweet and secretive, and I realized she was glad I had asked to hear the music she liked. I made a mental note it was important to her.

I could tell she was nervous about showing up in town. The plan, despite wanting to keep her to myself, was to meet up with my brothers as soon as possible, because it would help her feel more comfortable.

"You're going to have fun." I assured her. More than once. A promise.

"I'm neither slipping nor sliding, just so we're clear." She swallowed, and I watched her throat and threw the truck into park.

"What is it you plan to do all day?"

"Walk around holding your hand. Get a killer tan. Eat good food."

Hell yeah. This was a plan I could get behind.

"Come on then."

I carried her bag and the basket despite her protests that she was perfectly capable of carrying something. I marched her through the crowd to the sprawling river oak on the far north side of the park. Beau had promised to secure a spot in a less populated area. That tree was as far from the festivities you could get while still at the park. Families were spread on blankets, children running wild screaming and dripping with melted popsicles, moms yelling about sunscreen, dads setting up portable charcoal grills and cracking open beers.

"Oh my goodness. Did you do all this?" Maggie came to a sudden halt and waved a hand at the set up.

"Nah, it was Beau."

"Mostly Elliot, actually." My brother admitted without a drop of shame, happy to pass the credit where due.

Beau popped up from out of nowhere and pulled Maggie away from me to hug her. In order to pretend I wasn't stupid with jealousy, I busied myself depositing her things on the corners of the blanket set out for us.

"Where is Elliot?" Beau kept an arm around Maggie's

190

shoulders as she inquired after his boyfriend.

"He went in search of frozen lemonade. He'll be back soon." I watched while still pretending to not watch, as Beau squared off with my girl. He studied her and her cheeks went pink. "Dom told us. About you and Cotton. We couldn't be happier. Cotton couldn't do any better than you, dear girl. Not to jump the gun, but when are you moving in and making babies?"

She gasped. Beau cackled. I grumbled.

"Maggie Peach, about damn time." Dominic sprinted up to her and scooped her up into his arms. It was proving difficult to stomach my brothers man-handling her.

"That is not her middle name. It's Jane."

"Magnolia Jane? And all this time you've let me keep guessing?" Dominic acted shocked, hand to his chest and the full drill.

"Jane is boring. I like your guesses better."

"I don't understand you two." I reclaimed her hand and thanked my lucky stars that she had fessed up earlier to wanting to hold hands all day. It was about to happen.

"You don't need to, brother." Dom sassed me and I flipped him the bird. Not missing a beat, he answered with one of his own. "Down to business. I am going to flirt my way through every female at the park, making sure to drop information to each and every one that Maggie Rose and I are only friends."

"What? Why?" Maggie looked confused, and if I wasn't mistaken, a little hurt.

"Because you are only friends." I said the words meaning for them to be obvious. Instead they came out like I was staking a claim. Damn.

"Obviously. But why the need to urgently spread the word?" She looked between me and Dom and back. "Oh! Is it Emily? She was acting weird when I was out with ... well, when I saw her the other day."

"She was pissed you were cheating on me." Dom shrugged, his mouth twisting into a rueful grin. They both danced around saying Vincent Berry's name out loud. The more they didn't say it, the more it popped into my mind. "Ludicrous. As if you would cheat on me."

"Totally. Wouldn't happen." She let out a small laugh and I clutched her hand tighter. "Also, Rose as my middle name? You think my mama named me Flower Flower?"

"Technically I think a Magnolia is a tree. So Tree Flower."

"That sounds like a fairy name."

"More like a dryad or nymph." Elliot arrived with hands full of frozen lemonade in cups. He dropped a quick kiss on Maggie's cheek.

We settled on the blankets in the shade of the sprawling tree. We ate the frozen too sweet too tart treats. Joseph and Missy showed up with the kids, depositing them to stay with us while they went back to the car for more supplies. Kids required too much damn stuff. Dominic immediately scooped Sarah up and swung her high into the air eliciting delighted squeals from her, while Michael waited and watched. She was four now, sure she was grown, and in love with her uncles. Mikey was calm, always keeping an eye on his surroundings, and less interested in being tossed about. After Beau and Elliot fed them both chilled berries and let them steal sips from their sodas, the kids were content to play on their own. They climbed the low wide spread branches of the tree, and Maggie watched them with a worried expression.

Joe came back and wrangled the kids long enough to ascertain they were appropriately geared up with swimsuits, hats, sunglasses, water shoes, the whole shebang. Missy ignored us for the most part, focus divided between telling Joe what to do and checking her phone. Then they wandered off in search of a Slip'n Slide to join the festivities.

I lay back and pulled Maggie to join me. I held her hand and we looked up into the green of the tree with the sun filtering through in dancing spots. The park was alive around us, voices a continuous chorus peppered with screams of delight. I could have spent the rest of my life there with her.

My brain registered the hit of water about the same time Maggie sat up and screamed. I sat up and scanned the area for the source.

"Alyssa! What the hell?" Maggie jumped to her feet, hands

192

out as if that could protect her, and playfully screamed at her friend.

Alyssa Hunter was a goofy flirty girl with a big mouth. She was fiercely loyal to Maggie, and for that I loved her. She had sprayed Maggie with the hefty water gun she held in her hands, a brightly colored plastic contraption with a sloshing tank. A mischievous glint in her eyes.

"You're asking me? What the hell are you doing hiding over here? And fully dressed?"

Two seconds later, Alyssa's face changed. She looked over our mass of blankets, Beau and Elliot playing a card game, and me sitting below Maggie checking out her long legs.

"Where is Dominic? Where is your freaking date? You know, Vincent, the guy you told me you were showing up with." The accusation was clear in her voice. I suspected she was upset being out of the loop more than anything, but the severe glare she angled at me told me she was concerned about my presence as well.

"It all happened so fast." Maggie, wringing her fingers, pleaded with her fuming friend.

"Too fast to tell me? No way."

"Calm down, Alyssa." I stood up and took Maggie's hand. "She broke things off with Berry last night. It was late."

"You are holding her hand!" She sounded mad, then she looked us over, and gradually her face transformed. "You're holding her hand!"

From pissed to squealing happy in no time. Girl was giving me whiplash. Maggie blushed. I didn't let go of her.

"I am stealing her." Alyssa grabbed Maggie and pulled her hard. I let her go, reluctantly, but kept my eyes on her.

They walked far enough away not to be overheard, but remained in my sightline. There was a range of emotions on their faces, back and forth, up and down, as they worked out how we got to this point. Several times Alyssa looked at me, sometimes with confusion, sometimes with excitement. Several times Maggie looked at me, each time with obvious happiness and disbelief. She had no idea how special she was to me, and I would spend my life showing her. I would make

193

sure she looked at me with confidence that she was mine, and not wonderment at how I could like her.

"Alyssa is part of the package, you know." Dominic dropped a tube of sunscreen into my lap. I'd asked him to track it down. For Maggie's porcelain white skin.

"I know."

"Do you? I mean, have you thought about what that means?" Dom's voice dropped low, and I was irritated that he was distracting me from peeping on the girls' conversation. "You have to share her."

"I have thought about that, yeah." I gave him a go to hell look. "Hard to miss the way she looks at you and touches you."

"You jealous of me?" He laughed, then sobered. "We weren't talking about me."

"I'm not worried about Alyssa. Are you saying I should be?"

"She doesn't think you're good for Maggie. You'll have to win her over to have her rooting for Team Cotton."

"Team Cotton? What the hell does that even mean?" I shook my head. "Never mind, don't tell me."

He laughed again and hopped up in a rush. I watched him stalk over to the girls, goose Maggie, then tuck her under his arm. He was doing it for my benefit. To teach me a lesson in sharing.

It was a long day. The highlight of which was Maggie stripping off her clothes and spending the remainder of the afternoon in nothing but her sexy bathing suit. The bane of which was not killing every fucker who checked out Maggie's body. I didn't piss on her, per se, but I damn sure made a show of giving her a rubdown of sunscreen, and of holding her hand at every opportunity. We talked, we joked with my stupid brothers, we ate her picnic followed by fair food from the trucks. We sat under the tree, we walked around the park and people watched, we were soaked by Alyssa and Jacob's water gun war. It was a good day.

194

Chapter Twenty-Four

Magnolia

I had known my mama didn't like Cotton MacKenna. She had been saying he was awful for as long as I could remember; since that first time he fought with Lucian. I hadn't known that Cotton fought with my brother in a misguided effort to protect me. An effort that became a habit for him. Even not knowing the reasons growing up, I had known that it wasn't Cotton's fault. Luke was antagonizing. He provoked people, then blamed them when they reached their limit with him. He was an excellent button pusher all the way up until the end. Blaming Luke for any of his actions was something my mama had proved incapable of doing; she said I would understand when I had my own children. Arguing on behalf of Cotton wouldn't make a dent in her residual hatred for him after devoting so much energy to the endeavor for the entirety of my brother's life.

Leaving with him, leaving my mama angry and on the verge of tears, was hard. More than hard, it hurt me. I was in tune with her moods and her needs, and I knew that she saw my leaving her - especially the who and the where - as a betrayal. I let Cotton's words roll through my head on repeat, that my mama was strong and smart and she could handle it.

He was right.

The strangling co-dependent routine we had fallen into was unhealthy. It was my fault for offering to take on her burdens and letting her needs dictate my life. It was long past time I stood up for myself. Only I hadn't. Cotton had done it. No one had ever done that for me. Not once in my whole life had anyone put me first and made a stand on my behalf. He may never understand what that meant to me, but if there was any doubt I was falling for him, it was obliterated.

I reflected on Cotton's reputation as he held my hand and secured me to the world. He was not the town Bad Boy per se. That title went to the likes of Danny Albright, who basked in being an insufferable jerk and player, or to Jason Wakefield, who was Fox River's not so secret drug connection. Cotton was seen as untouchable. Of the MacKenna kids, he was the one with the temper, the one to watch out for, and certainly the one you didn't date. I knew firsthand about his propensity to start fights. But if I filtered through the last twenty years or so, all those fights happened back when we were still in school. In fact, I couldn't remember him getting into a brawl since high school. I wasn't sure the things we did during those years should be used to define who we were now. He'd told me himself he had a temper, and he worried about losing it not with me but near me. By all accounts, that should scare me. I couldn't rustle up any fear over Cotton and his rumored temper.

I was aware my intense feelings for Cotton were too soon. In the moments I managed to look at things with cool detached logic, I knew I should slow down. We needed several dates, not to mention lengthy verbal sharing, before I said I was his and all his consequences be damned. What had I even agreed to? Most of the time I drifted far off shore from logic and reason, into the land of my heart and my libido. They told me without doubt I was right to be with Cotton. He was strong, he cared about me, and I felt safe with him. More than that, I felt cherished. Physically we had wild attraction that begged to be explored and given into.

My biggest fear when it came to Cotton was that he'd leave. That he would decide it was for my own good. It was early enough in our relationship, if you could call it that yet, to walk away mostly unscathed. The idea of him turning away, changing his mind or opting to end it on grounds of protecting me from himself, plunged a spike of fear into my chest. Right at the base of my rib cage above my gut, a sharp and splintering pain took up residence. I would have to hold back with him. If I let myself fall deeper for him, I wouldn't recover when he left me. I hated that I was so sure he'd be the one to end it, that I didn't have enough faith in him to stick it out. Cotton's reputation aside, what I knew of him was the way he held himself at a distance, and the way he could so easily walk away. His only loyalties were with his family. All I could be certain of was that he saw things as black or white, and he lived his life accordingly. He either cared not at all, or too much with a fierce devotion. He either didn't notice you existed, or you became his world. His life was in extremes, where you were nothing to him, or you would become the target of all his attention. I came to the conclusion that Cotton's reputation of being a Bad Boy was unfounded. His tendency toward all or nothing was what scared me, and likely other people, and that was what garnered him as someone to avoid.

The entire day together at the park had been surreal. We had all loaded up and gone back to the MacKenna's house before heading to the bonfire. It was about an hour until sunset, and the boys all wanted showers and to pack a big cooler of beer to bring along. I sat in Cotton's bedroom while he showered down the hall, and I was in a daze. Exhausted from being outside in the sun, surrounded by people, and keeping thoughts of my mama at bay. Anxious about my ever growing feelings for Cotton that stood less and less chance of being something I could escape unscathed. Excited, if not also nervous, about going to the bonfire with this guy that kissed like a devil and wanted me all for himself. I was happy to give myself to him, to be his. The idea of it thrilled me. Every time the thought crossed my mind - which was exceptionally often - my heart bounced in my chest. I had been a freak all day, too quiet or else rambling, because the simple feel of Cotton's hand wrapped possessively around mine knocked me sideways.

I distracted myself checking out his bedroom. His private space that he so willingly invited me into and left me alone to do as I pleased. He trusted me. The knowledge was weighty, in the good way. On one wall he had dozens of ribbons hung, announcing a first, second, or third place victory at some fiddle convention or another. Some were from years ago, which wasn't surprising. Some were as recent as months ago, which I did find surprising. I knew he played banjo, obviously, as I'd watched him covetously at the local jam for many years. I knew people said he was good, but he was far out shined by Denver and his fiddling. I had no idea he did these competitions and walked away with awards. Below the ribbons sat a desk littered with photographs, handwritten lists, and random nothings like mints and rubber bands. The sidewall had a closet door and three tall bookcases lined up side by side, overflowing with books. I sat on the edge of his bed, which shared a wall with a tall chest of drawers, and looked over his book titles. The bed was covered over with a quilt, soft and worn like mine, in rich colors and a log cabin pattern. I fisted the material in my hands and breathed in the concentrated scent of him.

"I like coming in to my room and finding you on my bed."

Cotton walked in and swiftly shut the door behind him. He wore only a thick towel wrapped around his waist and beads of water on his shoulders from his still wet hair. Before I could process the full on glorious sight of him in only a towel, his chest and stomach exposed, he was upon me. He leaned over me until I laid myself backward across his bed. His hands came down on either side of me, bracketing me in, while he hovered over me. Soap, minty toothpaste, manly warmth were all my body could sense. My eyes locked on his, sharp blue and seeing right inside me.

I lifted both my hands and placed my palms flat on his chest. His muscles were defined and firm to the touch, his skin extra warm from his shower, and I forgot how to breathe.

"Mmm." Cotton made a soft humming sound as my hands made full contact with his skin. He lowered himself further and brought his lips to mine, soft but greedy, inviting yet demanding.

I was lost in him. Time had no meaning. His house full of brothers and our plans for the evening had flown my head. My hands slipped down to his stomach, then around his waist and to his back. My fingers scrambled to touch every inch of him. I lifted my hips without thought, to find the fullness of him right there behind only a towel.

"I would very much like to let this happen." Cotton nipped at my jaw line and I gasped for air. "However, we have a bonfire to attend."

He was pulling away mentally before physically, shutting down his desire for me. I watched it happen, as he reeled himself in and regained control. I let one hand slip lower, to barely graze the towel and what was behind.

"Oh, Magnolia." Quicker than I could follow, he caught my hand and pulled it away. He took both my hands and pressed them into the mattress on either side of my head. His eyes were all heat, the center of the flame, blue at the hottest point. His lips lowered to move gently at my ear, his whisper a tickle. "Be careful what you wish for sweetheart."

He stood so fast I wasn't prepared for it. I was still panting and struggling to contain my own rampant hunger for him. I slowly sat up and watched as he went to the chest of drawers, dropped his towel, and pulled on boxer briefs. Cotton MacKenna's bare butt was a shock, a thing of beauty, and not something I was likely to ever wipe from my memory. He threw a half smile over his shoulder at me, knowing the effect he had on me, while pulling a t-shirt from another drawer.

"Aren't you changing?" Cotton tipped his chin in my direction. I looked down at my clothes, my swimsuit still my base layer, my high waisted cut off shorts, and my now terribly wrinkled white button-down shirt tied at my waist.

"I didn't bring anything." I shrugged. It wasn't a big deal. "And I can't ... can't go home."

Cotton's eyes locked onto my mouth, my chin that threatened to wobble with an onslaught of emotion, then on my hands that fisted his quilt. Next time I walked through the door to my home, I had to face my mama. Between now and then I had to figure out what I would say to her. I had to find it within myself to draw a line, to make boundaries, and to do it hopefully without causing a massive breakdown of either party.

"I'll go in and get whatever you need, Mags."

My lips found a smile and showed it to him. Mags. He was sweet and familiar, and my heart told me crazy things about love.

"No. I'm okay in this." I gestured to myself. He nodded as his eyes roamed over my body for the thousandth time that day.

A loud knocking on his bedroom door made me jump. The door flew open before Cotton could answer it. Dominic was framed in the doorway, all red blonde hair and twinkling eyes, mischief and mayhem wrapped up in laughter and generosity. How did I get there? How had I landed firmly in the MacKenna house with devotion of one kind or another all around me?

"Oh good, you're decent." He gave me a wink and tipped his head to his brother. "Time to go, folks."

Dom gave the doorframe a rap with his knuckles, then turned and flew down the stairs. Cotton had managed to pull on jeans and looked ready to go. His reluctance to leave his room had little to do with our destination or his state of ready, and everything to do with an obvious desire to press me into his mattress again.

I hopped up and stood in the doorway. The doorway that had looked too small to hold Dominic, then conversely made me feel small with space on each side and yawning above my head.

"Come back here with me tonight." Cotton moved into my space and pulled me in and up, pressed chest to chest, and his hands firm at my waist. His voice was intense, and sent a shiver along my spine and right down to my fingers and toes. "Spend the night. We'll go to your mom's place in the morning so you can change for our hike."

"I can't stay the night." Fear warred with yearning and filtered through my voice. It sounded like a question.

"Yes. You can." He pressed his nose into my where my neck met my shoulder and his breath over my skin was distracting. "Stay all the nights. I can't let you go."

"I have to face my mom sometime." If he was trying to

keep me from having to go home, deal with the hurt feelings and argument that waited for me there, it wasn't possible. I couldn't run from her. He couldn't always be there to step in and stand up for me.

"You will. Tomorrow morning. I'll go with you." His lips guided his way up to my face, where he paused and left his forehead to meet with mine. "That isn't why I want you to stay. I can't bear saying goodbye to you. Not after sharing you all day. I want to hold you in my arms tonight."

His words were thick with emotion and my whole chest burned. I didn't think about it being too soon. I didn't think of all the reasons I should say no and go home like a good girl. I only thought of lying in his bed with his body warm and close, with his arms holding me to him, and waking up to him.

"Okay." It was a whisper. I tilted my head so that I could press my lips to his.

"ARE YOU TWO COMING OR NOT?"

I shook with restrained laughter at Dominic's demand coming from somewhere downstairs. My face heated, knowing Cotton's brothers were well aware what we could be doing up there alone in a bedroom. After a long sigh, Cotton took my hand and led me downstairs.

Chapter Twenty-Five

Magnolia

We all rode together, in Beau's giant SUV. He drove and offered to be our designated driver. Elliot sat shotgun and messed with the radio, never happy with one station more than the length of one song. We didn't get many stations in the middle of nowhere of the mountains, so he cycled through the options fairly quickly. Cotton climbed into the back row, a bench seat, leaving captain's chairs in the middle row for Dominic. I immediately appreciated the benefits of a bench seat. Cotton slid my body as close as possible to his without my being on his lap. He insisted I wear my seatbelt, because my safety was paramount. Our nearness allowed for ample touching, and his hand rode higher and higher up my thigh until his fingers met with the thick material of my swimsuit that I still wore under my shorts. He managed to keep up his end of conversation with Dom - they were discussing whether they should renovate the big barn into a living space since they don't use it as a barn - all while his fingers moved against me in a delirious pattern. I had a harder time keeping a straight face and acting like I wasn't about to come apart.

"What would we even do with it after it was renovated? You moving into it?" Cotton asked, clearly not keen on the idea.

"No. I like living in the house. I figure it will be good for whoever couples off next. The house is Denver's and he doesn't care how long we stick around. But at some point, we'll all be settling down." Dominic was making too much sense, and it was weird that he was being so logical.

"Yeah. If Beau doesn't move in with E, they can live out

there."

"Beau is moving in with me." Elliot said the words casually, over his shoulder. "He'll see the wisdom of my ways eventually."

Beau didn't answer. He tapped his fingers on the steering wheel to the rhythm of the obnoxious dance song Elliot had left to play on the radio. I gasped when Cotton's fingers moved in a smooth circle, providing delicious pressure to my most sensitive point. Holy hell. Dom squinted at me in question; I re-worked my face into a hopefully casual smile.

"If it's not Beau, then that leaves you." I answered sweetly, trying to mask my mounting pleasure in Cotton's fingers as they continued to build me up.

"No. That leaves Cotton." Dom shook his head and then his body, like he was shaking off the idea of commitment. "You two can live out there."

That time when I gasped it was in reaction to Dominic's words. Cotton's fingers pressed harder, his movements made more intense by Dom's assumptions, or by my answering gasp. I placed my left hand over Cotton's thigh and squeezed. Beau and Elliot chimed in, but I missed what they said. As soon as Dom turned to face forward, Cotton finished me. He flicked his hand in a way that tore me apart, released all the bits of me that had built up into a quiet explosion. I sucked in a sharp breath, tried not to move or react outwardly, other than to dig my fingers harshly into Cotton's thigh surely leaving behind moon-shaped fingernail marks. He slid his hand back down to a decent place on my leg and his half smile gave away how pleased he was with himself.

I let my hand slide up his thigh. I had to do it. If for no other reason than to feel him hard beneath my hand, evidence of his physical longing for me. He let me have only seconds of soft exploration, before taking my hand in his and holding it away from that long hard part of him. He wouldn't let go of my hand or let me touch him again. I couldn't ask him why or press the issue.

Beau was parking barely a minute later, aligning his ridiculous big SUV in a field of vehicles. Rows and rows filled the grassy pasture, a flat spot surrounded by rolling hills. Someone had set up flood lights, vaguely marking the ends of the impromptu lot and giving us just enough light not to trip. It was easy to follow the other people, the sounds of laughter and music, and the flicker of firelight. We had to maneuver down a steep slope, back and forth on switchbacks cut into the side of the cliff that fell to the creek. The bonfire was huge, people milling all around the clearing at the side of the creek, fanning out in all directions but remaining central to the flames.

Cotton held my hand and helped me get down there without falling. His brothers carried the supersize cooler of beer to the bottom.

It was beautiful. Enchanting. Mesmerizing. My eyes locked onto the ebb and flow of the fire, caught in its trap of light and heat. Cotton led me around to a large felled tree with plenty of room saved for the MacKennas. They were royalty enough in our town to have warranted the people at the bonfire saving them prime seating. Cotton sat on the trunk and pulled me between his knees, my back to his chest. He was content to hold me and let me get lost in the powerful pull of the bonfire.

I think I laughed and smiled and talked, but time passed in a manner I couldn't keep hold of, and I didn't try to keep track. I stayed squarely held by Cotton, happy to lean into him, to feel his steadiness at my back. He held a beer in one hand, and me with the other. The party raged all around us, loud and chaotic.

I was so caught up in my own happiness and warmth that I didn't see him approach.

"Maggie." Vincent was suddenly standing in front of me.

I focused my eyes on him, and hated that he looked unhappy. His head was dipped to look at me, his hands stuffed into the pockets of his knee length cut off skinny jeans. He was adorable as ever, all his tattoos blurring together in the darkness and dancing light of the fire.

"Hi." I sat up straight, pulling myself off Cotton's chest. If he hadn't been alerted to Vincent's presence yet, he was then. Cotton's hand on my waist tightened.

"Can I talk to you? For just a minute."

"Yes, of course." Cotton didn't release me when I moved to

stand. I peeled his hand away from where he gripped and held me.

I turned to face Cotton before I went with Vincent. He didn't bother to hide his feelings, anger and jealousy on full display. I leaned in a little closer to speak without having to yell.

"I'll be right back. I owe him an explanation."

I didn't look back at Cotton. I didn't want to see the barely contained rage that might lurk behind his eyes. I knew his eyes stayed on me. I felt the pinpricks of his staring on my back. I saw that Vincent was aware of Cotton's glare in our direction, too. I wondered how well they knew each other. They had been in the same grade in school and surely had talked or hung out at some point. I couldn't remember.

"I'm sorry about the way I broke our plans." I led with that simple truth and offered up an apology.

"Me too." He looked down at me, his face cast in shadow, his expression pained. "I woke up thinking we had plans today. Then I saw that you cancelled. I didn't know what to think."

It was shitty the way I had cut things off with him. I knew it, and I didn't have a good explanation. But we'd only gone out once, and weren't in a relationship, so I knew too that he wasn't crushed so much as maybe disappointed.

"I wasn't expecting to ..." I turned and looked back to where Cotton sat, movement and life all around him, still as his focus never wavered from me. "Cotton and I ..."

"It's okay, Maggie." He shook his head and I could tell it was an effort to help me not feel so bad. "I was disappointed is all. I also wanted to make sure you were alright."

"I am. Thank you." I reached out a hand and touched Vin's arm, a brief reassurance. It was sweet he was worried about me. I hadn't handled things well. "I want you to know that I had a good time with you. It wasn't you."

I heard the cliché nature of my words too late. I hung my head and rolled my eyes at myself. Vin chuckled.

"So, you and MacKenna, huh?"

"Cotton? Yeah?" I felt the need to clarify given the sheer

number of MacKennas and my known relationship with Dominic. "It was kind of sudden."

He opened his mouth, as if he wanted to say something, then closed it. His eyes were framed with creases of concern as he looked me over. I opened my mouth to explain, but then closed it. I didn't need to defend myself to him. The pause between us was heavy, awkward. I wondered what else could be said and decided there was nothing left.

"Listen, just ... just be careful." Vincent stepped in close to me and said the words low.

He moved in to give me a sort of one-armed hug. I reached an arm his way, to have it snatched back. Surprise came first, then a trickle of fear. Before I could settle on one or the other, I was behind a solid wall of person. Cotton. My heart began to slow, my fear receding, as I took in the familiar sight and smell of him. I wiggled to free myself and shift from where he'd moved me out of the way. He didn't let go or give me an inch of wiggle room. I settled for putting my free hand firmly on Cotton's shoulder blades, to let him know I was there, solid and waiting.

"I don't want any trouble, man." Vincent proclaimed, trying to diffuse the situation.

"Don't touch her again."

"Cotton. Let me go." I pounded my hand on his back, as if he were choking and needed me to dislodge something from his throat.

He adjusted me so that I was at his side, but he did not let me go.

"Look, I was just checking in with her, making sure she was okay." Vincent's words were casual, placating even. His posture was relaxed, seemingly unaffected by the angry beast of a man that confronted him.

"She is none of your concern, Berry." Cotton's voice was laced with a threat. His posture gave away how easy it would be for him to snap and cause a heck of a lot of trouble.

Once again, Vincent looked like he wanted to say something, but refrained from following through. His eyes met mine and his concern was clear. I tried to look happy in order to relieve his worry. I didn't think it was effective. But Vin shrugged and walked away. I watched him join a group of people not far away. He didn't look back.

"Cotton Alexander MacKenna." My voice laid out a demand, and he answered by looking down at me. His face was still a storm. "What was that?"

"He doesn't get to touch you, Maggie."

I made a sound of protest, a funny noise from the back of my throat. What had happened with Vin was nothing. Truly innocent and friendly. Did he not trust me? Was this what he meant by not being willing or able to share me?

"Hey." I placed my still one free hand to his cheek. He was so tall, it was a reach. I took in the fear in his eyes, the worry that overtook the anger. "I ..." choked on the words that almost came out, swallowed roughly and tried again. "People might hug me, and that's not a bad thing. I'm a hugger. You have to trust me."

"It isn't about trust. I trust you." Cotton still radiated violence and restraint. I pressed forward, my breasts to his chest, reminding him I was right there with him. His eyes drifted closed for a second before he refocused on me. His inherent gentleness toward me came through.

"When you stood up for me before, to my mama? I liked it. Too much probably. Because no one has ever done that for me. Put me first, not for their own good but mine." I sighed and stretched up onto my toes. His breath staggered in reaction. His riotous jealousy and anger shifted to tenderness laced with hot flames of desire. "When you came over just now, and pulled me behind you? I didn't like it. I didn't know what to think because I didn't need protecting."

My voice was soft, and even as I lifted higher, he bent his head lower. I knew he heard what I said because a deep line formed between his eyes and his hold on me increased.

"I don't want to scare you. I will try to control the all-consuming need I have to intervene when another man touches you." He ground out the words in a low harsh whisper and hovered an inch from our lips touching. I shivered. "I did warn you. I won't be good at sharing you."

"Don't worry, Cotton." I clutched at him and my breath hitched. I wanted him to close the space and kiss me. "I only want you."

His lips met mine with a fury. A tumultuous desire that came out in his rough hands, his possessive claiming of my lips and my body, and a rocking of my foundation. Vaguely I heard hoots erupt around us, a delirious mix of voices calling out in support as well as mock disgust. I paid attention only to Cotton's lips on mine, my hands on his solid shoulders and arms. I was aware of the heat building inside me, the summer night and the bonfire come to life as an inferno of need. He lifted me, easy as if I was weightless, and I automatically wrapped my legs around him. I secured my body to his as he walked us through the crowd until we were shrouded in darkness. The people partying faded into background noise. The night was suddenly cooler away from the fire, the press of bodies, and out into the relative open. Finally, without everything else, I could hear the babble of the creek that ran alongside us.

"Magnolia." My name was a prayer on his lips, a break in the concentration he applied to kissing me. I gasped and panted and moaned in turn. He held me and I clung to him. His lips professed their devotion to my skin as he licked and kissed every inch he came to. "You are mine," more kissing, more groping, "as I am yours."

If he hadn't held me, I might have swooned. A lack of oxygen mixed with a fluttering heart left me light headed.

"I am yours," more clinging, more lust, "as you are mine."

More. More. More. My lips begged his to never stop. His hands asked me to surrender, and I did so willingly. Every kiss, every touch, every shared breath brought us together. Until nothing could tear us apart. My heart beat against his chest, finding the rhythm of his equally pounding heart, so that they joined in harmony.

I stayed that night with him. As he had asked, I spent the remaining hours of that night curled into his body, as he held me close. I slept with his fingers tangled in my hair, and my knee hooked over his legs. He was too warm, vital even during the night, and I craved the closeness we shared in those moments. I never wanted to give it up. I had found a home there, tucked safely into his side, without rhyme or reason, trusting only my heart. I woke to his watching me, his eyes both sad and happy, his embrace both tender and fierce. I recognized the fear in him, that he would do something to cross a line and scare me away. As I'm sure he saw the fear in me, that he would leave me for my own good. There was no need to voice those fears, only a need to hold on tight to one another. So we did.

Chapter Twenty-Six

Cotton

I didn't sleep for any real stretch of time. Not with Maggie there in my arms, not with a chance to observe her so closely and with no recrimination. She surprised me when she agreed to stay with me. When I'd made the request, it had been a need so strong I couldn't hold back asking it of her. I was sure she'd shoot me down, tell me to take her home. After I played the role of Jealous Asshole at the bonfire, I was more sure than ever she'd want to be done with me.

I couldn't sit there, just sit there and let him touch her, not when I saw how much he wanted her. Maggie felt bad for how she broke their plans, and I knew she would want to apologize to him. Vin's eyes had flicked to me, past where Maggie stood before him, and he hated that she was with me. I could see it in him, the disapproval, as if he had a say in her life or mine. I didn't give a shit what he thought about me, or my relationship with Maggie, but putting his hands on her was taking it too far.

The thing of it was, after, when she yelled at me, I liked it. That spark in her eyes and whip in her voice. Then she immediately softened, caressed me, and called me down from the place I had gone. She should have shoved me away and sent me packing. At least read me the riot act. Nope. Maggie pulled me into her and let me devour her with my need for physical contact with her. People were watching us. Partly that was a good thing, as it cleared up any doubt that she was with me, and only me. But Maggie's reputation was precious to me, and it wasn't something I was willing to throw away.

Only tarnish. A little.

I pulled her away from all those eyes and ravished her

mouth with my mouth and her body with my hands. I kept her away from everyone as long as I could and went as far with her as I could without crossing a line. Then she said yes, yes she would come home with me and spend the night.

It was a gift. Those hours with her pressed to my side, her limbs greedy to tangle with mine. I watched her sleep. I spent hours breathing her in and slowing my breath and my heart to match hers. I let my fingers softly glide along every bit of exposed skin. I had convinced her to take off her clothes from before and sleep in one of my t-shirts. The fabric swallowed her small body and pooled around her while she slept. She smelled like Maggie, sweet and haunting like burnt sugar and gardenias, and also like me. It was the convergence that became toxic to my sensibilities. I didn't stop touching her all that night.

I thought to get up and start coffee and breakfast for her, but was reluctant to leave the bed we shared. When I shifted and went to peel one of her arms from around my waist, she woke up. Her dark lashes fluttered as she looked at me and remembered where she was. I was struck with sudden sadness that came from knowing I couldn't keep her forever, not really. She would grow tired of my shit at some point and set me free. But when I looked into her sleepy face, her eyes brazen and challenging, her hold on me was one that told me she wasn't letting go. Her biggest fear wasn't that I would continue to be a jerk, but that I would leave her.

I pressed my face into her hair and cradled her head in my hands.

"I will never leave. Not unless you tell me to go." I mumbled and whispered and she didn't hear. She hummed and snuggled ever closer.

"Are we still hiking today?" She asked, her body wriggling and stretching beneath my hands.

"If you want."

"I want."

I smiled at my ceiling as she trailed fingers over my bare chest. It was already after seven, and by the time we ate, went by her house, and drove up to the trail, it would be midmorning. If we waited any longer, it would be too hot to be enjoyable.

"I'll go start coffee." I kissed her forehead, not daring to taste her lips. We would not leave the bed if I let myself start kissing her in earnest. She let me move away from her, and stayed there curled up in my bed. In my sheets. Where she was mine. "Come out whenever you're ready."

She nodded, and her wide eyes followed me as I pulled on a clean shirt and left the room.

I saw Beau was out on the deck with a steaming mug. I checked the pot and found it mostly full. Good.

"Morning, Cotton." And there was Beau joining me in the kitchen.

"Morning." I pulled mugs from the cabinet, taking time to pick one for Maggie I thought she'd like best.

"What are you two doing today?" I liked his assumption I would spend the day with my girl.

"Hiking up to Raven Falls. It's her favorite spot."

"Good." He nodded and smiled into his coffee. "I'm happy for you. She's a sweet girl."

"Yes. She is." She was so much more than that, but I got the feeling my brother knew and I didn't need to explain. I also got the feeling he had more to say on the matter.

"Are you worried?"

"About?"

"Mrs. Porter."

I looked past where Beau stood, and made sure Maggie wasn't on her way down to the kitchen yet. Just in case, I leaned across the island on my elbows before I voiced my answer.

"Honestly? Yes." I pulled in a breath, tried to sort my thoughts, then shook off my worry. "She hates me. I never cared before, but now, it matters."

"She will always hate you. And I suspect she will always have a strong hold on Maggie."

"You're not telling me anything I don't already know."

"I think that girl has been waiting all her life to step out of the role she's played." Beau's lips curled into a sad smile as he shared his thoughts. "All she's ever been was Luke's little sister, the good one of the Porter kids. She wants to be more than that. Needs; she needs to be more."

I gave a stiff nod. He was right. Everyone knew that Luke was the bad one, and Maggie was the good one. After Luke died, and it was just Maggie, I thought she could shrug off those expectations. Then I realized it was too late because she'd already spent too many years being that girl - the one that put everyone else first, that always worked to keep the peace, the girl that shied away and people forgot about. I saw all of those things in her. I saw that they weren't bad qualities. But she needed to know also how to think for herself, to make decisions based on what she wanted rather than what was expected of her. I could stand with her, and I could help her. I loved Magnolia Porter, and I wanted what was best for her, and I was more than happy to put her first.

"You're right." I stood and checked again for Maggie's arrival. If she didn't come down soon, I'd bring coffee up to her. "We're stopping by her place this morning. I imagine there will be an opportunity for her to stand up for herself. If she can't do it, I will."

I remembered her words the night before, that she liked it when I stepped in with her mama. She liked it because no one had ever done that for her. I didn't know the whole story with her daddy, just that he'd been gone since we were little kids. I knew that what was left of her family, between her mama and her brother, neither of them would be putting Maggie first. It was a wretched feeling all over my body, a sickness, when I thought about her growing up that way. It was that whole squeaky wheel gets the grease thing. Where her brother was the squeaky wheel. There was nothing left for Maggie - no time or energy or grease. It was time she was seen, that her wants were made important, and that someone put her first. That was a role I was happy to step into.

"Good morning, Beau."

"Ah, good morning, darling girl." Beau patted Maggie's shoulder and looked at her with wonder. She blushed and looked all around the kitchen.

God damn, she was a sight. She still wore my t-shirt, but she'd rolled the sleeves up to her shoulders, and knotted it at her ribs. She'd pulled those short shorts back on, the ones that cinched up her waist and showed off her figure. Her hair was messy, falling out of a halfhearted ponytail, and she looked more amused than afraid, and I counted that a victory.

"I'm going to cut right to the chase." My brother got down right serious with my girl, while I poured the coffee. "First, I'm real happy for you and Cotton. I think you'll be good for each other."

He paused. She smiled and ducked her head down. I placed her mug of coffee, cream, sugar, and a spoon in front of her.

"Is there a second? To follow that first?"

"Yes, hon." Beau waited for her to move, to start fixing her coffee. "Second, I don't know how it really is, only how it seems ... it won't be easy to put yourself first. But I think it's time."

She was quiet so long, I didn't think she'd answer. Beau waited patiently. I placed English muffins in the toaster to make a quick breakfast, and busied myself finding plates, cream cheese, and bananas.

"I think so too. That it's time." She was speaking softly. We stilled to hear her. I sensed a deluge coming. "I don't know how to put myself first. It isn't the way I'm programmed. In my head, I know what I want to do, and I know it's the right thing. When it comes down to it, I revert back to what I've always done."

Her eyes flashed to me. She wanted me to help her. I assured as well as I could with my face that I was in it with her and would be right there to remind her that she was important. She was worth standing up for.

"Good girl." Beau smirked. She rolled her eyes. "You need anything at all, and we're here for you. The whole lot of us, we're on your side."

I watched the pink crawl up her cheeks. She tried to hide behind her coffee mug. Beau gave her a wink before letting himself back outside to sit on the deck. I sighed and placed a plate of food in front of her.

214

We ate, and we talked about anything other than her mama or what lay ahead of us. She told me she liked staying with me too much. I told her I'd like it if she made it a habit. Days ago, I was torn up over her. I knew that I was in love with her, but I held myself away from her. I knew that I was bad for her, and she deserved better than me. There we sat, together, after condensed time with each other, and longing for more. What I knew, what I thought I knew, changed. I saw that what she needed was someone to bolster her, to hold her hand and not let go, and to push her to take lead. I could do those things. There would never be a time I wouldn't put Maggie first, and it was the opposite of her whole life experience. She would still try to avoid confrontation, automatically trying to smooth the waters. I would teach her to be a skilled sailor; she couldn't change the water, only what she did with her ship.

Chapter Twenty-Seven

Magnolia

Talking with Beau gave me an ounce of courage. Cotton looking at me like I was strong, and holding my hand like he would never let me go, gave me the rest of what I needed. What they gave me wasn't an easy way out. It wasn't that I gave my power to them or asked them to fight my battles for me. I was stronger for having them in my life.

Going home, I was nervous. I couldn't be sure what my mama would say or do. I only knew it was time - long past time - to show her that I could stand on my own two feet. I steeled myself, aware that she was skilled at employing tears and twisting facts to be laden with guilt. I steeled myself so that I wouldn't fall prey to her.

I loved my mama. For all her quirks, I loved her more. Some of the things that drove me crazy were also things that helped make me who I was. Growing up in my house, it wasn't all bad, and I knew that my mama wasn't either. She had done the best she could, and she did want what was best for me. It wasn't fair to think of her as the bad guy, or to think she manipulated me on purpose. She was trapped in a pattern, driven by her own grief and guilt, and I let her have too much control over my life.

"You got this, Mags." Cotton whispered in my ear, as he held my hand and stood at my side. A solid thing I could lean on if I needed.

My head nodded and I still worked at securing the protection I was building up inside me. The walls I might need to shield myself. I paused at the door, the idea of knocking crossed my mind. Which was odd. It was my house. I lived there, and had always walked right in. Already, I was distancing myself from this part of myself that accepted the role I'd been handed, and I had become a visitor. Definitely time to move out, to find my own place and land on my own two feet. The knob turned, the door unlocked, and I entered my mama's house.

"Mama!" I called out to her when I didn't find her in the living room.

"Oh, thank goodness." She came around the corner from her room, hands clutched at her chest. Her eyes were red rimmed. "Magnolia Jane, don't do that again. You said you'd be home last night. You didn't answer your phone. I've been worried sick."

I paled. I had to take time to think. I'd come in ready to defend myself, my walls fortified. But in this, she was right to have been worried. This wasn't her twisting things.

"I'm so sorry. You're right. It was so late when we left the bonfire." I looked at Cotton, and his lips held a secret and powerful smile just for me. I stayed strong, even knowing I was in the wrong. "I haven't even looked at my phone. The battery is probably drained."

That would explain the lack of contact from Alyssa after she and Jacob didn't show up at the bonfire. Hmm.

"Can I assume you spent the night with ..." She flicked her hand toward Cotton, standing sentinel at my side. "With this boy? Honestly, Magnolia, what will people think?"

"They'll think I'm an adult and that I can spend the night with my boyfriend if I want."

It was not lost on me that was the first time I'd said that word. Boyfriend. Cotton squeezed my hand. My heart was lifting, choking me with its insistence I pay it due attention.

"Your boyfriend?" My mama was legitimately shocked. Her face reflected a myriad of worries along with her surprise. "Yesterday he was taking you out, and I was under the impression it was your first date."

"Well, yes." That was true. How could I explain the depth of our feelings? From her perspective Cotton came out of nowhere. "That was the first time we went out, and I know it seems sudden."

"Ma'am," Cotton interrupted. "I wasn't exaggerating when I said I loved Maggie. I've loved her since the first time I stepped in to protect her." He didn't say Luke's name. Still, it was there, blossoming into a mushroom cloud of poison. I chose to focus on the other L-word, the one that had nothing to do with my brother.

"I love you, Mama. Don't doubt that." I reached out my hand, which she took into both of hers. "I am sorry I worried you last night. I'm going to change clothes, then Cotton and I are hiking up to Raven Falls before it gets too hot."

"Will you come home after?"

There was fear in her eyes. She was afraid I'd stay away again, without telling her where I was. It was past time for me to set my own schedule, to live my own life, but I knew her concern was real.

"If you want me to." I shrugged, though I was anything but blasé about the exchange. I would come home, but it might not be alone, and I needed to make that clear up front. "Cotton will be with me. Maybe we could have all have dinner together."

She dropped my hand, and I watched her throat move as she swallowed. I saw in her face that she knew she'd lose me, she knew if she threw a fit, I wouldn't come home. My mama had gotten up to speed fast, and she knew the way things would be. Perhaps my unintended worry in not showing up was the perfect catalyst to set us on the right path. I didn't like the fear I saw in her, and I'd do better keeping her in the loop. So long as she made an effort as well, to let me live my life, and to accept the changes coming. To her credit, she stood strong, even with the worry trying to bow her shoulders. She rallied, and it relieved some of the pressure that had squeezed my chest, that had been suffocating me for years.

There was a shift in the way things were with us.

"That sounds nice." Her voice was falsely polite. I had to give her credit for trying. "I'll run to the store and get ingredients for lasagna. Yes."

"Thank you, Mrs. Porter."

My mama gave Cotton a curt nod. She held herself in check, and turned her back to me. She shut herself in her bedroom. I was flooded with relief, but also guilt. She was upset, whether she said so or not. I'd made her worry by not telling her I was staying out all night. I pulled together the pieces of the wall I was building, focused on the effort she was choosing to make in order to let me go. I focused on letting myself go.

The hike was beautiful. It was a shady trail, which turned the glaring sunlight into streams of gold flickering through the leaves. We stood at the base of the falls and watched the water plummet. Water was a strange entity. I could rake my fingers through with no resistance, splash it and feel an unearned sense of control. Yet it was powerful enough to shape the earth, to carve stone, and to carry me away if I slipped into its hold.

It wasn't weird being with Cotton. I kept thinking it should be more awkward. Spending so many hours in a row with Cotton should have been too much too soon. I should want to send him home so I could think and shower and be alone. I'd always loved alone time. Instead, I touched him every chance I got. I blatantly stared at him and marveled at how I was not at all tired of him.

I loved him.

That had to be it. Love was a strange and powerful thing, and I had been swept up into its hold.

My mama wasn't home when we got back from the hike. I texted her to let her know we were there. She was at the grocery. I took a shower, hyper aware of being naked while Cotton was in the other room. Smarty-pants brought a change of clothes and showered off the hike in my bathroom. I was equally hyper aware of his being naked, in my shower, right on the other side of the wall. I thought I might combust. He came out smelling like my honey and gardenia shampoo.

"Hmm. You smell good."

"I smell like you." He didn't sound the least bit put out about it. I got lost in the amused light of his eyes.

"You smell like me plus you. I like it." I snuggled in close and breathed him in.

He held me in his arms, strong and secure. The house was small around us, time ticking the seconds away, counting down until we faced my mama again.

A thud rattled the back sliding-glass door. I jumped, and Cotton's hands smoothed over my back to calm me. We walked together to the door and looked. A little brown bird was on the concrete pad just outside the door. Tiny and frail, and looking so broken and amiss lying there on the patio.

"It's a sparrow." They nested above the light outside the backdoor. The little bird wasn't moving, and looked particularly tiny lying there.

Cotton pulled me into his chest and turned my head away. He buried me in his strength.

"I'll go out and check on it."

I nodded. I didn't want to see, but I couldn't help looking and hoping it would be okay. That it would fly away after hitting the glass door. We had talked about putting something on that door for years, because this wasn't the first bird to hit the glass.

"Go grab my water bottle from the truck."

"What? Why?" I looked at his stoic face and knew in an instant he was trying to distract me. "That won't work. You're going to move it, then tell me it flew away. You're trying to protect me."

"Yes, Maggie." He pulled me into his hold again; the full severity of his face aimed my way. "I will always try to protect you."

"It's too late this time." I whispered the words that came out, and he leaned in closer to catch them. "I'll know it couldn't be saved, and it's my fault."

Cotton's face changed to reflect my own pain. He swiped the tears from my cheeks. I thought he would say, *it's just a bird*. He would surely think it was silly that I was so sad about the itty-bitty brown bird.

"Don't blame yourself, Mags. This isn't your fault."

"But it is! I should have done something to prevent it from

happening. They make stickers you can put on your windows so the birds can see them better."

"I love your heart. You feel so deeply." He still crushed me to him, and looked at me with such adoration my heart faltered, restarted, then beat stronger than before. "There's no use feeling guilty over something you have no control over. You don't know that stickers would've helped. Accidents happen, sweetheart, and this isn't your fault."

"I can't stop it. The guilt."

"Yes, you can. I'll help you."

I nodded and he pulled my head into his chest. I breathed in his warmth, and I let his hands tell me of his gentle strength. He held me, and I knew then that he wouldn't stop. The worries that he would leave me slipped away. The flimsy attempt I had made at holding back with him crumbled, and I fell instead into trusting him.

"I've always liked sparrows." He said, and I listened to his voice as it rumbled through his chest right into my ear. "They're said to symbolize good things coming in small packages, and that the loudest voice isn't always the most powerful."

I knew what he was saying to me. I had always been the quietest voice, especially in my own family. I went mostly unheard. Not with Cotton. Not with his brothers. They saw me and heard me, and I didn't need to raise my voice for it to happen.

"I always heard they represent love and commitment." I said, my heart swelling and pushing at my ribs.

"It can be all of those things." He petted my hair and I sank deeper into his embrace.

When we turned back to the door, the patio was empty. The little sparrow had flown away on its own. I was flooded with relief. A sound caught between a laugh and a sob left my mouth. Cotton and I shared a secret smile, happy for the bird, but also the wave of assurance that rolled over us.

"I'm home, kids."

My mama voiced her arrival as she came through the door laden with grocery bags. Far more than was necessary for lasagna. Cotton mouthed the word *kids,* questioning my mama's use of the word. I shrugged and giggled. I knew it meant she was accepting Cotton in my life, or at least making the attempt. It wouldn't be all smooth sailing. There were many old grudges to overcome where the two of them were concerned. My mama and I had our own issues to work through. But she smiled at us, and I saw in her a sense of intense relief when her eyes found me. Although I did feel bad about not coming home the night before, it had shown her that I wasn't always going to do the right thing. Instead of getting mad at me, she gained appreciation for when I did show up and try to be her good girl.

We would be okay.

Cotton helped with the bags. I put on sad music and watched my mama move gracefully around her kitchen. And I came to appreciate her too, as her own person, as someone I could love separately from our roles of mother-daughter. It was a start.

Together we shared the evening and a meal. We got to know each other in these new roles, feeling them out and discovering how they fit. It was a relief to know that I could grow and change and still come back home. That I could be my own person and my mother's daughter at the same time. Cotton was there, at my side all the while, happiness and pride radiating from his whole being. I let myself get lost in his smiles, his sharp blue eyes, his hand holding mine. I fell in love with all of him, even the dark parts. And I let him love all of me, even the broken bits. Together we were stronger.

Fantastic Books
Great Authors

CROOKED
CAT

Meet our authors and discover
our exciting range:

- Gripping Thrillers
- Cosy Mysteries
- Romantic Chick-Lit
- Fascinating Historicals
- Exciting Fantasy
- Young Adult and Children's
  Adventures
- Non-Fiction

Visit us at:
www.crookedcatbooks.com

Join us on facebook:
www.facebook.com/crookedcatbooks